PENGUIN BOOKS

THE ELEPHANT TROPHY AND OTHER STORIES

Paul GnanaSelvam is an Ipoh-born writer and poet whose work often focuses on the experiences, issues and identity conflicts of those in the Indian diaspora. Writing since 2006, he has published both locally and internationally in anthologies, literary journals and e-magazines. His first collection of short stories, a mixed bag of themes on the slice-of-life stories of Malaysian Indians, was published in 2013. He currently teaches writing while undertaking research on instructional communication and L2 writing in Higher Education at University Tunku Abdul Rahman in Kampar, West Malaysia.

The Elephant Trophy and Other Stories

Paul GnanaSelvam

PENGUIN BOOKS

An imprint of Penguin Random House

PENGUIN BOOKS

USA | Canada | UK | Ireland | Australia
New Zealand | India | South Africa | China | Southeast Asia

Penguin Books is part of the Penguin Random House group of companies
whose addresses can be found at global.penguinrandomhouse.com

Published by Penguin Random House SEA Pte Ltd
9, Changi South Street 3, Level 08-01,
Singapore 486361

First published in Penguin Books by Penguin Random House SEA 2021

Copyright © Paul GnanaSelvam 2021

All rights reserved

10 9 8 7 6 5 4 3 2 1

ISBN 9789814914017

Typeset in Adobe Garamond Pro by Manipal Technologies Limited, Manipal

www.penguin.sg

Contents

Komalam and the Market Women

Seven ATMs, four cash and two cheque depositors. And every one of them is occupied by customers, awaiting their turn with patience. As if there was any more standing space, more people continue to pour in until the entrance behind me is invisible.

No! You listen to me, I tell the cash deposit machine as I force-feed it the last fifty ringgit note to end my transaction, even tempted to give it a kick. With the long queue heaving about, the machine, an onslaught of auto-programming, refuses to accept any new notes, causing much delay. Each time it rejects the transaction I push a new, smooth note in as I do not want to make another trip to the bank.

'Technology nowadays . . .' I begin to complain to the person standing behind me but get a rude shock instead. A young chap, probably in his twenties, stands so close to me that I can feel his warm breath over my shoulders. I turn and stare him down for coming too close. I have to be careful when I deposit the cash.

In the midst of the mayhem, I notice two hands extending from one side of the huge glass door, each time somebody walks in or out. They are brushed away by clumsy thighs and knees or by other weary hands.

I am not all that perturbed by beggars as they have become a common sight at banks, Sports Toto and Da Ma Cai outlets I frequent. But my heart does pity the hands that seem perpetually optimistic.

I let out a heavy breath and remember that I have to buy dinner for the family later as it is payday. The banking chore is the most prominent out of all the others on payday, when the loans and bills have to be settled. But it is also a day when the family gets a treat for dinner, either an outing or a takeaway.

The beeping sound from the teller signals that my transaction has been accepted and it takes another few seconds for the receipt to emerge. I pull it out and turn to walk towards the door. Outside, it is already dark and the road is teeming with cars and motorcycles. As I step out, the same pair of hands shoots out towards me almost immediately. She looks up from where she sits, smiles and calls out 'aiya'.

I scrutinize its owner. They belong to an old woman. She could be in her early sixties and has fair complexion. Her closely cropped hair suggests that she might have just fulfilled a vow. She does not have any jewellery about her except for the three glass bangles shimmering on each of her twiggy wrists. The loose end of her sari gracefully cascades down the lower steps of the bank's entrance like a peacock fantail. Her eyes, almond and hazy, are enchanting, I think, for a woman of her age.

A sudden thought crosses my mind. I recognize this woman. Yes, I do know her; not personally, but from my childhood days when I used to walk to the market. She had a name. I ponder for a while. *Komalam*. Yes, she was known as Komalam by the market women, the vegetable vendors, municipality workers and shoppers alike. She had been present throughout my growing-up years.

'Aiya,' Komalam pleads again. I decide I could spare her some loose change. I pause to open my wallet and find fifty and one hundred ringgit notes in it. Her eyebrows are now raised in question. I run my fingers into my jeans and shirt pockets to look for smaller denominations, ten ringgit or five ringgit bills that can be parted with. But they are not available. Not knowing what to do, I walk away quickly, without throwing another glance in her direction.

The restaurant is located at the end of the same block from the bank. I place my order and sit down, my heart pounding with guilt. I am still mesmerized by those droopy pair of eyes and the sarcastic grin Komalam gave me. I shouldn't have opened my wallet and then changed my mind. Poor Komalam, she must have been terribly disappointed. I tricked an old vagrant, someone who I knew by name!

* * *

Years ago when I attended the afternoon session at school, I was beleaguered with marketing chores after breakfast at nine, something I hated as a young boy but began to cherish later on. I left with the shopping list my mother gave me each morning. To reach the market, I had to cross a river and walk for almost ten minutes on a road that veered upwards. A village ran along the main road that branched out into many smaller roads dotted with homes, vegetable patches and a confectionary. At the end of the main road was a cross junction, at the top of the hill, and the market was on the immediate left turn. The entire Buntong population was always either going to or returning from the market.

That was when I would see Komalam cycling past me on an old chopper, labouring hard as she went up the hill. She was almost always dressed in a sari, those thin, soft and bright coloured nylex ones popular at that time. The pleats were neat and perfectly tucked in right at the centre. Her favourites were saris that had gigantic black coils that could make one dizzy. If it was not these mosquito coils, she had prints of savanna grass or ferns and leaves. On rainy days, it was a sky blue sari with candy-floss clouds streaked across it. On sunny days, it was a bright sari with cherry polka dots or giraffe patches or simply lines of different colours. On at least two occasions, she walked into the market flamboyantly, looking like a zebra and a tigress. If I was late, I would see her swooshing down the hill with her goods hanging from either side of the handle bars. She was always proud and self-assured. I admired her agility and ever-smiling face. I didn't know where exactly she lived, but she would slow down and vanish into one of the smaller lanes by the main road just before the Sungai Pari bridge.

Sometimes I waited to pick up brinjals and tomatoes beside her at the market stalls. I was attracted by the subtleness with which she chose the vegetables, the time she took to smell them and the way she tested their texture with her long fingers. There was such grace in her movements as she pressed the onion knobs or pricked the top ends of ladies' fingers or left faint nail marks on bottle gourds.

The market women did not talk to her, though they had tried to befriend her once. 'What is your name?' they had asked. Komalam did not answer. Then they wanted to know where she lived. Still, Komalam focused on picking the fresh red and green chillies. The market women stopped smiling. One day, they asked her where her husband worked. Komalam dropped what she was doing, looked up at them, turned towards me and sniggered. Only, her chin tightened like a pouch. Then she handed the chillies she had gathered to one of them behind the counter, paid and left.

The bewildered women were left guessing. Whenever Komalam approached their stalls then on, they were subdued into silence and they communicated with each other from the corner of their eyes. They spoke only after she had left.

I couldn't care less. Neither could Komalam.

Unlike Komalam, the market women did almost everything from their respective counters. They made all kinds of loud noises; talked, bullied each other, laughed, quarrelled or even farted. Komalam came and left as daintily as a doe. Sometimes I saw her talking to people. Most of the time, she walked alone through the different sections. By the time I finished buying the items on my list and turned into the street that took me downhill towards the bridge, Komalam too would be zooming down with her merchandise. However sometimes, she left the market with strangers, different men on different days. They were the men I saw at the coffee shop behind the market having coffee or cigarettes after unloading goods at the stalls. Some of them wore the bright orange t-shirts that the municipality women wore. If she was not alone, she did not pedal. The men took over the driver's seat and they would go in different directions with Komalam and her goods. She, on the other hand, would sit sideways on her bicycle carrier and put one leg over the other, holding the seat with one hand. She would maintain her balance perfectly, head held high.

When I was twelve, I started cycling to the market myself and the market people soon became a blurry image. They did not matter; I was too fast to notice them anymore. That's when I noticed that Komalam wasn't cycling to the market, but walking. This time she had a little girl by her side.

'She found her,' reported the municipality women. 'Starving and abandoned by the rubbish bin. The red ants had already swarmed into the eyes of the girl, she is blind in one now.' One day, when I was pressing my nails into bitter gourds, I was near enough to see the girl. She was about eight, and had a black strap of leather covering one eye. She was neat and ready for school. Her pinafore was ironed, her hair plaited and her forehead sported a black pottu. She carried a school bag and a water bottle. One of the market women handed out a piece from a Tamil newspaper to her and asked her to read it. They were amazed at the clear and fluid rendition that followed.

They told Komalam to make her into a teacher. Komalam's cheek bones rose and she shook her head. One of the market women then gave her two carrots for free and told the little girl to be kind and gentle with Komalam when she grew up. Of course, all this talk was absurd to an eight year old.

I hardly saw Komalam thereafter. If she was not walking with the girl, she was seen talking to the scruffy looking men; either near the coffee shop at the corner of the street that took everyone downhill to the bridge, or at the turning before the bridge which led to her home.

Years had gone by since my mother decided that a big man like me shouldn't be going to the market on a bicycle anymore. I was given a motorcycle the day I turned seventeen. The ride on the motorbike was swift, making my trips to the markets short and quick. The market people I grew up seeing almost every day now vanished from my sight and I got busy with school, studies and exams.

I still saw Komalam every now and then. When I came back from university one day, I noticed that Komalam was now walking with a grown-up lady. The young lady looked like a typical teacher, with an umbrella in hand, a lunch box and a leather bag. The girl did not have a leather strap across her eyes. Probably she had consulted an ocularist. I smiled for Komalam. I bet the market women were not making eyes at her now or dropping free capsicums and peas into her shopping bag.

I spent almost five years away at the university and then work took me to a different state. Whenever I came back for the holidays I shopped hand-in-hand with my proud mother and the trips to the market had become an exotic getaway from the humdrum of city life.

The road that led to the market had been widened and it is now infested with lorries, buses, cars and motorcycles. No more pedestrians and cyclists. I did not see people anymore. The market women, on the other hand, had aged and most of the stalls had changed hands. The old people were gone and so was Komalam. Familiarity had faded.

I am now a married man. It has been two years since I have moved back to Buntong for good. I thought it will be good for my daughter to grow up around her grandparents, uncles and cousins.

* * *

The order arrives, piping hot in plastic bags.

I change a fifty ringgit note. I have a balance of eighteen ringgit. *I should go and give it to her*, I tell myself. But what is eighteen ringgit? Would that suffice?

I keep wondering. What really happened to Komalam? What pushed her into the streets? I deliberate on these questions with a kind of inexplicable pain. Where were the men she used to leave the market with? And what happened to the one-eyed-girl who read so well and grew up to become a teacher? Wasn't she there to take care of old Komalam?

Should I give her only a ten ringgit? Five or three?

I walk up to where Komalam is sitting. This time I can see her well. She has really aged. Her cheeks are shrunken and her eyes hollow. She is resting her chin on her knees. *Why she is not putting her hand out?* I wonder. She is kneading the edges of her sari and presses her lips together. Her blouse has patches under its sleeves and the sides are worn out. Her sari is almost a bleached blue. She just sits there and looks up at the people walking in and out of the bank.

I know that I can't do much for Komalam. I'd like to sit and talk with her like an old friend, but we are not friends. She wouldn't understand if I told her I used to see her on my way to the market all my years of growing up. And what difference would it make? I wish the market women were here to help her or tell me what happened. I wish the little girl had helped her out. But that was Komalam's world. I don't know how it looks from the inside, but it definitely isn't the same as mine.

As I approach, Komalam looks up at me and gives a desolate sigh. The least I can do is keep her from begging for the next few days. Yes, I can do that. Keep her off the street. I won't give her an eighteen, ten, five or three. So, I take out a hundred ringgit note, purple and flashy like the brinjals we picked at the market and shove it towards her.

She gives it a furtive glance. At once her eyes brighten up. She smiles shyly. I almost expect her to clap her hands. She doesn't. She takes the money, and clasps the tips of my fingers in her palms. Then, she drags them along with the money and presses them ceremoniously against her left eye and then the right.

With folded hands, she utters her gratitude and says that my kindness will be returned by God.

I turn and leave without a word.

The Ride

Arasan despised the irony of his name. It meant 'king' in Tamil, but he was hardly royalty or could afford anything a king would want. Burning the midnight oil with his elbow resting on a pile of books and papers, he dreamt of things that made him salivate. A bigger house, good clothes, branded accessories, continental cars and travelling the world over. Things that the boys at the mission school he went to often boasted about. Although he was among the top students in his class, admired by both his parents and teachers, the ruthless real-life comparisons often reminded him that a mere name did not mean anything. He concealed his embarrassment behind hard work and good grades. Often he brushed away the present state of affairs, creating a make-believe euphoric world of possessions and persons for himself.

In school he was used to being at ease in the company of the richer students. A boost for his ego. Acceptance, he reckoned, could only be maintained by indulging in their interests. And almost always their conversations were loaded with what they, or rather their fathers, possessed; business or professional practice, landed or leased properties, cars and gadgets, foods advertised on television, European breeds of pets and security guards or maids imported from the Third World.

It had been some time now that Arasan felt his own 'my father' stories were not keeping up with the rest. His clothes were presentable, his bag was new and he managed to use his stationery with care. But his stories could not be too grand, otherwise his friends would expect to see proof which did not exist. The expansion of this circle of lies agitated him.

He fervently wished for a pair of new shoes. The pair he regularly wore had already developed three holes and become too tight. His big toe would flash out like a tortoise head if he wasn't careful. Keeping it tucked inside hurt so badly that it swelled up, and walking daily two miles to the Methodist High beyond Pudu was quite painful. The merciless road tore through the thin soles of his worn shoes under the unforgiving midday sun, and when it rained his socks soaked enough water to leave his feet smelly with peeling skin by the end of seven hours of school.

However, with prom night around the corner, the boys' conversations were laced with adult pleasure. Girls and parties, movies and alcohol, late night dates, shopping at Pavilion, Tropicana, or The Curve, arriving in posh cars. They kept piling on to these lists. Several had already obtained a driver's license and drove to school in their own cars. Others had drivers to drop them off. A new pair of shoes seemed so petty.

With cars now the main subject of discussion among his schoolmates, Arasan's own fascination with them peaked. He made it a point to memorize and jot down fancy car names, makes and models, so that he could speak knowingly about them with his peers. Just before going to sleep at night, he would forward divine petitions to all the gods he knew, hoping that by some miracle he too could be chauffeured to school in a nice car. With the luxury a car provided, his skin would not burn under the sun, develop sore feet or muscle cramps. The corns that grew on his feet would no longer be an issue. He would not be jolted out of sleep in the middle of the night.

One night his foot ached so badly that he couldn't sleep for hours. He had prayed in those waking hours with so much fervour that he thought he actually heard the sky rumble in response. It did rain that night; a violent thunderstorm heralding the early arrival of the rainy season. The scary flashes of lightning and the deafening sound of thunder convinced Arasan that God had heard his cries. He slept.

The restless night transitioned into a cool morning full of promise. The notorious San Peng flats where he lived were abuzz with the usual morning activities. One could hear the flushing of toilets and splashing of water, clearing of throats and smell the aroma of coffee and breakfast from the adjoining units. Of course, traffic had already clogged the roads by this time. Pulling apart the curtains that partitioned the one-room flat, he stretched his arms and yawned. He dressed and drank a cup of black coffee, munching slowly on a leftover chapatti before slipping into his school shoes. He examined the holes and sighed. The hardened thick layers of the white shoe polish did not prevent them from showing, and the thinning soles already looked like a world map.

'We'll have to get you a new pair of shoes soon or you won't be able to walk in them,' he heard his father say.

School wear or casual wear, he smiled unkindly at his father's concern.

Arasan carried two plastic bags of trash down with him to deposit into Mulot, the community elevator.

This isn't the coolest chore to do, he mumbled, being dressed so well. He had protested but to no avail.

'It's a boy's job,' his mother had pronounced judgment.

He had to descend four flights of stairs to reach the ground floor, carefully manoeuvring himself around the gloom-stricken drug addicts and drunkards who made themselves at home in the corridors and stairway landings. He reached the building's elevator, officially christened by the flats dwellers as Mulot.

Mulot had been given its name since it behaved like an erratic human. It worked and rested as it liked and sometimes it played pranks by trapping unsuspecting passengers. It would stop midway between two floors or ferry ghosts, ascending and descending random floors at odd hours of the night. But most of the time it stood idle with its doors fully open, half open or closed. The residents treated it with suspicion, as they had lost their trust in its mechanics and converted it into a trash heap by dumping malfunctioned electronic items, household goods and used clothes inside if its doors were open.

Over the years Mulot had coughed up a number of dead bodies too, including overdosed drug addicts, a homeless vagrant and an unfortunate but clumsy resident. It soon became a realm of spirits and unscrupulous people began to feed it with offerings; sireh, pulut kuning and kafir limes, bits and pieces of silk and vermillion, fruits and whole roasted poultry accompanied by joss sticks. Mulot became the source of any jinn and phantom stories that circulated among the residents.

A slight drizzle had started by the time he reached the ground floor. His neighbours had gathered at the bottom of the stairway to wait out the rain before setting off in their vehicles. A large group of children also waited under the awning until their school buses arrived. The stench from the wet garbage nearby was overpowering, and many stood about with their noses covered.

'Look at this rain. It isn't subsiding,' a man complained.

'Such a drizzle will not stop soon,' the others nodded. They helped themselves to a pile of old newspapers stacked along the wall, using it to wipe off their muddy shoes. With more people trying to squeeze into the tiny space right next to the garbage deposit, Arasan decided to go on his way, covering his head with an old newspaper he picked from the pile.

Come rain or sunshine, I have to get to school on time, he warned himself, *or get in trouble with the Discipline teacher.* He would suffer the shame of being asked to pick up trash at the school field with the other delinquents or have his sideburns pulled at the staff room. *Another wet day to contend with*, he sighed, fully aware that no matter how carefully he steers his feet away from the small puddles, water would steal into his socks and remain there throughout the day. He shook his head, dreading the smell his socks would render his feet when he finally releases them from their soggy abyss.

Arasan had walked the entire length of Jalan Kenanga and was about to cross the Hang Tuah intersection when a flashy Mercedes Benz stopped a few yards in front of him. By then the drizzle had reduced to isolated drops. He paused to scrutinize the brand's series and was impressed with the car's polished alloy sports rims. As he waited for it to move on, the tinted windows by the rear seat wound down, buzzing smoothly. *Probably someone wanting directions*, he assumed. But a familiar face greeted him. It was Ishvin, beaming like the morning sun, his bright orange turban peeping out from the window. He called Arasan over. A gust of cool, perfumed air blew out, infusing Arasan's senses with life as he bent down to talk to Ishvin. Before he could say anything, Ishvin had already pushed open the door and made room for him to get in. Arasan quickly dropped the newspaper sheet he was carrying and kicked it towards the pavement.

'Next time, you just hop into my car. I usually reach the Hang Tuah junction at a quarter past seven,' he said. 'Where do you live?'

Arasan maintained his silence. It was the dreaded question. He closed the door, mindful of the tranquil silence that filled his ears, away from the noise of the city bustle and construction sites. The car slipped into the flow of traffic with ease.

'Where are you coming from?' Ishvin asked again.

'The LRT station,' Arasan answered disinterestedly and pointed to the back of the car.

'I see.'

The interior was more posh than he had expected. He ran his fingers along the wood trimming and the upholstery. Soft music played in the background and the leather seats showed class.

'You like my car?' Ishvin asked.

Arasan nodded, still in awe of its grandeur.

'I like the colour,' he admitted. 'Metallic pearl black . . .'

'Obsidian black metallic,' Ishvin corrected him, his eyelashes flickering at each syllable.

The driver, who wore a long-sleeved batik shirt, did not turn around to look at them but fixed his eyes on the road. Arasan could not believe his luck; his prayers had been answered so soon. Being offered a ride every morning made it all the better.

A quarter past seven, a quarter past seven. Arasan memorized the time schedule and he couldn't contain his excitement at the prospect of surprising his friends. *It would be an awe-inspiring feat*, he thought.

The car easily weaved in and out of the morning traffic, climbing over humps, gliding over pot-holes and the gravel-filled roads like a hovercraft. From the inside of this car, even the otherwise monotonous city landscape looked vivid and attractive. It was like watching it on an HD screen. Even Stadium Negara looked like a carefully framed work of art. The windows darkened and brightened automatically. Arasan wondered what it would be like to drive around the town with an open sunroof.

What model?

'S-400L Hybrid . . . *Hybrid*,' Ishvin emphasized. 'Keyless Go,' he chuckled. 'No need key to start.'

'When bought?'

'2017. My father's birthday. Only a few in the country.'

'How much?'

'A little more than half a million. About 600k. The insurance costs nothing less than 5,000 ringgit a year. Imagine that,' Ishvin explained, almost mesmerized himself.

Arasan didn't say a word as he was too preoccupied with his new obsession. Ishvin aborted all conversation when he realized he could not comprehend Arasan's demeanour. Ishvin leaned on the arm rest and yawned.

Although Ishvin did well in school, he did not make it to the top students' list like Arasan did. But he was rich. His father was a well-known and well-connected lawyer. Unlike Arasan, whose six family members had to share a 750 square metre single-bedroom apartment and take turns to use the bathroom, Ishvin lived in a plush house. It even had a name, *The Cove*. His house was taller and bigger than his, had segmented facades and numerous tinted windows with air-conditioning. The boys who had been to his house reported seeing a sports car, a swimming pool, rooms with attached jacuzzis, along with Dobermans, security guards, gardeners and servants.

After turning at Stadium Negara, they arrived at school. The car drew everyone's attention as the morning sunlight reflected off its polished exterior, as if commanding the world to stop momentarily.

'Remember, tomorrow at 7.15 a.m.,' Ishvin reminded Arasan, as he slid out from the car and walked off. Arasan remembered to thank the driver, who did not acknowledge him and drove away as soon as the doors were closed.

Thereafter, the perils of walking were replaced by the comfort of being chauffeured to school. And over time, the two boys became good friends. The news of his new found ride had also reached the ears of his parents. Although they were happy, they were also apprehensive. A few weeks before payday, Arasan's father told him that once he got his new shoes, he would have to start walking again.

'It's not good to take kindness and favours for granted. One day they will be exhausted,' he advised his son, and promised to buy him a bicycle to help with the commute to school.

Ishvin, however, kept turning up at the junction right on time and Arasan was always there waiting for him. When Arasan left for school a little earlier one day, Ishvin caught up with him at Wesley Road. He was very annoyed with Arasan. 'You can wait for me if I am late. Or I will wait for you if you are late. What are friends for?' assured Ishvin as he turned on the massage mode on Arasan's seat.

In school, Ishvin began to hang around with him during recess. Arasan was shy at first, afraid that Ishvin might give out information on where he lived and how he got a lift from him, but the discomfort eventually subsided. He enjoyed his company, along with the other wealthy students. Arasan noticed too that Ishvin brought food from home, much like the other rich kids. They usually brought bread, but layered it with condiments that the local markets did not sell, fillings that never quite made up the middle-class menu. Their version of roti came with cheese, butter, mayonnaise, lettuce, ham, bacon, sausage, floss, preserves and/or scrambled eggs. Because bread was a popular choice, Arasan started to bring his own as well. His bread, however, was lathered with nothing more than margarine or sugar, and fitted neatly into a square, plastic container. Ishvin and the other boys never took any interest in what they ate. They did not trade or share their food. Each boy had his own Tupperware, and their mouths were simultaneously occupied with munching and talking about gadgets, laptops and video games, private tuition, parties and girls. They would even talk about end-of-the-year break travel plans. Ishvin remained a jolly, carefree kid, and always smiling. He was the joker among all of them and through him, everyone got an update about the private dealings of all the rich men in town.

The year-end exams were around the corner and it rained nearly every day. The sky, streaked in dark and gloomy shades, warned of more thunderstorms. Arasan hadn't walked to school for nearly two months and had forgotten about the poor condition of his shoes and the way they used to hurt his feet with all the walking. If Ishvin was late, he faithfully waited at the LRT station. Ishvin said the main road was too dangerous for an expensive car to stop. There was always the chance for ruthless motorcyclists brushing against the car's surface (because they are jealous) and according to the law, motorcyclists can never be in the wrong.

'Actually,' he further explained, 'there is no point asking motorcyclists for a compensation, they simply cannot afford it and the touch ups would only end up like an unsightly sore on the car.'

Once, Arasan's ride was delayed and they both reached school late. They giggled when their sideburns were pulled and made to pick up trash at the school field.

Exams started as the monsoon heightened and rain pelted Kuala Lumpur without mercy. Flash floods and heavy downpours became frequent. *The car is such a life saver,* thought Arasan as he walked up to the Hang Tuah station, delayed briefly by the rain on Jalan Kenanga that had stranded the entire population of flat dwellers in San Peng all the way to Seri Sarawak. The obsidian black metallic Mercedes was already parked at the main entrance of the LRT station with its hazard lights flickering. Arasan walked up the other side of the platform from the back of the station, a shortcut he used to avoid suspicion from Ishvin.

He noticed a break in their normal routine. Ishvin sat slouched with his fingers arranged neatly on the dash board, half-smiling but anxious. Without looking at him directly, he pointed backwards with his index finger crossed over his shoulders, instructing Arasan to sit at the back. The doors did not open to welcome him as they usually did. Not suspecting anything amiss yet, Arasan pulled at the handle and slipped onto the seat, pulling it shut as gently as possible. The driver surprised Arasan by turning to look at Ishvin and then at him, revealing a scraggy face. Outside, it had started to rain again. Arasan caught a glimpse of Ishvin staring at him from the side mirror with a worried expression.

Is he all right? he wondered. *Was it the exam yesterday?*

Just when Arasan was going to utter his concerns, the ruffling of newspaper pages distracted him. He realized that he was sitting with a very large, burly man on the other side. The armrest was missing. He looked exactly like Ishvin, only multiplied by four in size. His shoulders reached the middle seat's mid-span and his arms were fat like those of the wrestlers on the WWE. He was dressed in a long-sleeved shirt and the tip of his necktie rested on his protruding belly. He sat at an angle with his legs crossed as they were too long even for the Mercedes. He sported a thick, long moustache that enjoined a bushy, dark beard that was restrained within a thin, netted cloth. He wore a black turban, which almost touched the roof of the car.

Must be Ishvin's father, the car owner, Arasan inferred.

Though he was nervous, Arasan made himself comfortable and sat as prudently as possible. He edged closer to the window than usual and became conscious of trying to conceal the big toe from sight and checking for other signs of wear and tear on his person. As the car turned onto Wesley Road, just a stone's throw from the school gates, the other passenger put the pages of the newspaper together, shook and folded it before placing it on his lap. He took out his phone and his fingers sailed over its smooth surface.

'So where do you live?' he asked Arasan.

'Flats,' Arasan pointed backwards. 'San Peng Flats,' he answered reluctantly, aware that this was an open confession.

'Where does your father work?' The gentleman's eyes were still fixed on the mobile phone screen.

'At the Immigration Department.'

'Yes? What does he do?'

Nothing grand. Something regular, immaterial. 'General . . .' Arasan coughed up.

'General? General what?'

'He's a dispatcher,' Arasan said, revealing his father's designation. Dispatchers were servants at corporations who bought breakfast and tea for their officers, carried suitcases for their bosses and ran around the town to pass important documents come rain or shine.

'What is his name?'

Arasan did not answer; it was immaterial. He pretended to be busy picking up his bag and adjusting his shirt.

The car stopped.

For once, he thought that the driver, clad in his blue and purple batik shirt, was stealing a glance at him from the rear-view mirror. Arasan thanked the man and the driver. This time, when the driver turned around to look at him, his eyes were softer and he managed a little grin. Arasan was glad to step out and closed the door behind him. Ishvin did not emerge from the car for a few minutes. When he did, he looked abashed, his cheeks flushed.

And from the moment they gathered in the school field and until assembly started, Ishvin spoke about his father, the husky man who had sat languidly in the car. That was all.

Nothing else.

Ishvin said his father chaired the school's Parent-Teacher Association and sometimes gave away certificates during the school's annual speech days. He was also the city's most capable lawyer who handled criminal prosecutions and was a wanted man by everyone; politicians, drug lords, thugs, gangs and criminals. His father, he admitted, carried a gun in his pocket unless he was playing golf with the Sultan. And when his father raised his voice, the entire courtroom shook.

'Why were you kept back in the car?' Arasan asked, intrigued.

Ishvin was silent but answered eventually.

'He wanted to know if you were better than me in studies,' he whispered.

'What did you say?

'I said yes. I told him you were among the top fifty in the whole standard,' murmured Ishvin, looking out for the school prefects.

'Top five!' Arasan screamed. In no time, the prefects closed in on them like hungry scavengers. Ishvin pointed to Arasan. Arasan got booked for talking during assembly! The boys completely avoided each other from then.

Arasan came home from school feeling uneasy. He had disliked the big burly man and his questions. He had disliked Ishvin's self-guarded behaviour. He had disliked the friendliness of the car's driver. Ishvin's betrayal that morning was too much to bear. He disliked even more the dirty municipality flats he lived in.

'Pigeon holes,' he declared to his mother.' Dirty pigeon holes, uncivilized, disgusting, with no sense of class.' He made a repulsed face at his siblings and found the food at home deplorable. He snubbed his neighbours and did not talk to anyone. He prayed that God would remove him from his present circumstances.

The next day he woke up to the deafening noise of police sirens playing cat and mouse with some criminal. He got ready for the last week of school and reached the LRT station just in the nick of time and waited.

He could see the obsidian black metallic Mercedes coming down the street. Its glow flashed into his eyes.

He smiled.

He waited.

But instead of stopping, the car zoomed by without even slowing down. It took a few minutes for Arasan to gauge the situation.

Was it the correct car? Was it Ishvin inside the car? Did he forget to stop for him?

Suddenly he was afraid. His hands trembled.

The chilly breeze brushed against his sweat-drenched shirt, making him shiver. A pang shot into his belly and an inexplicable feeling of despair began to fill his chest. His heart seemed to be crystallizing rapidly.

Unable to gauge the situation, he took a few steps backwards and slunk down on a bench in front of the LRT station. He remained there, forgetting all about school. Hunger struck his stomach an hour past noon. He stirred from his daze and staggered home.

The next day Arasan repeated the same routine he had got so used to. The cool morning had already started to absorb the warmth of the sun by the time he reached the pick-up point. The road that led up to the LRT station was speckled with shadows of the Angsana trees. He kept his eyes wide open and watched the traffic, scanning the cars like a hawk. Then the glorious machine appeared, rolling swiftly up the hill. Arasan descended the steps of the station, stood at the edge of the road and exhibited himself. His heart warmed at the familiar sight.

But the car swooshed down the road, glinting like a knife against the morning sun. It had passed close enough to reveal Ishvin in the front seat, looking straight ahead without turning to even look in his direction, and the open newspaper sheets in the back seat.

Just as the car slowed down at the intersection in front of him, Arasan expected it to reverse, waiting hopefully for Ishvin to roll down the window and wave for him to climb in. Nothing happened. Arasan gathered himself and started to walk forward. The car, however, turned round the corner and vanished behind a wall of thick traffic.

'Why?' he mumbled, his voice shaking. His earlobes heated up. He looked around, realizing there was nothing he could do. People walked about. The Indonesian nasi lemak and goreng pisang sellers tended to their customers. The taxis lined up at the pick-up area and waited.

'Why?' Arasan whispered again. Agitated, he crushed a snail under the thin soles of his shoes and walked towards the school, defeated and broken.

During recess Ishvin was erratic, not friendly yet cordial. He stood with the other boys and spoke to them. From time to time he glanced at Arasan, but kept his distance. Arasan did not ask why, he knew. The burning sensation from the morning walk gnawed at his feet and plugged all his senses. He threw away his sandwich. He slammed his plastic container on the floor in front of the bewildered boys. Ishvin let out a shriek and ducked his head.

'*That*,' he shouted, 'that . . . was *mine*. That was *my ride. My ride!*' Arasan shouted at the top of his voice. The boys were stunned for a moment. Only the thud of the container hitting the dusty canteen floor could be heard.

Ishvin and the boys took a step back. In their eyes, glassy from fear and shock, Arasan saw himself and backed off. He saw his school bag hanging from his shoulder, tattered clothes on his thin frame and a pair of the most dreary-looking shoes.

He laughed.

Slowly the boys murmured, *scary . . . psycho . . . possessed . . .*

Arasan walked away.

The journey home after school was difficult. He noticed that another hole had appeared on the sole of his left shoe. There were four now. He walked slowly, burdened by desertion and reality. The ground floor of the flats was empty at this time of the day. Most of the children were at school, and the housewives were busy napping or doing their chores. Only Mulot stood in welcome, like a metallic pitcher plant.

Filled with fatigue, Arasan smiled in return. He stood near the narrow opening of the elevator and peered into its dark interior. He stared at the mound of discarded clothes, sofa cushions, Styrofoam boxes, mineral water bottles amid the rice cookers, old TVs and fans.

He touched Mulot's rusty doors, cold but comforting. He felt lighter. His feet gave way. He needed to rest.

A gust of stale air hit him, as if Mulot had whispered consent. He pried open the doors with a little effort, stepped inside and stood on the mound of decay.

He felt the elevator shaft vibrate slightly. Clanking noises of the tired chains interrupted the peace Arasan was seeking. He turned as voices approached Mulot's mouth, but before he could step out again Mulot closed its jaws.

The voice of his father travelled through the rusty holes. He was talking to someone.

'A new bicycle and a pair of shoes for my son,' he was saying.

The pulleys laboured. Arasan sensed that Mulot had awakened. The hell notes and melted red wax littering the floor frightened him. He hit at the door, but it made no difference.

'It's not my ride,' he shouted.

Marigold Wedding

This must be how it feels when one is zonked, thought Anu, a funny smirk tightening her jaws. *Must have been the tuna sandwich at Changi, or the cabin food. The amount of trouble I've gone through. Escaping is easy, living as an escapee is much tougher.*

The room was no comfort, the cold bit harshly into her bones. *Saravanan must have cursed me,* she thought. Or maybe mother. Tears filled her eyes as she was helped onto the examination table. A stinging pain shot through the right side of her skull and an unexplained numbness settled on her palms and feet. She raised her hands slowly, but her left palm was immediately caught by someone. *A nurse,* Anu realized, slipping in and out of consciousness. She looked Chinese, but tanned. The other nurse was Caucasian, and had an expression that matched the cold tiles of the examination room. The Vietnamese nurse, Nguyen, her name printed in bold on her name tag, looked down on Anu with soft but regretful eyes. She held her palm in hers and stroked her knee with another. She nodded each time the other nurse whispered something and observed Anu from time to time.

But Anu's mind raced against the doctors and the nurses. She tried to recollect the day's events.

* * *

Anu handed her husband the silver tumbler that contained milk and crushed almonds. She sat with her back towards him, feet still on the floor, and had not taken off her wedding apparel. *Thank God for the air-conditioner*, she breathed in relief, when she felt the mattress depress on the other side. Though nervous, she assured herself, *it won't take place*.

'Menses,' she said as she turned around to look at him. 'It is unfortunate, it is happening on our first night,' she expressed regret.

'Relax,' Saravanan replied, and gently turned the other way. Anu noticed that he too was perched upon the edge of the mattress, his buttocks pushed only halfway up the smooth bed sheet. He was turning his head this way and that, cracking his knuckles and stretching his hands. The mattress quaked with every move. Finally, he yawned loudly, suggesting that sleep was unavoidable.

'Would you mind switching your phone to silent mode?' he asked politely without looking at her.

'Oh, sure.' Anu picked up her mobile phone from the desk beside the bed. On it laid a large tray of sweets, a bunch of grapes and three bananas on one of which an incense stick burnt.

'Lots of congratulatory messages from well-wishers and friends,' she told him.

'Really? At this hour?'

Anu did not reply. A few minutes passed.

'Safety guaranteed, good things can wait. I'm sure you are tired,' he chuckled softly.

Anu welcomed the idea.

'Let me know if you need anything. I know how you must feel . . . new place, new people . . .'

Anu lifted both her legs onto the bed and leaned against the cushioned headrest. The humming of the AC filled the void between them. The mattress shook again and this time it caved slightly towards her side of the bed.

'You're very beautiful,' Saravanan whispered to her. He was lying on his side, facing her. Their eyes, still shy of each other made brief contact a couple of times. Saravanan squashed the jasmines and rose petals on the bed distractedly. In no time, he dozed off.

Anu caught a closer glimpse of the face of the man she had married that morning. It was round, peaceful, and solemn. His head rested on his right palm, spread like a fan under his ear on the pillow, while his left hand laid neatly over his pelvic bones and thighs. She noticed his hair, so prudently cut, and the curls disciplined into perms along the sideburns. Even his clothes behaved themselves, with his veshti neatly wrapped around his silk jippa. *A sleeping Buddha. His closed opal eyes could rival even a baby's.* She started to yawn.

She woke up to the humming of a tune from the shower. It was half past eight and the after-effects of a million ceremonies the days before seemed to rattle her bones. She waited. The whistling stopped and out came Saravanan, wiping his head with his hands, a modest towel wound around his waist.

'Good morning,' he greeted her cheerfully. The previous night's shyness seemed to have coiled away from him. Standing bare-chested in front of the dressing table, he began to grease and comb his hair. Then he powdered his face and armpits, rubbed down his chest hair and powdered them again. Lastly, he fastened the gold bracelet gifted by her family on his right wrist.

'Mother wants you to be dressed in a silk sari; and wear your jewels,' he told her as he slid into a maroon silk shirt and jeans. 'There will be visitors,' he said. 'Spare towels in the bathroom.

Don't forget the jasmines for your hair. Come quickly. We'll be waiting for you.'

'Are we going somewhere?' Anu enquired.

'No,' said Saravanan. 'We have to pray and eat breakfast together, see you in ten minutes.' He left the room.

'Ten minutes?' Anu protested softly and proceeded to check her inbox. 'Twenty-one messages and five voice mails,' she counted.

When she stepped out of the bedroom, Saravanan's house was abuzz with sullen, disapproving glances from the womenfolk— especially his mother. She tried to be civil, but Anu could sense her reticence. Had *they found out she was menstruating?* It *would be considered unclean*, she knew.

* * *

Aided by Munesh, Anu had planned everything to the last detail. She was going to get out of this marriage, no matter what. The suitcase was packed and ready, hidden from the entire family under her bed at her house.

'Your mobile is ringing again. You have a lot of admirers,' Saravanan smiled. 'What colour do you like?' he asked, as he looked about the huge wall cabinet of their bedroom.

'Red,' Anu answered disinterestedly, clutching her phone tightly.

'So, what would you like? I mean, would you like to go for coffee or a movie before I take you to your parents' house?' he asked, having picked a red cotton shirt pockmarked with small black stars.

'No, no, I'm quite full now. Mom would want us to stay for lunch too,' she turned down the offer.

Munesh must have sent a hundred and one text messages by now, Anu giggled. *I'm so sorry to have to put you through this.* Her heart softened at the thought of him despairing, waiting nervously at the airport in Melbourne. He lived and worked with his uncle in the suburbs of Narre Warren, Victoria.

'Do-NOT-stir-the-hornet's-nest' a message beeped from Munesh.

Anu was careful not to get too occupied with texting. This was something she had disciplined herself to do, to avoid her parents' suspicions. In the beginning there were the casual ones. 'I'm worried', 'I love you' and 'I'm missing you'. Then they changed to more paranoid ones. 'Are you safe?', 'What's happening?' and 'Did anything happen?'.

If only he would relax, she wished.

Saravanan belched quietly as the car stopped in front of Anu's house. She was nervous as she knew brides were not supposed to visit their parent's house until the third day after marriage. She knew preparations were under way for the farewell dinner at her home when she officially leaves her birth home. She got down and walked towards her mother, who was staring from the doorway. 'Don't worry, no returned goods,' Anu said.

'No need to be sarcastic,' her mother raised her voice.

Her father was not at home. Saravanan came in a few minutes later and took his seat in the living room. Anu served him tea and left her mother in the living room and went to her bedroom.

She pulled out the big trolley bag from under her bed and started to pack her clothes.

'Oh, and why couldn't you wait for tomorrow?' Anu's mother questioned her as she walked into the bedroom. 'Your mother-in-law allowed you to leave the house on the second day?' she asked disapprovingly.

'What's cooking?' Anu changed the subject. 'And where is appa?'

'We only have leftovers in the fridge,' her mother started. 'He's gone to settle the payments for the wedding expenses,' she said. 'I'll ask him to come home now, since Saravanan is here.'

Alarmed, Anu nearly tripped over her large bag. 'It's all right mother,' Anu protested. 'We are planning to go out for lunch and a movie later.'

'What? What has gotten into the two of you?' her mother rallied. 'No outing, I'll talk to Saravanan,' she said and left the room. Anu smiled coyly as her mother diverted to the kitchen and not the living room. The rushed clanking of the wok and cutlery signalled she was engrossed in heating up the leftovers. 'Phew, no disruption,' she sighed in relief.

The bag was ready. Her father was out. She had to get Saravanan out of her way now. She had to calculate first. Her flight to Melbourne was to depart at 6 p.m. in the evening from Changi International Airport. Check in time was two hours before the flight, so she would have to check-in by 4 p.m. She would have to call for a taxi that would take her to the Johor Bharu immigration complex and through the Woodlands checkpoint, up to the airport. But the checkpoints could be disastrous as she could get caught in the after office hour traffic. There could be a delay. The clock showed 10 a.m., she needed to act fast. She unlocked her trolley bag and very discreetly took out her tote bag. She unzipped it, and found the air ticket, cash, her passport, and the call cab's company number. *Ten minutes waiting time for the darn taxi!*

Mumbling to herself she set her mind on devising a way to send Saravanan away on some errand.

The movie, she remembered. *He suggested a movie and coffee*, she recalled.

Anu emerged from her room and found Saravanan alone, napping on the sofa. He looked pale. She shook him gently.

'You done packing? Shall we leave?' he asked.

'Not yet.'

'Why?'

'Everything is ready, but I wonder if we could catch a movie and coffee before going home,' suggested Anu.

Saravanan smiled gleefully. 'Yes, of course,' he said. 'Let's go.'

'No, nope, wait, mother is getting lunch ready for us,' she lied. 'In the meantime, why don't you try booking the tickets? I'll wait here. I could spend time with my mom and sisters.'

Saravanan's voice quivered a little. He was unsure, but agreed.

'Thanks,' said Anu apologetically, remembering that the journey to the Tebrau Jusco Mall would take at least an hour and a half from where they were.

Ten minutes after he had left, Anu called for the taxi and told her mother that Saravanan's car had broken down and he had asked her to take a taxi home.

'I'll call your father,' she said and started dialling his number immediately.

There is no stopping after this, is there? Anu murmured. She pushed her trolley bag to the porch, hugged and kissed her sisters goodbye, her tote bag slung across her shoulders.

A large blue taxi arrived at the gate. The taxi driver came out, opened the door and waited for her. One of her sisters ran inside the house to inform her mother. By the time her mother came out, the driver was tucking the trolley into the boot, and Anu had already climbed into the passenger seat. She wound down the window, took one last look at her family and her house, waved and instructed the driver to go.

If there was one thing she could never forgive herself for, it was the look on her mother's face, the confusion she could not grapple with.

* * *

L-e-a-v-i-n-g, Anu texted Munesh.

And that ended all communication that she would have from then on. She switched her mobile phone off. Taking a deep breath, she removed the sacred yellow matrimonial string from her neck and slid it carelessly into her bag.

She took her purse out and opened it. A passport-sized coloured photo of a smiling Munesh appeared from inside the plastic folders, dashing in a blazer and tie. A dimple appeared at the base of his chin and he was his jolly self. *I'm coming, I'm coming for you my sweetheart, I can't wait to rest in your arms*, she articulated to the picture. *Be patient*, she said, *nothing will come between us.*

'Miss, Miss, what did you say?' asked the taxi driver, perturbed by Anu's uttering.

Interrupted from her melancholy, Anu shifted her gaze.

'I need to reach the airport by 4 p.m.,' she said.

* * *

Dressed in a blue cotton shirt and jeans, a feeble-looking Munesh greeted Anu at T2.

'Raman,' a tall man who came with Munesh introduced himself sternly and proceeded towards the exit.

'Uncle,' whispered Munesh. Raman had sponsored Munesh's trip to Melbourne and absorbed all his living expenses too. He would pay off Raman once they settled down.

It did not matter anymore for now, she was safe in Munesh's arms. 'I'll go and get the car,' said Raman hurriedly.

Munesh had very few things to ask her despite the numerous text messages he had sent. Nor was he exhibiting much affection. He did not run his fingers against her cheeks or offer a kiss on her forehead. He was struggling with the bag but *he sure could ask about the events that had unfolded, about her parents and Saravanan*, deliberated Anu, disappointed.

'I'm fine,' he said, finding her looking at him enquiringly, and busied himself being on the lookout for his uncle's car coming up the ramp.

'Are you hungry?' he asked, when Anu enquired about their wedding.

'Yes,' Anu nodded.

'Here take this,' he said. 'It's not *Wrigley's* but it's chewing gum,' he said.

'When is the wedding?' Anu asked, burying her nose into Munesh's shoulders and inhaling deeply.

'Soon. There are some formalities to be completed. In a week,' he assured her.

The car arrived. Its boot opened and the trolley bag was dumped into it. Anu sat at the back and Munesh joined her, his arm around her.

The car rolled up an overhead bridge and into the adjoining Monash Freeway.

'Where is the gum?' he asked.

Anu showed it to him. He unwrapped it and popped it into her mouth.

'Won't make you hungry. Most eateries close by dusk and its past midnight. It will take us almost an hour to reach home,' Munesh told her.

* * *

Nurse Nguyen looked like a child under the flashy cornice lights of Dr. Hanson's Women Clinic. Anu had read the label while Munesh helped her to walk in. She had doleful eyes, straight hair tied in a ponytail, a round face, and a small frame. *She is a good nurse*, Anu deduced. The Caucasian nurse, who stood two times taller than Nurse Nguyen, did not look pleased and kept looking at her watch. But obviously they were waiting for something

'Shall we start the IV drip or not?' she asked Nguyen, who shook her head.

'*Owh*, come on, it's almost the end of the shift,' she groaned. 'There is nothing wrong with her, why don't they send her home?'

Anu realized that her mouth had been emptied of the chewing gum.

'Just wait,' said Nguyen, looking up. 'I hear them coming.'

Three shadows stood by the door of the examination room, their images magnified like eerie humanoids on the glass partition of the door by the fluorescent lights outside. Only the voice of a stranger could be heard, for it was louder and determined. Nguyen and the Caucasian nurse looked up and listened.

'I disagree, I will not do it,' said Dr. Hanson. 'As far as I am concerned, it's a violation of privacy and I will report you if you do not leave. This is insane. One finger or two fingers, you keep your Dark Age prejudice and take it home with you.' He pushed the door open with such force that it banged against the wall.

Munesh looked adrift as they followed the doctor into the room. Anu held out her hand to Munesh.

Dr. Hanson looked into a file handed by the Caucasian nurse.

'There is absolutely nothing wrong with this girl,' he said. Looking into Anu's eyes and taking her pulse, he smiled with his lips pursed to one corner. His blue eyes shone tender and kind.

'Go home now,' he told them. 'You'll be fine. Take the medicine and drink lots of water. There was minor food poisoning.'

The Caucasian nurse bolted from the room, and then Dr. Hanson. Raman was missing.

Nurse Nguyen helped Anu down from the cold examination table.

'I can manage,' said Anu, locking her arms around Munesh's elbow.

* * *

Anu woke up to the buzzing noise of a large group of people. The floorboards around her were creaking in many directions. There was a wonderful smell of biryani and the sweet tinge of barbecued meat accompanying it. She was in a large bedroom. Sunlight stole into it from a large window and shone on the yellow and orange wallpaper filled with autumn leaves. She was hungry and cold despite the warmth around her. She drew the blanket up to her exposed breasts and lay still, feeling feverish. Cold sweat ran down her face and neck. She wiped the sweat with the edge of the huge blanket and looked about for water. Small red pockmarks had appeared on her elbow and arms. *Is it a rash?* She wondered.

The shower was on and someone was whistling a grand number from within its walls, interspersed by the noise of children calling out to each other and bouts of laughter exchanged between the men outside the window.

There was a knock. The door creaked open and to her dismay, Munesh came into the room. She noticed that the whistling stopped.

'I love you,' he said, peering into her eyes.

'You're back to yourself,' Anu replied, thinking of his detachment the day before. 'I missed you,' she said.

Munesh sat down on the bed's edge and looked out of the window thoughtfully. The yellow wallpaper cast a golden hue on his smooth, fair skin. Anu patted playfully on his shoulder. He arose from the bed and took a deep breath.

'Get up, we're getting married,' said Munesh, getting himself into an embroidered cream coloured cotton *jippa* and a pair of black slacks. 'There is a small temple down the road, and uncle managed to get hold of the priest. We'll tie the knot today. He pointed to a silver tray that held a sandal paste-coloured sari, a rose, and costume jewellery. 'That's for you. Ten minutes,' he said, clicking his wrist watch tight and leaving the room.

Anu felt so tired that she was tempted to ask for a postponement. *But isn't this what I came for?* She checked herself. She caught sight of a rolled-up yellow thread on the tray, similar to the one that Saravanan had tied around her neck in three knots and declared that she was his to behold, for good times and bad times, in life and in death.

As she was about to move, she felt a sharp piercing pain shoot up into her abdomen from between her thighs. *I have to get up, nonetheless. The knot must be tied, three times with a yellow string,* she told herself. *It's only jet lag, or a fever, or an allergy.* The pain persisted. As she moved her legs off the bed's edge, she felt a slimy wetness on her inner thighs. Pinch marks had mysteriously appeared on her arms and breasts. *Strange,* she told herself while scratching them. Instinctively, she pushed her hands gently down and felt about the liquid. Her vagina burned to the touch, like an exposed blister. Shocked, she withdrew her hand. *What is this? What happened?* she wondered.

There was a knock on the door again.

'Are you ready?' Munesh's voice enquired from outside.

Anu did not answer, figuring out the source of the whistling from the adjacent bathroom.

The door opened wider revealing Munesh with a gold-laced turban on his head and an orchid corsage. Anu clutched the blanket tightly.

'Now, now, what is happening to you my darling Anu? We need to get going dear, before the auspicious time passes,' he said.

This time she heard the shower stop. Munesh turned to look in the direction of the bathroom. His voice almost choked. He mumbled something and sat by her side.

Anu remembered the red marks and pointed them to Munesh.

He smiled wryly and looked away.

She took his hand and put it on her forehead.

He gently pushed aside hair from her face.

She touched her lips and he caressed them softly with his thumb.

By now, she was genuinely afraid. Her hands shivered. Trembling, she withdrew her other hand out from under the blanket, and brought it close to her face. It was bloodied. She screamed and screamed and screamed, her writhing body embraced tightly by the warm and gentle hands of Munesh and her course shouts, muffled against his loving heart.

The Identity Bargain

The air-conditioned ground floor of the National Registry Department headquarters was a welcome after having survived the craziest trip Saras had ever taken in her life. Like a thirsty camel, she gulped down the last few mouthfuls from the mineral water bottle she held, scrutinizing the lone cactus that stood like a trident on the bottle's label. As the water soothed her dry throat, she thought thankfully that she was now safe from the glaring sunlight that had rendered her almost blind after hours of aimless driving. She sat down on the nearest available seat, staring at the words *LIFE GOES ON* printed below the picture on the water bottle. *What irony*, she thought again.

'How could you?' she asked her husband, Sunder, a thin wiry man looking about the signboards of the vast complex, lifting his spectacles to read the bold letters and arrows. The trip had also given him cracked lips and a tan, Saras observed.

'How . . . what?' he asked her, half listening, his breath stale and thick with a small pod of saliva gathered at the corners of his mouth. He repeated the question, trying to comb his dishevelled hair, his eyes now fixed on the people who were going about their business, wondering if he should stop someone to ask for directions.

Saras got up and walked towards a nearby bin to throw the empty bottle. Dusting her new *baju kurung*, she came back and stood close to Sunder.

Looking up at him, she said, 'How can you be lost in your own country?' She was rather annoyed. The sound of the announcer calling after the tokens rang out in the background.

Sunder was still engrossed in his mission to locate the right counter. A few seconds passed.

'Wait,' he told her and their sons. 'Wait here.'

With the right counter in full view now, he gently plucked an envelope from Saras' hand and walked towards it at the furthest end of the complex. His sons trailed behind him, forgetting their father's orders. They left a bewildered Saras to wait alone. This area of the NRD was clean, cool and soothing, balanced perfectly by cream-coloured tiles and blue cushion chairs arranged in many rows. Several people were waiting patiently for their turn. Some were seated on the chairs provided, while others stood in small pockets in different corners. Some had their fingerprints being taken, some were scrutinizing forms that were being shown to them and others were busy getting their particulars and identity cards verified and computed.

Sunder emerged from the crowd with both the boys. In his hand he held a token with numbers printed in bold. He seemed pleased and smiled.

'We have to wait, the interview will start in twenty minutes.'

Together, they walked to the other side of the big hall and took their seats. Here, the crowd was not as thick and the women behind the counters looked unruffled.

'It's normal,' said Sunder.

'What? What's normal?' asked Saras.

'Getting lost,' he said curtly, his voice now coarse.

'I kept telling you it was k-a-y-l-w-a-r, k-a-y-l-w-a-r, but you went on driving ahead. Like you had the map in your head,' Saras snorted.

'But this is Malaysia. One would never get lost in his own backyard,' said Sundar, managing a little grin.

'K-e-l-u-a-r, amma, k-e-l-u-a-r,' said her younger son, correcting her pronunciation. It was the word for 'EXIT'.

'Whatever it is, you should have listened. The Google map was correct, it said exit 26 and I saw the board saying k-a-y-l-w-a-r, and it just didn't register. And we have reached this complex two hours, two hours late, Sunder.' Saras fumed at her husband's sense of direction.

'It's okay,' Sunder comforted her, 'we are here and the interview is still happening.'

'Appa, can we go to Alamanda later?' their eldest son asked. 'I'm hungry, they would definitely have McDonald's there.' He sounded optimistic.

Sunder shook his head. He had seen Alamanda somewhere, as they had travelled in and out of the maze called Putrajaya, the administrative capital.

His younger son pulled at his sleeve. 'I'm hungry too,' he said.

'Yes, yes, we will go, but after amma's interview,' promised Sunder.

'Look appa, two more numbers to go now,' their younger son pointed to the huge counter.

'Do you still have the google map and directions?' Sunder asked as an afterthought.

'Yes, why?' asked Saras, surprised that he wanted the directions again. 'What do you want it for? Shouldn't we just look for the signboard for Kuala Lumpur and drive straight out?'

'The boys are hungry, maybe we could take them to the shopping complex we saw on our way in precinct 1A or 1B?' he tried to ascertain.

'Alright,' agreed Saras. 'We'll have to read the directions bottom-up I suppose. Putrajaya—*Victorious Son*—isn't that what it means, in Tamil?' She asked to clarify, 'or Sanskrit?' she asked again.

'We all spoke Sanskrit and re-wrote it in Pallava, I suppose it is,' said Sunder, still trying to figure out the route that they had taken to reach the NRD.

'Do you remember any landmarks on our way in?' Sunder asked Saras.

'The bridges and the lakes,' said Saras, 'and of course the thematic street lights,' she added.

'Too many, almost identical,' surmised Sunder, 'and the Precincts all too close for comfort.' *16, 15, 2, 1A and 1B*, he repeated. *Where is the rest*? He wondered.

'Of course, you can't miss the building with the green dome and the pink mosque,' Saras remembered. 'Yes, according to the map, that's Precinct 2. Putra *Pra—Perdana—the grandest son*,' Saras translated again.

'Just count the lakes and bridges,' Sunder tried to help, getting confused, 'but we kept going back to the same place again'.

'We should pass two lakes and two bridges, drive straight out to the cross junction and turn right into L-ay-b-o-h *Pradana Timur*. After that, it's Jalan *Alamanda*, and *Alamanda* complex. See, it's so easy,' Saras giggled. 'We'll have to continue our *saga*, with the directions bottom-up,' she summed up their return journey.

'Really, it's that easy?' Sunder asked, doubtful if he would make it to *Alamanda*, hassle-free and if he should really ask Saras to drive this time.

As he exited the highway this morning and drove up the long ramp that emptied them into Putrajaya, he became a little overwhelmed. The sky was exceptionally wide and empty. The sheer vastness of the new and empty roads, the small pockets of greenery intentionally left to complement the cleared lands of humongous construction sites left him disorientated and perplexed. Only the sign boards stood to welcome, to direct and to bid them farewell. *It was a delirious drive*, he reckoned, having arrived at the same spots again and again—Precinct 2, then 1A and then Precinct 16, even with a map in hand. From every corner, only the chequered dome of the lotus-pink mosque served as a beacon of hope, minimizing the feeling of abandonment.

'Relax,' Saras tried to cheer up Sunder, 'this is Putrajaya, our country, and after all, everything except for the numerous huge domes, are all written in Sanskrit. We'll be fine,' she assured him.

Though she had resided in Malaysia for almost fourteen years now, Saras was apprehensive about her citizenship application. This was the first time she was applying. She knew she fulfilled most of the criteria, but she was not confident about speaking in the Malay language, which would be tested during the interview. 'Elementary Proficiency' level was all that was required, but finding the right words and pronouncing them correctly still posed a challenge. She had been prohibited from using some words by her family, for they sounded inappropriate. And she had to be careful with her vocalizations, especially vowels that she uttered in her strong south Indian accent. And in this country everyone seemed to speak so many different versions of the same language that it veered completely from its original. Homonyms were the easiest, as the language was composed of borrowed words from English and contained a rich array of words etymologically linked to Sanskrit and Arabic. She had mastered some important ones that interviewers liked to ask.

Sunder and Saras were distant cousins. His parents did not want to cut their links to the motherland completely and felt that a marriage of convenience would bridge that gap. But such things were to change after marriage. Sunder had given up on the yearly visits to Madurai, discontented with the weather, water, food, the rising costs of travelling and having to put up with the exhaustion due to excessive hospitality from his in-laws. *They are overdoing it*, he had protested quietly to Saras. He was a man of simple needs, well-educated, and trouble free but timid, too afraid of his mother even now. He was a man of few words, choosing to speak only if the need arose, or else he was buried in his magazines or spent time with his orchids that he was so fond of. An accidental horticulturist, he cultivated hybrids, took part in competitions and spoke to his flowers in the language of nocturnal creatures.

Saras, on the other hand, having graduated with a Master's in Arts, taught full time at a private university and had been pretty much acclimatized to the Malaysian way of life, its triumphs and its peculiarities by now. She was mesmerized by its gastronomical wonders, three-quarters of which she did not consume as she was vegetarian. The accessibility to the rich cultures, celebrations and all things non-Indian were exotic and exhilarating. Malaysia Boleh, she likes to rhyme, throughout her trials in adjusting to life. Her sons, eight and six now, were very much Malaysians who went to national schools, spoke fluent Malay, and had been her strength and support.

Sunder turned towards her, his face taut with anxiety. He would be accompanying her to the interview as per the requirement to meet the Registrar of Citizenship.

'Do you remember the names of fruits?' he quizzed.

Cheeku, ram-button, durian, langsat, eppal, orange, strawberry, lychee, cherry and . . . and . . . cats eyes . . . mata, mata kuching.

'Names of flowers, national flower?' Sundar implored.

Rose, dahlia, orchid, hibiscus . . . bunga . . . bungah raya . . . as in Hari Raya?

'Hari Raya is Eid, it's a celebration, remember?' Sunder reminded her. 'What about Malaysian food?' he posted the last question.

'Nasi l-a-y-m-a-k, nasi champur, and kari I-am.'

Sitting cross-legged and rolling up the Google map, Sunder seemed satisfied and tapped the rolled paper against his elbow. The boys were gleeful, laughing at their parents' relic.

The soft bell sounded and signalled a change in turn, and their number appeared on the large screen.

Asking the boys to behave, Sunder and Saras got up from their seats and left for the interview room, led by the smiling clerk from the counter.

The pretty lady with the most elaborate *tudung*, complete with sequins and origami pom-poms, walked ahead and opened the door. They had to climb a flight of stairs and then they reached a room that said M-A-S-U-K. It was nice and cozy, with elaborate looking chairs and satin table covers, adorned with plastic flowers and a tea set kept on a silver tray. One part of the wall had a big bay window, proudly showcasing the splendour of Putrajaya's main boulevard. The clerk motioned to them to sit down on the chairs and wait. She then produced piles of papers placed in plastic files and arranged them on the table. She also brought in two bottles of mineral water and a box of tissue paper and placed them neatly in front of the vacant chair.

Saras looked about and pointed at the exit sign to Sunder.

'Look, k-a-y-l-w-a-r, again,' she said. 'Must be an obsession to find one's way out. The words are posted all over the place.'

Peering from behind his lenses, Sunder tapped his wife's shoulder gently and said, 'We all want a way out, don't we?'

Sunder has been especially apprehensive about this interview. He can't imagine Saras failing the interview. The citizenship issue has remained sticky all these years, like standing on loose ground under a climate of uncertainties. Sometimes he reports of having vivid dreams of peering over barbed wires outside tall and thick concrete walls, or waving off goodbyes during deportations at the airport departure gates, to which Saras would burst out laughing, dismissing them as inflictions caused by National Geographic. *Thank God it's not a boat Sundar*, she once scoffed. Though the potent situations were invisible all these years, the possibility of Saras taken apart from him and his sons made him anxious. Flouting immigration rules and matters could complicate matters and pose all kinds of nefarious endings, he knew. But he also believed that life cannot be sustained or contained forever by these constant struggles between the state, identity and belonging either.

It had been an arranged marriage and he had tried very hard to make it work during their early years. Like his mother, he had expected to marry a girl who would only stare at her feet when she walked, a traditional girl who would not lift her eyes or her voice in front of anybody. And so he had agreed to resign himself to his mother's wishes. He had only met Saras on his wedding day, a lavish, extravagant affair organized by his in-laws in India. The feasts lasted for three days. And of course, being a foreign groom, he was gifted large amounts of gold and a five-acre paddy field complete with a house. He had turned them away at first. *What will I do with them?* he had asked. *It is supposed to be a summer home, your house in India*, his mother had said. Rather it became a monsoon home, when they made their year-end trips to India as the weather was cooler then.

Culture shock upset Saras the minute she arrived in Malaysia. She could not get used to the food, water, climate, its people and their way of life. Homesickness took a toll on her and Sunder's introvert demeanour did not help, either. And she was no easy feat too. She was opinionated, robust, independent and highly educated. It was not until recently that Saras revealed that the paddy field was a security plan for daughters to rely on if and when a marriage withered.

'The world has changed, India has changed, have you?' she had asked him on his passive confrontation one night, unable to withstand the cold war taking place between his wife and mother. 'I did not come here to cook and clean after your mother and siblings,' she told him point blankly. 'If you think I would mope around the house chiming with an anklet, wrapped in six yards of textile, you are wrong,' she had incessantly warned him. 'And I can always go back to where I came from,' she seemed to have perpetually prepared for the one-way trip. But she was a good wife and mother, loving, caring, and dutiful and at the same time career focused, despite her threats. She did what she could in housekeeping and cooking, but she drew the line. She did not tolerate complaints or orders. In time, she had taken up a full-time job, and was currently doing her postgraduate studies. But there were problems.

The work permits were becoming a pain in the neck, with more stringent rules devised by the Ministry of Higher Education and the accreditation boards. Its confusion of what was standard, legal or recognized in its bid of controlling the ever-available pool of professional expats flooding into the private educational sectors seemed perpetual. Of course, the idea of returning to India was still rife and inviting, with the technological and infrastructure boom in the South. And for their two children, Saras had not given up on her ideas of enrolling them into institutions with English or French-based curriculums with full boarding. She had even suggested that Sunder moves to Tamil Nadu, assuring him that her family would support them, and the returns from the property that she itches to lay her hands on was promising. Sundar ignored such propositions altogether. He pointed out that Saras hardly spoke of such things when things were progressing for her. After all, a wife is obligated to follow her husband and not the other way around.

The door opened.

A short stocky man walked in, followed by the clerk. He was dressed formally, complete with a tie and blazer, though the tie was too short to reach his belly button. He had small eyes and a cheerful face. His hair was well greased; he was a little tanned and sported a shabby beard and a moustache. He seems to be a jovial man, and offered a benign smile.

'Selamat Petang,' he greeted them. Sunder exchanged the greetings.

Saras smiled, for she had been told not to speak unless she was asked to and only if she understood the question.

One of his teeth is enamelled in gold on its three sides, observed Saras.

The man bent down, took out a black and gold placard from a drawer and placed it in front of the files. It spelt out his name as Z-a-m-a-n-i. He sat down, and looked up to smile again at both Sunder and Saras. He rubbed his hands together and asked if they had taken their lunch.

'Ya, sudah,' answered Saras confidently.

A few minutes passed and Zamani had not started the interview. He busied himself and flipped through the files but did not seem to have found the correct one. He pressed a bell on the table and in came the pretty clerk again. Zamani murmured something to her and she rechecked the files. Zamani was at ease, joked with her, at which she laughed. She said sorry to him and rushed out. Zamani looked up, smiled again and tapped his fingers on the table top while he waited.

Saras drew Sunder's attention to the multiple rings he wore. All of them were either silver or brass and were mounted with stones, red, black and off-white. She counted three on the left hand and two more on the right. These were complemented by an expensive watch that hung loosely on his wrist.

'Rolex,' she tried to stir interest in Sunder.

'Yes, yes,' Sunder gave a flat reply.

'I'll ask my father to present one to you when we go back to India at the end of this year.'

'I don't wear watches.'

The door opened again and the same clerk walked in with a file in her hands. Zamani said something and burst out laughing, while the clerk smiled sheepishly. Sunder smiled too.

'You must be Saraswathy Muthuvel and Sund-e-r-a-moorthy,' Zamani said as he read from his file. 'This is your wife?' he asked.

'Yes,' said Sunder. Zamani looked up to them from his file and smiled again.

'Very convenient, he speaks in English,' whispered Saras.

'I will read all the arahan first,' Zamani said.

'Rules,' explained Sunder. 'Requirements.'

'I will read them in English,' said Zamani. 'This is an application by a married woman, whose husband, in this case Mr Sunderamoorthy, is a Malaysian citizen. And you,' he turned to Saras, 'Sarawathy Muthuvel, have fulfilled these syarat-syarat.'

Saras nodded.

'How long have you resided in Malaysia? Zamani asked the first question.

'Fourteen years,' answered Saras.

'Try to use Bahasa Melayu, please,' said Zamani.

'Belas, a-m-p-a-t belas tahun.'

'Do you intend to stay in Malaysia permanently?

'Ya,' she answered.

'Have you been of good character? Errr . . . errr . . . like . . .' Zamani seemed to be lost for examples seeing a frowning Saras.

'Like police reports, overstaying on visa . . . criminal records?'

'None, tidak ada,' answered Saras, though she knew she could have done some damage to her mother-in-law and sister-in-law who had made it known to her that come hail or thunder, she had to make chapattis for dinner seven times a week. *What's so difficult in rolling up a few doughs with loose flour and baking them on a non-stick pan?* She could not find an answer.

'Okay, very well,' said Zamani as he pondered over the file's contents. His rings gleamed in the cornice lights as he took a few sips of the mineral water and continued.

'Now, we must know if you can speak in the Malay language. Can you or can you not?'

'Can,' Sunder assured the interviewer.

'Buah-buahan, fruits you like,' Zamani asked, with a little help.

'Mangga, nangka, betik.'

'Bunga kebangsaan Malaysia,' he stated.

'Kebangsaan?' *What's that?* Saras wondered. Did the tuition teacher leave that out? She knew the word 'K-a-y-s-i-m-a-s-a-n,' it was written all over buildings and ambulances. But what was the word again? She wished she could hear it again.

'Kebangsaan, kebangsaan, national, national flower,' Zamani translated at last.

'Owh,' Saras tapped on her forehead, relieved. 'Hibiscus,' she blurted. 'I mean, sorry, bunga, bunga raya,' she let out her words confidently.

'Awak datang dari mana?' Zamani asked.

A few seconds passed. Dating, dating, dating . . . Saras recited, hoping to catch its meaning. Then, datang means 'come', she recollected in time.

Sunder was whispering something to her now.

'K-e-l-l-a-n-g,' she said. Then she remembered that she was from India. *Klang or India, India,* she decided.

'Oh, India?' Zamani's eyes lighted up. 'Bollywood . . . *kah?*' he asked. 'Amitabh Bachan, Dixit Dixit . . . Dimple Kapadia, Rajesh Khanna, Dharmendra . . . Shah Rukh Khan . . .' He enlisted the names of his idols. 'Datok Shah Rukh Khan,' he murmured.

'No . . . no,' Saras corrected him. 'Me, saya . . . Kollywood, South . . . South . . . Rajinikanth, Kamal Hassan, Sri Devi, Aishwarya Rai . . .'

'Aishwarya Rai, Kollywood?' he seemed puzzled. 'You know, Bobby, you like?' he asked.

Bobby? Like Bobby what? . . . Who? bemused Saras.

But then Zamani was enveloped by an aura of excitement and he was cheerful. Clearing his throat, he looked about his voice for the right pitch, an octave . . . *'tum syair, toh nehiiii . . .'* he recanted, hitting creakingly on a high note, and climbed even higher, '*magallll*' . . . and stopped, and started to cough profusely, panting heavily.

Saras sat, almost shocked and puzzled by his relics.

Zamani's cough had not ceased and he was trying very politely to clear his throat again. He struggled in his seat, and touched his pockets, produced a pack of Marlborough cigarettes, a lighter and a handkerchief, and placed them on the table.

'Excuse me,' he said, pleased with his demonstration.

Sunder leaned closer to her and said, 'Play along . . . play along. Help him with the lyrics.'

'What do you mean? Sing along?' She protested. *I did not grow up singing Hindi songs, I'm South Indian*, she wanted to emphasise. And she had no obsession for cinema either.

'*Tum pass aiye, kiu mushkuraiye . . .*' Zamani continued with another hit number, this time gracefully moving his hands in the air and pointing towards Saras. '*Kuchu kuchu hota hai . . .*' before bursting into another spurt of shy but loud giggles.

Saras raised her hands and clapped. For once, her anxiety faded. Sunder was smiling too, and had now straightened his legs.

'Kahwin cinta? Or arranged,' Zamani asked about the nature of their marriage.

'Ya,' Saras answered, hoping to end the interview as soon as possible.

'Arranged,' Sunder butted in time.

Then Zamani checked himself, drank some more mineral water, and pulled himself together.

'Suka makan apa?' he asked.

Makan, that's an easy word. Everyone used it at work. And she too had learned to use it with ease. *Probably he's asking for my favourite food.*

Satay, r-a-i-n-dang, kari-pop, pau, puttu mayam. Should she add Teh Tarik, Neslo and kopi kaw-kaw? But she dropped the idea.

Zamani looked into his watch and his expression became serious.

'Suka tinggal di Malaysia?' he asked.

'Ya, chukka,' she answered.

Didn't he want me to sing the national anthem? she thought.

He looked at the watch again, and quickly turned the pages of the completed forms in the folder. He took another form from the table, made a brief note and put a legal stamp on it. He did not say much thereafter.

He pressed the bell for the clerk, turned to Sunder and said something. Sunder got up to go and shake hands with him.

Zamani looked at Saras and said something unintelligible.

Saying goodbye, she thought.

Not wanting to be rude, and wanting to demonstrate some leave-taking cues in the local language, she got up and said, 'Saya mahu p-o-o-r-k-i.'

Both Zamani and the clerk stopped for a while. Sunder frowned at her.

Poorki means to go, to leave, what's wrong with that? Saras thought. *Oh dear, I'm lost for words, again!* And she had totally forgotten to hear herself before she uttered anything. Peki, puki, peki, peki . . . *oh yes*, she remembered, *pergi* . . . and she corrected herself.

'Saya mahu p-e-r-g-i, saya k-a-y-l-w-a-r,' she said.

Zamani laughed hysterically. So did the clerk as she pointed them the door.

Closing the door behind him, Sunder shook his head.

'You just called him a bloody c-u-n-t!' he said gravely.

'Aiyo, kadavuleh, I did? I should have been careful,' she regretted. 'Shiva, Shiva,' she prayed. 'Should I go in and say sorry? Mintak maap?'

Sunder took a deep breath. 'Let's get ourselves to Alamanda, shall we?' he said, picking up the rolled Google map on their way out and into Putrajaya.

Kari Curry

Vijayakumar slouched in his chair. The workers scuttled about, carrying rolls of fresh banana leaves, platters of side dishes and curries and vegetables. 'Plain rice or parboiled?' the waiter asked in Tamil. Not receiving any reply, he repeated, 'Plain or parboiled, *saar*?' Alice, Vijayakumar's client, pinched his elbow. Startled, he shook off his temporary daze and rubbed his eyes.

'Parboil,' Vijayakumar replied, watching lumps of steaming rice being served on a large banana leaf before him with an assortment of vegetables. The aroma refreshed his dull mind and stirred his appetite.

Should I tell them about the mango tree? He wondered.

'Sorry, been sleepless for almost a fortnight,' he apologized to the young Chinese couple, running his hands over the sharp stubble on his cheeks. Dereck Ho, Alice's husband, nodded gently. His eyes were fixed on the waiter serving his food, as if it were a live art performance.

'Alice, why not use your fingers?' Vijayakumar suggested. 'That fork is going to tear the leaf.' He pointed to a trickle of saambar already running towards the edge of the table. 'Look at Dereck,' he chuckled, even though there was curry all over his palms. 'Well done.'

'I'll be gentle,' said Alice, turning the fork sideways to gather the rice.

A small plate of mutton curry appeared in front of Vijayakumar. He looked up questioningly.

'I ordered it,' Dereck said, smiling.

'Oh, no problem, Dereck. Enjoy the food. If you'd like to try something else, let me know.'

'Thank you,' said Alice. A thin smile appeared on her small, clear face. 'So, how much is the property going for?' She tucked her hair behind her ears. 'Can we bargain?'

Dereck grunted softly, nibbling at a piece of chicken *varuval*. 'Sure *lah*,' he gurgled.

'The market price of a single bungalow unit at a strategic location is 2.95 million ringgit,' said Vijayakumar.

'Fine, fine,' Dereck replied. 'But we have to see the property first. You know, we need to get that feeling, that comfortable feeling, that the house wants us kind of feeling.' He turned to Alice, his lips coated with a thin film of oil. She shook her head and passed some serviettes to him.

'No problem,' Vijayakumar assured them. 'We'll go immediately after lunch, the property is nearby,' he said.

'Is there a lot of work that needs to be done?' asked Alice, splitting a crispy masala pomfret's head into two.

'The house is about forty years old,' said Vijayakumar. 'Most of the furniture is gone. The plumbing and wiring needs to be reinstalled.' Grabbing the opportunity, he blurted out nervously, 'There is a rather large old mango tree in the front yard . . .'

'Oh, that's lovely,' said Alice, clasping her palms together. 'We don't mind.'

Dereck laughed. 'If we buy the house,' he said, 'could you arrange for a bank loan?'

'Yes, yes, of course,' Vijayakumar responded. 'The current interest rate is 4.6 per cent, I can arrange for that.

Also, the lawyer's S&P and insurance, if you like,' he said with some excitement stirring in his stomach. 'But let's enjoy the lunch first.' He wondered again if he should elaborate on the mango tree.

It had been Vijayakumar's habit to have lunch at the Lotus Restaurant at Jalan Gasing before he brought clients over to view his properties. *A good meal makes happy customers, and happy customers make promising buyers*, he believed. Though he was an engineer, real estate had been so lucrative in Petaling Jaya that he had ventured into it on a part-time basis for the last five years. The handsome commissions were enticing and occasional free stays at the new luxury properties were very welcoming. But despite all these, he had another purpose: to do away with a part of his past. It was Aunty Deepa's property, trailing him like a shadow. It held memories that had started revisiting him lately, with strange streaks of blurred visions during the day and stalked him in his dreams at night. His wife believed they would drive him mad very soon. *Your uncle's spirit is restless. You are holding on to something that was never intended for you*, she had warned him.

Vijayakumar finished eating his lunch, and washed it down with a tumbler of rasam. Alice and Dereck sat like obedient children, nibbling quietly on the *appalam* as if Aunty Deepa stood watching over them with a cane. *No talking with your mouth full.* Dereck licked the gravy off his fingers. *Aunty Deepa would have smacked him,* Vijayakumar thought. Alice was more prudent. Her fork and spoon lay on the folded banana leaf. 'No, fold it towards yourself, Dereck,' she told her husband. Dereck merely flipped the folded leaf, spilling curry from its open end. Like children, they giggled. *Aunty Deepa would have smacked him again*, Vijayakumar chuckled at the thought.

'How far is the property?' asked Dereck, slurping the last bit of his mango *lassi*, his eyebrows knitted.

'It's about 600 metres from the main road,' Vijayakumar told him. 'Quite visible, too.' He was aware that nobody invested three or four million ringgit on a half-century old decaying house to live in. Most were converted into business properties, either urban spas or showrooms for luxury cars, boutiques or galleries to cater to the rich, upmarket residents. Alice and Dereck were art collectors. They were planning to open a branch in Kuala Lumpur, with one already established in Johor Bharu. They had been his only clients so far who had not grumbled about the price. It was the location they were after.

But I must inform them about the mango tree.

* * *

It was an old wives' tale that adopting a child would bring a baby to one's own womb. Vijayakumar did not remember his parents. He had a fleeting memory of the tranquil moments before the loud, shuddering noises came and the shrill cries of women pierced his ears, when he was five. The bloodied, headless bodies of unknown people floated into his dreams.

It was through Shanta, Aunty Deepa's live-in maid and confidante, that Vijayakumar pieced his life's puzzles together. He relied on Shanta's oblique narration as Aunty Deepa never talked about his adoption. When the army shelled his village, he was placed among the dead bodies, swathed in a bloodied canvas and besieged by flies, in the hope that a relative or an NGO would pick him up. Luckily, his birthplace remained almost as a caste mark, Aunty Deepa's ancestral village of Kilinochi in Jaffna. She found him through an agent, rather a child trafficker. He was six years old when she christened him Vijayakumar, officially becoming his legal guardian against her husband's wishes.

'Why won't you learn to be a mother?' Shanta used to question Aunty Deepa.

'I'm a child myself, I have no time to mother a child,' Aunty Deepa lamented, turning to her seeps of chamomile tea, waiting the late nights out for Uncle de Silva to return from the club.

Uncle de Silva, Aunty Deepa's husband, was edgy, most of the time. At the most, he nodded or shouted impatiently to communicate. He left for work early in the morning after a short hike up Gasing Hill, once he had filled his belly with three glasses of warm water. At 8.30, the servants carried his black cloak and briefcase into the Bentley and waited until he was chauffeured away. Shanta told Vijayakumar that he was old enough to be his grandfather. Throughout his life, Uncle de Silva had only spoken to Vijayakumar in sibilant sounds or curt noises.

'*Shooo . . . hush . . . sheeesh . . .*'

The year Vijayakumar turned twelve, Aunty Deepa completed her PhD and the mango tree appeared in the front yard. *It is a male tree*, Shanta declared after two seasons. *No fruits.*

Uncle de Silva stayed home on most Saturdays, and if he was in a good mood, he chatted with Aunty Deepa and made dirty jokes. Aunty Deepa was pleased, grateful for the casual air that filled the house. Uncle, dressed in his chequered sarong and white pagoda bunion, sometimes tattered with holes and patches. *Keep the mutton coming*, he would screech until he let out his signature belch that almost shook the house.

'PhD in what?'

'Etymology'

'What is etymology?

'Study of words, WORDS, Alfred de Silva.'

'Haven't you anything else to study? Poppadom?'

'Fry your arse and pop-a-dom, Alfred!'

On such Saturdays, they would talk and laugh sonorously over gin and tonic until they staggered to their bedroom. Uncle de Silva did not raise his voice. Nothing broke or tumbled to suggest a quarrel. But the wee hours of a particular Sunday morning carried a strange muffled crying from their bedroom.

'Alfred, how could you? Not attend our own party? Why on earth do you have to be away? Of all places, Fraser's Hill on a Saturday? Has this marriage become so stuffy?' Aunty Deepa sniffled.

That's when Vijayakumar heard the inevitable news.

'He wants to marry his mistress. He wants a child.' The servants smacked their lips, their faces grey between approval and disapproval.

'A child of his own,' Shanta whispered.

* * *

Vijayakumar took a left turn after the restaurant at Jalan Gasing and announced, 'We're here, Section 5.' Alice nodded thoughtfully.

'Very near to the main road,' Dereck announced, somewhat gaily, shaking his head.

'Isn't it? And near to many other facilities, too.' He brought his car to a halt and got down. It was half past three; a pleasant breeze brought down the afternoon heat. He wiped away the sweat on his forehead and lifted the latch over the rusty gates and entered. Alice and Dereck followed Vijayakumar into the compound, taking in the sights and smells.

Old memories, like pitcher plants, threatened to trap and dissolve him once he entered the compound. A grove of banana plantains crowded the left side of the large lawn. A large mango tree guarded the right side of the porch. The one and a half storey bungalow sagged between them, almost eaten away by time. The missing cast iron grilles have left gaping dark holes where they once guarded the house's privacy. The walls were pockmarked with cracking plaster while rotten wood hung about the adorned door frames. Faded plastic wires competing with evergreen epiphyte ferns dangled about freely like arthritic fingers all along the porch. He checked the verandah where Uncle de Silva sat in the evenings to smoke his cheroots. Nothing stirred despite the breeze.

Dereck kicked a pebble and rubbed his hands, observing the decayed roof tiles. Alice ran a finger along the inner walls of the gate post and plucked a hibiscus.

Good, they are already talking to the house, Vijaykumar assured himself. 'The property is also very near to a number of facilities,' he repeated, aware that most customers made investigations prior to their visit, and proceeded to the main door of the house.

'Such as?' asked Alice, looking up the mango tree. 'Does it still fruit?'

'Yes, it does, occasionally. Shall we look around the house first?' Vijayakumar suggested.

'What's the built-in size of the house?' asked Dereck.

'4,300 square feet, on a 10,300 square-feet land size.'

'What kind of facilities?' Alice repeated.

'Owh, Asuntha Hospital and EPF are down the road. KL is fifteen or twenty minutes from here, depending on the traffic, and from Jalan Gasing, we are accessible to a number of city link roads, the KESAS, LDP and the Federal Highway that connects to the KLIA and the North—South Expressway. And PJ Newtown too is only five minutes from here.'

Alice nodded, her hands wound around the thick, calloused tree trunk. The hibiscus now rested at the base of the tree like a peace offering. Vijayakumar wanted her to get away from it, but dared not dampen her interest. *The tree and master need their space*, he reckoned. 'Let's go,' he said as he ushered them towards the house.

Dereck helped Alice brush away the silky cobwebs that came undone and floated towards them as they walked onto the large porch. Vijayakumar then unlocked the padlock that chained the grilles of the main door. Dereck extended one of his hands and helped to push the front door open rather impatiently.

A rusted chandelier hung from the ceiling, shrouded by yarns of cobwebs. Alice and Dereck took small steps, as if they were spiritually connecting with every part of the house. They inhaled the musty air, felt every tile and paint, pressed old switches and scampered barefoot on the dirty but cool terrazzo. Then they paused. A huge stuffed head of an elephant stared from the wall in the dining area. Alice giggled excitedly and pointed to it. *It's yours*, Vijayakumar signalled. Not having to explain and show around, he slumped against a wall himself. Feeling its vibrations, he entwined his heartbeats with the rhythmic story it held. He closed his eyes, lulled by the disembodied voices echoing around him.

* * *

Two weeks before the party, a strange scrawny man with an overgrown beard appeared at the gates with a woman, one who made Uncle de Silva fold his papers and retreat into the house. Aunty Deepa gave them a snooty welcome. The hawk-eyed man, called Naren, stood away from the woman, smoking his *bidi*, but engulfed in deep thought. They were given the gardener's shed to settle in. Sometimes Naren came back from short outings and locked himself in the servant's latrine. Or he curled up in his room and slept for hours on end. Unperturbed by Aunty Deepa's and Uncle's show of displeasure, the woman, his wife, lounged about the house like a tourist, much to Shanta's annoyance. 'Every one hour want coffee. Every one hour want food. Is she the new boss?' she sniggered.

'I'll get that drug addict jailed,' Uncle de Silva said after a week. 'Get your prodigal brother out of my house.'

The servants did not like him either because of his lecherous stare. But he was good use in the kitchen. It actually stopped the servants from manhandling the poultry before they were slaughtered. Under Naren's hands, both knife and animal obeyed. Chicken, geese or turkey stopped squawking or thrashing about, but stood hypnotized under his glare. During Deepavali, he had the honour of slaughtering the Boer goat Uncle de Silva had bought. *Only Naren knows*, the servants agreed, *to pull down the goat's ears to its neck; the point where the glinting knife slices the jugular vein, painless and soundless.*

* * *

'The mosaic is still intact,' Alice's voice echoed from one of the five bedrooms. Vijayakumar moved away from his thoughts. 'I like the terrazzo.'

'We need to polish it,' Dereck murmured, his attention clearly on something else.

Vijayakumar was not pleased. Anyone would be charmed by an old bungalow. They were hardly anything like the flimsy houses built these days. The concrete was solid and the timber stood with time. The plumbing was more efficient, except for the rusting pipes. Wiring and switch boards needed attention. But there could be termites, too. And the renovation would cost a bomb. The dust from the floor rose and tickled his nose.

'Very nice barbecue pit,' Dereck said as he came up the hallway.

'My aunty used to have parties in the garden, her lamb kebabs were a must,' Vijayakumar said, feeling squeamish. 'But . . .' he began and stopped. Dereck was already stepping outside to make a call.

Damn, just when I was about to talk about the mango tree, sighed Vijayakumar, gently punching his arm.

* * *

On the day of Aunty Deepa's party, Vijayakumar woke up to the sound of footsteps on the patio bordering his bedroom and the garden. Looking out, he found the Bentley missing from the porch. Aunty Deepa was pacing about with Shanta, waiting for Naren to return from the market. It was raining heavily.

Though Uncle de Silva had left, his leather shoes remained in the shoe cabinet and his pungent cologne lingered over the breakfast table. If he was not at home, there were only two other places he could be: at the Country Club or his mistress's condo in Ampang.

Lately, Aunty Deepa had stopped brewing her cup of chamomile tea. Instead, her conversations had increased with Naren, while he smoked his bidis like an active volcano. Naren looked agitated as he entered the house in a clumsy stupor, balancing a bulging sack of groceries on his shoulders. Shanta thought his pupils were dilated.

'He's mad,' she reported.

'Of course he is mad. Don't step on his toes. He was imprisoned in Pudu for gouging out the eyes of an opponent. He swallowed them,' Aunty Deepa sneered at her complaint. Naren chuckled.

Aunty Deepa took over the food preparations for the party. Much to Shanta's annoyance, she was reduced to scraping three halved coconuts for the kerisik while the other servants peeled, cut, and ground the ingredients. Naren prepared the meat. By the time he was done with the cleaning, slicing, dicing, cubing and mincing, his elbows were soaked in roasted spices, ground chilli and turmeric paste. Pepper and coriander powder wafted in the cool morning air. Onion and garlic peels, lemongrass stalks, curry leaves and pudina stems littered the kitchen. By late morning, when the masala had been churned into two large lumps and the meat had marinated in large silver cauldrons, Aunty Deepa dismissed the servants.

'Come back next week,' she told them as they stood about, bewildered. Little did they know only Shanta would remain employed, come Monday.

Silence engulfed the house thereafter, eerie and foreboding. Naren was fidgeting around the kitchen, smoking so many bidis that Aunty Deepa had to ask him to stop. She left the kitchen late afternoon, filling the house with the smell of curries, soraputtu cutlets and sweet caramel. A caterer delivered naan and a huge cauldron of vegetable biryani.

'Look at this smart young man,' said Aunty Deepa, pinching Vijayakumar on his cheeks. 'Purple looks so good on him, right?' she asked a smirking Naren. 'Now, Vijayakumar,' she said, straightening the collars and pulling the sleeves of his jippa. 'Wait for the guests at the gate, shake hands first, address those you don't know as sir or madam. Then, bring them to me,' she instructed. 'Don't eat in front of the guests, we are the hosts, remember? Ask Naren to give you something to eat if you get hungry.'

The faculty members, except for the Dean and Uncle de Silva's family members, arrived first. Aunty Deepa's close friend, Sally, arrived last with her family. Soon, they surrounded the twelve-seater dining table, filling their plates with skewered lamb kebabs, mutton curry and kurma, lamb kheema, vodka-lime-mint cocktails and liquor, as well as pastries that glowed golden under the glossy chandelier.

Vijayakumar walked into the kitchen and found Naren's wife gorging on fried chicken. She pointed to a KFC barrel sitting in the middle of the table to him. 'Eat quickly,' she said with her mouth full. The kitchen table was already messed up with discarded skin and bones, sauce sachets and spilled carbonated drinks. He looked around for the home-cooked meals he looked forward to eat, but they were not served here. KFC proved to be uninviting amidst the lingering smell of spices and curries of the day. Vijayakumar arranged two drumsticks and a few potato wedges on his plate. 'Stay here,' Naren's wife almost screeched unkindly. He would rather hear the adults talk than be in her company. He walked off to the living room.

'Hey Deepa, why no salad?' Sally asked from across the table.

'Because we are *kari* people. So, we focused on kari,' Aunty Deepa said, smiling mischievously, looking resplendent in a violet dinner dress, with a large butterfly brooch pinning her breasts tightly.

'Kari?' Sally asked perturbed. 'Isn't all these curry?' she asked. A few guests had gathered about, listening to the conversation.

'Well, kari simply means meat. Meat swimming in a condiment of spices is "curry",' Aunty Deepa explained.

'True,' the Head of Department chipped in. 'In south India, people tell you that they are off to the market to buy kari, in other words, carrion.'

'But there is much confusion here,' Aunty Deepa continued. 'Kari also meant charcoal, it also connoted grease,' she said.

'And in some instances,' the Head of Department continued, 'if you had kari smirched on your face, you've euphemistically got shame on your face,' he said, chuckling.

'But curry is curry, where is the confusion?' asked Sally.

'The curry we refer to is the anglicized term for the Tamil word kari. It's been used to denote carcass, until the British generalized and termed the colloquial kari, curry,' she said, her eyes twinkling. 'Dewitt and Gerlach have much to be blamed for.'

'So, what do we have here? Lots of kari curries?' asked Sally.

'Exactly,' Aunty Deepa snapped her fingers. 'Or kari kolambu.

'Etymology,' she explained to her neighbours. 'I did a study on the origins of words, et-uh-mol-uh-jee,' she said, moving her lips in circular motion.

Her neighbours stood tight-lipped. 'Waaah, a degree just to study one word eh, good for you, good for you,' they patted her back. Aunty Deepa laughed heartily.

Everybody wanted to know where Uncle de Silva was. Aunty Deepa jokingly told them that he was at his mistress's house, shocking them with her indifference. She walked about, making constant eye contact with Naren, who was diligently dishing out the kebabs, mutton curry, lamb kheema and the bone in mutton kurma. Apart from uncle's whereabouts and her dress, the ladies were inquisitive about where she had gotten the kari from. They pestered her for the secret ingredient. *Papaya leaves marinate? Candlenut? Or simply crushed poppy seeds? How could mutton and lamb be cooked to such perfection?* 'It simply melts on the tongue, like sashimi,' another guest complimented her.

Only one guest complained about the food. It was Uncle de Silva's father, bent on a walking stick as he moved around the dining table.

'Why isn't Alfred here?' he asked with fatherly concern. His family members ignored him, busying themselves with the cocktails and food.

'Is this mutton,' he asked, 'or venison? It's sweet and tender, a little too pink for red meat,' he said, suckling the pieces of meat and then spitting them onto his plate. He lifted a bone from the *kari* curry and inspected it.

The Head of Department seemed to agree. 'It has a burnt taste, like the crispy tops of siew yok,' he said.

'Senile,' Uncle de Silva's brother brushed off his father's burlesque behaviour and whispered something into his ear.

'No, look at this. The bone marrow is missing, the cartilage is too hollow for a goat. Is it beef? Pork or a horse?' he deliberated loudly, drawing laughter from the guests.

'The kari in the curry has the consistency of beef, but the kebab has a musty taste, like mushrooms,' added Sally, turning about the thin bamboo skewer.

'Give him some whiskey,' Aunty Deepa instructed Naren. 'On the rocks,' she said, her eyebrows rising in a sharp arc.

'And the lamb shanks, Deepa,' the Head of Department butted in.

'What about them?' Aunty asked sullenly.

'They come off so easily, bittersweet and soft,' he said. 'And there is no odour in these meats. That's the best part. I really want to know how you managed to reduce the greasy odour,' he crinkled his chin.

The old man thanked Naren when he passed him whiskey with a few ice cubes in a short glass. He took a gulp. In a few minutes, he sat hunched on the dining chair, his dentures exposed in a scary grin. Naren deftly moved him into one of the rooms.

Aunty Deepa moved away from the table, occasionally nodding her head to the guests and raising her glass to compliments she received from them. She was extremely pleased when Naren came sniggering towards her.

'The kari curries, all finished,' he announced.

'What about the kurma?' she asked.

'A few shanks are left,' he said.

'Kebabs?' she checked again.

'I've fed it to the dogs. No one touched it,' he said.

'Good. Make sure nobody packs anything home,' she instructed. 'Tell them we are running short ourselves and we expect more guests to come,' she said, her eyes, cold as steel.

'What about the curried kari?' he asked.

'We'll finish that last, thank God we buried the innards earlier' she said, releasing a puff of air.

'Who's that?' she asked Naren, alarmed. 'Somebody is vomiting in the toilet.'

'It's Sally,' he said. 'She must have had too much kari masala.'

The toilet flush gurgled and out came Sally, her cheeks flushed.

'I'm feeling unwell, Deepa, I think I'll call it a day then,' Sally said, her face twitching in pain.

'Come, let me help you,' Aunty Deepa reached out to her and held her close. 'Shall I take you to the clinic?' she asked, concerned.

'No, no Deepa, I'll take leave for now,' Sally stuttered, dabbing tissue paper on her forehead. 'Where is Vijayakumar?' she asked. Naren found him slumbering on the sofa in the hall. 'Get up lazy head, *akka* is calling you,' he said. Sally picked up a red envelope from her handbag and gave it to Vijayakumar. 'It's ok, I did not buy anything for him on the way, this young man is very tall now,' she complimented when Aunty Deepa gently pushed away the gift. Vijayakumar only accepted it when Aunty Deepa nodded.

'Say thank you,' she chirped. 'Walk Aunty Sally to her car,' she instructed as the two women embraced in a warm hug.

Vijayakumar returned to find Naren whispering to Aunty Deepa.

'What about the head?' Naren asked, his voice breaking as Aunty Deepa moved out from the dining room.

'I'll take care of it,' she said, a smug smile on her narrow face.

Naren cleared the tables as the guests began to leave. The head that Naren mentioned had been packed. 'Roasted head of the goat,' he told Vijayakumar cockily. It looked like a large oval ball, rather a pineapple in an aluminium foil. Naren twisted the top loose end of the foil and fastened it with a raffia string. Not knowing where to place it, he left it to sit on a large porcelain tray in the middle of the dining table.

'Touch it, you will die,' he warned Vijayakumar. 'Now, go and feed these to the dogs,' he pointed to a large brass pot.

'But you've already fed them,' Vijayakumar protested. 'Not them you idiot, the strays outside the gate,' he said, dumping the unfinished lamb kebab and kheema onto the leftover biryani rice and naan breads before giving the kari pot a good shake. 'Now, go,' he ordered, raising his eyebrows.

Vijayakumar did as he was told. By the time he returned, Naren was feverishly scrubbing the pots and pans and cauldrons with his wife.

'You can go back to bed,' he said.

'But I have had no dinner,' Vijayakumar pleaded. 'I'm hungry.'

'He had KFC,' his wife butted in.

'That was dinner, now go away before I pull your ears,' he warned.

The clock showed 1 a.m.

'Aunty told me not to touch the food,' Vijayakumar tried to reason, disappointed.

'I will ask Naren's wife to make you hot Milo. Maybe there are cakes and fruit left on the table. Take them to your room,' Aunty Deepa's voice assailed somewhere from the living area.

Uncle de Silva's father's snores echoed across the dining area from the servant's quarters where he had been left for the night. With moist eyes, Vijayakumar scanned the dining table for leftovers. He managed to pick up a scone, slices of watermelon and splotches of custard pudding. Naren was busy in the kitchen, flipping the brass and silverware. Aunty Deepa walked into the dining room and ruffled Vijayakumar's hair.

'Go to your room, eat and sleep well. Go get your Milo in the kitchen,' she said, and picked up the wrapped goat's head.

She did not notice that Vijayakumar had returned from the kitchen after fetching his drink and was standing at the staircase between the hall and the dining room. She returned to the living room and slumped on the rattan sofa. She nestled her head on a soft brocade cushion propped against the wall and held the goat's head close to her. Vijayakumar wondered if she was going to eat it. She pulled the knot and it began to unwind like Hershey's chocolate strips. An acrid smell arose from the package and dark grease flowed away from its folds. Suddenly, Naren let out a shrill cry. Shocked, Vijayakumar dropped his plate and cup. The smashing china broke the silence. Aunty Deepa turned to look at them, her face shrivelled into a taut ball. Vijayakumar stood gawking until Naren pulled his collar and slapped him hard.

Aunty Deepa lodged a missing person's report, two days later. A week after, the police found a decomposing torso, arms and feet packed into an old sugar sack in the thickets of Bukit Gasing. Naren identified Uncle de Silva's wrist watch. The Bentley was found parked at the Shivan hill-top temple. The innards were missing, so were the thighs and buttocks. The gruesome murder of the famous prosecution lawyer shook the town with terror. The police returned a box, tightly wrapped and secured with duct tapes that was transferred into a gilded coffin and cremated. After the sixteenth day, when prayers had been offered for the soul's official departure into the netherworld, a mango sapling let out its first leaves. Naren knotted a red saffron thread around its stem, to ward off evil eyes.

'Who planted the mango tree?' asked Shanta when she came back to work the following week.

'Nobody,' said Naren. 'Maybe it grew from a seed you carelessly threw away,' he accused her.

'I swear I don't do such things,' Shanta raised her voice.

'Just leave it there,' Aunty Deepa interrupted them. 'Would be nice to have mango chutneys made from our own fruits,' she said.

* * *

The narrow leaves of the mango tree rustled in the evening wind. Alice and Dereck had taken almost two hours to scrutinize the property. Vijayakumar was aware that Dereck had made a number of discreet calls. He walked towards the couple, who were now standing under the tree, deliberating.

'They are the KL Towers,' Vijayakumar pointed to the tall pink building that gave off bright lights from its single pillar. The sky had darkened over Kuala Lumpur, promising a heavy downpour.

'Beautiful,' said Alice. 'I bet the scenery is better from the balcony,' she said.

'We'll take it,' Dereck decided on his purchase. 'You can process the papers.'

'The mango tree . . .' Vijayakumar began. He was still unsure of unravelling the story. He knew it would detract his sale, or worst fail. These were promising customers.

'What about the mango tree?' Dereck's face tightened.

'It's a male tree,' Vijayakumar mumbled nervously. 'It has not yielded any fruits in almost thirty years,' he said.

Alice looked confused.

'And,' he took in a deep breath, 'the neighbours have reported seeing something.'

'Oh dear,' Dereck said gravely. Alice moved to his side.

'Neighbours have seen a fat man, looking for something around the tree after midnight,' he rushed his words, short of breath. 'He was headless.'

Silence ensued. A car passed by slowly. Vijayakumar wondered if this was another mistake.

Then, Dereck burst out laughing. Alice laughed too. 'We'll keep it. It's part of the landscape, we'll keep the ghost, too.'

Alice pointed upwards. And there were the unmistakable dark green twigs, protruding from the foliage, heavy with light green flowers.

Vijayakumar shook hands with Alice and Dereck. He was sure there would be no more hazy daydreams. No more sleepless nights. The house in Section 5, Jalan Gasing, PJ, was *SOLD*!

Shooting the Breeze

I'm not sure why I consented to this meeting, I think to myself regretfully. The afternoon sun is at its pinnacle and the roadside cafeteria is being pummelled by hot dust. The noise from the incessant traffic with the vehicles' metallic glares reflecting on the only vacant table where I'm sitting is not helping either. Sometimes, when friends and family say that I am too soft and my ever-ready heart that embraces other people's problems is the weakest spot in my character, I refuse to accept it until I am put in a spot like this one. It's 1.15 now, three quarters of an hour have passed since I've been sitting here. The sweet-looking waitress has approached me twice to take my order. She kindly says I can call her whenever I am ready. I'm sure she's baffled at my business here. There is no sign of Kugesh. On top of all this, I have come to meet a friend who has never heeded my advice and warnings and who has only made matters worse for himself, like a rogue elephant throwing sand on its own head!

Just when I have finished my second glass of warm water and decide to call it a day, Kugesh walks hurriedly into the cafeteria, wearing a long-sleeved tee and short khakis. He comes straight towards me and pulls a chair. The sound of his flip-flops lingers long after he is seated. His eyes are bloodshot, it's obvious he's overslept. I can see stubble spread in uneven patches over his oval face, the white outnumbering the black. His curved sideburns are a sign that he has not been to the salon for some time. I'm annoyed that he fixes his gaze at the traffic building up the road instead. I choose to remain silent, afraid that my own mood would misbehave. *I'm here for an old friend*, I tell myself, *so sit tight*. A few seconds pass. Neither of us speaks.

'Hello Jeevs,' Kugesh greets me, extending his right hand for a handshake. 'How are you? Sorry, I am late,' he apologizes, as though he is reading from a script. 'You took a drink without me?' he asks jokingly, pointing to the two empty glasses on the table.

'You came late, mister, what do you expect me to do?' I reply. 'I'm drunk on water now.'

Kugesh chuckles shyly, covering his mouth. 'Really Jeevs?' he asks worriedly, while toying with the plastic flower on the table. 'Shall I locate the gents?' he asks. 'It can't be that bad, right, Jeevs?'

We both laugh and my mood is pacified.

I signal for the waitress and order a cappuccino, aware of gastric building up in my empty belly. 'Another cappuccino and some chips,' I tell the waitress, noticing that Kugesh is not responding with any orders.

'You want something or not?' I frown playfully. 'Have you had your lunch, Kugesh?'

'Yes, I had brunch. Quite hungry now,' he says and rubs his stomach. 'Will you get me a muffin? Vanilla.' He quipped.

'Of course, I'll get you anything you want, my friend,' I tell him. I swallow hard, my annoyance drowned by rising sympathy for my best friend. I smile quietly, reminiscing our old school days. It was Kugesh who used to drag me to the canteen during recess time and buy me a glass of soy milk and prawn fritters at ten cents each, during the five years we were together in upper secondary. I realize how much time has changed everything between us, especially the course of our lives.

A few minutes pass. The periodical silence has engulfed us again. I'm not sure how I should start the conversation apart from the repeated exchange of greetings.

'How are you?' Kugesh asks, again.

I nod, feeling silly. I keep thinking of the office files I've left behind at home. 'As usual, busy with work and more work. How have you been?'

'Sorry, I have not been taking your calls or replying to your text messages,' he says apologetically. 'The medication . . . it's the medication,' he whimpers. 'Look what's happened to me. My life is defined by Seraquel 50 mg and Eticim 100 mg, but the doses are just too much. It keeps me groggy all the time; it's been difficult to stay awake, even now Jeevs.'

'I understand,' I reply, empathizing with him. 'But here I am, Kugesh. What's the matter? You sounded frantic when you called last night.'

'I don't know, Jeevs,' Kugesh sighs. His eyes are slightly squinting; I could sense his speech slurring. I encourage him to drink a glass of water, which he declines.

'It's been a hectic month,' Kugesh begins. 'The doctors prescribed a heavier dosage of Eticim. I stopped taking it altogether. Two weeks later, I found myself at the Psychiatric ward at the GH. I had progressed into manic depression, the nurses told me.'

A sudden pang fills my heart. I don't know if it is safe to be sitting here, not knowing how to handle the situation if Kugesh turns manic. I remember manic depression can translate into aggression. Kugesh was put under observation last year when he threatened his family members with a machete.

'Don't worry, I am fine now,' he declares with a chuckle as if he has sensed my paranoia. 'Only sad,' he says, looking downcast.

'Why Kugesh?' I implore. 'What's making you sad? You're back at work, salary is running, and you look healthier now,' I compliment him, leaning over the table and giving a pat on his shoulders. 'Cheer up,' I tell him warmly.

The orders arrive. Without hesitating, Kugesh starts chomping on the muffin and my share of the potato chips. *He's never had such an appetite*, I remember. He had never been a good eater between the two of us. In fact, he used to be my worst critic where vanity was concerned. He was almost six feet tall and represented the school in swimming. His tanned complexion and athletic build made the girls tipsy. On the contrary, I was an ordinary next-door guy until I met him and started taking grooming seriously. Kugesh took me into his party circuits and friendship circles and exposed me to the world—his world, more like it. That's how I became Jeevs.

'You can have this, Kugesh,' I slowly push my plate of potato chips towards him.

'What about you?' he asks, concerned.

'I had one while I was waiting for you,' I lie to him. 'But I think I'll order two chicken burgers now, I'm hungry as well,' I tell him and signal for the waitress to come.

He nods, thoughtfully.

'So, what have the lawyers advised you,' I ask cautiously, 'about the divorce?'

'Getting her to consent for mutual dissolution, but climbing the Everest is easier, I think.'

* * *

Five years ago, I was taken by surprise when I got a call from Kugesh. We were both working in separate states, but kept in touch occasionally. He had agreed to an arranged marriage. The most outgoing party animal I'd known had resorted to a match-make? I was baffled. We talked it out and I agreed to accompany him on the first official visit to the girl's home with his family. Looking resplendent in a parrot-pink silk sari with green and gold borders, Wani was pretty, elegant, and exhibited pleasant demeanours when she presented the tea. She stood tall enough to match Kugesh's height, sensually proportionate, and was extremely fair in complexion. She was a school teacher and the youngest in her family. Kugesh was a teacher, too and the eldest. *All being indicators for a perfect match*, the elders agreed. Kugesh was smitten. It was love at first sight, I reckoned immediately and even remember congratulating him as we left her home.

That was all Kugesh had seen before consenting to marriage. Though I had advised him, he did not feel the need for Wani to respond to him, his ideas and thoughts when they went out, nor did he want to know why she even liked him. And everything took place very quickly after that, the engagement and the wedding arranged a fortnight apart. After marriage, Kugesh and Wani worked in different states but spent the weekends and holidays together for the first two years. When the transfer letters finally arrived for them to serve in the same state, the real challenge started. Kugesh was a good, obliging husband. He made her coffee, allowed her to wake up late, cleaned the house and tidied after her. He bought everything a man could for a woman. He celebrated her birthdays with pomp and show and in no time, had turned her into an empress. She, on the other hand, went to work, returned home, ate, slept, watched TV and spread her legs like an automaton when her whims took over. After a year,

Kugesh began to notice she was becoming indifferent to a lot of things, her duties towards home-keeping and his needs. He felt this marriage and his one-sided dedication was beginning to choke him. Slowly, the excitement dwindled. He left her to her devices, as he felt it avoided conflict. They began to grow apart from each other. Lacking sex and attention, Kugesh increasingly became attracted to the exhilarations of his old life. Clubbing, drinking and acquainting himself with *happening people* took him further away from his domestic commitments. That's when the late nights started and Kugesh got 'involved'. Or probably that was when Wani took notice of their estrangement.

* * *

Kugesh looks up from his plate and stops chewing his food when the burgers arrive. He scrutinizes me. I wonder what he's thinking about. I remember asking him about the lawyers. Or does he want to start on the burgers? I gently push his plate towards him. He doesn't seem interested. After thinking for a while, he speaks.

'They told me I could not do much as long as my wife did not comply with the divorce notice. So, they told me to cure myself first. This is despite telling them I've got bipolar disorder,' he laughs. 'They said bipolar disorder doesn't hinder family life. I can carry on with my wife's support.'

'Yup, what would they know? Where is Wani? Have you seen her lately?' I ask.

'I returned home. I think she was shocked to see me.'

'You went back home? I thought you had moved out when the troubles started with Wani. How did she react? Was she welcoming at all?'

'Not welcoming at all, Jeevs. Cold as Antarctica. My mother has been calling me up almost every day. She was worried about my health. A bit concerned too that the neighbours and relatives have started enquiring about my absence from home, but I couldn't put up with Wani anymore,' he says. 'I am afraid of her,' he confesses, his voice suddenly breaking.

'Did you try talking to her?' I ask. 'Did you call her?'

'This is the problem, Jeevs. This is the problem. She has shut me away from her world. I have no inkling of what's coming from her these days. Not even the divorce. She just lives in her pressure chamber and refuses to come out. Burning us with her release of hot steam. Spouting venom. Can't she know a man will make mistakes? I am not perfect, Jeevs. Why doesn't this get across to her? Why can't she be more like Anna?'

'Oh my god! Do you know, that is the source of all your problems? How can you ask her to be like Anna?' I blatantly slap my forehead a few times. 'These are two very different things Kugesh,' I try to reason with him.

'Wait, wait a sec, Jeevs,' Kugesh lifts a finger, probably dismissing my opinion. 'Let me explain,' he says, straightening himself up on the chair.

'Right now, at this very moment I am sitting with you, I feel very, very sad,' he stutters. 'If you ask me why, I cannot explain to you. I just feel so heavy. I feel everything is wrong. My head is heavy, my body has given up. Imagine this, Jeevs. I just have no explanation, apart from continuing with it, carrying this sadness on my back. The medicines wear me down. I wake up to this despair, desperation if you want to call it, for which I don't understand at all. I live everyday struggling,' he explained, a blob of saliva welling up in the corner of his mouth. 'Nobody seems to accept this part of me, especially Wani. What I did was not rational thinking. Anna was just a shadow in which I hid my oblivious self.'

'And is that how it all started?' I ask him quietly, aware that the waitress now has her ears turned towards our table, like an antenna.

'I had no one to turn to, Jeevs. Nobody understood me. Wani's absence drew me away from all my attachments. I was left to function in my own world, carrying out my duties as a husband and a teacher on my own. But I did not realize that ultimately, depression would intensify my detachments from a familiar world. I lost myself first,' he emphasized, thumping his fingers at the edge of the table. 'I started coming to an empty home. The loneliness was terrible. The sadness was engulfing me like dark fog. I could not explain it to Wani, at all.'

'Oh dear,' I sigh.

'I started drinking. I needed solace. I began to stay out late. I met Anna at the snow beer place in Old Town. We've been there. Yeah, yeah, I know what you are going to say. But she kept me company during the many empty, long weekend nights.'

'What kind of company, Kugesh?' I asked, masking my intrigue with a smile.

'Not of the sort that you think, Jeevs. All of you are the same. The lawyers, Wani, even my parents! But everyone in town saw us together. I went to bunk in with her after the late nights,' Kugesh covered his face and remained like that for a while. 'I can't drive when I'm drunk, can I?'

'Hey,' I try to distract him. 'People are watching us.'

Kugesh lowered his voice. 'Life went on like that at least for a few months. Only then Wani began to take notice. She started complaining that I did not sit with her and massage her legs. I did not talk to her about school or plan holiday trips.

That we had not gone to the movies. She asked if three years of marriage had lost its sizzle. I just played along, denying them flat. The roof came down finally, when she pointed out that I did not engage in eye contact while I was fucking her!' Kugesh confessed, almost bursting out laughing.

I feign a laughter too, trying to suck up the information. At this point, my shoulders are heavy and I am experiencing a slight headache. I wonder if all this is too much for me. Am I even qualified to save a drowning marriage? I massage my temples as Kugesh continues to talk. I think I must have missed out a few things until he stops to check on me.

'Jeevs?'

'Yes, yes, you were saying something about sex,' I mutter out.

He raises his eyebrows and lets out a sigh.

'Her detective instincts picked up very fast after that. I forgot that we had exchanged our pin numbers for the hand phones during honeymoon. She had actually written it down. She rummaged through my phone logs, Whatsapps and picture galleries. She found Anna and me.'

* * *

I was drunk, Kugesh had tried explaining. *That was the bleakest hour of my life.*

I am not stupid, she had told Kugesh. *I can see it in your eyes. Why do you have the photo of a she-male in your hand phone? Such intimate close-up photos. You are disgusting. You are a cheat!*, she had retorted.

I will not let you live. I will kill you like an insect, inch by inch.

* * *

Kugesh wipes his face a few times with a serviette and continues.

'She wouldn't let me speak. And my whole family is on her side. They are asking me to go back and live with her, but I can't, you know,' he says. 'She is not willing to forgive, compromise or change her attitude.' He begins to massage his temples. 'Why can't they understand?'

'Don't know, maybe they want you to change,' I say, but I wonder what does he need to change from? Only friendship, but intimate? I suppose some form of intimate friendship. Like fire and cotton in close proximity, only incombustible.

'Why are you shaking your head, Jeevs?' Kugesh asks, biting into the burger.

'Nothing, nothing, just thinking,' I tell him, observing his protruding Adam's apple, sinking and rising. Kugesh places his burger on the plate.

'Anna was the only person who was willing to listen. She actually did everything to help me to patch up with Wani. I met him . . . I mean her, only once after that, to offer my gratitude. It was her birthday party. I sat in a corner, watching the guests gliding in and out of the apartment hall, balcony and the kitchen. Then the charade game started. I joined in reluctantly. One by one, we were taking positions in front of the TV and gestured with pointy hands and velvety lips of famous politicians, athletes and artists. There was so much laughter and happiness. I was euphoric, having left my perfect world behind.' Kugesh stops talking momentarily and gulps down his coffee.

'"Take life with a pinch of salt", said Anna. "Or treat it as a joke," said another man, chuckling like a parakeet with a beer in his hand. My spirits lifted at once. After a long time, I laughed. I laughed and I felt lighter.

'I've tried playing my cards well, keeping my excursions a secret, but it did not last and the woman began to sense my detachment. It's her fault, you know. She never treated me like a husband. I gave up on her,' Kugesh says, looking around the cafe. 'She knows it's a mistake on my part. And she knows I've gone the extra mile to make it up to her. But she prefers to believe I am not a man anymore, so why is she holding on to the marriage? To make me miserable? And she has succeeded. Look at me now.' His eyes, by now, have turned red and watery.

'I'm sure your parents stand by your side, Kugesh,' I blurt out, hoping to shed some hope.

'Wani was all nice, obliging and sweet in front of my parents and the in-laws. Once in the bedroom, she worked me up like a bullock. I felt embarrassed. There were weird fetishes that I found noxious. Turning them away meant I had lost my manhood. She would slight me in the middle of lovemaking, at the height of ecstasy. She would bring up Anna, tell me I've entered the wrong door, cover her face and burst out laughing, or push me away roughly, kicking and slapping. Or she would wake me up in the middle of the night, pelting me with vulgarity, curses and wailing that lasted till the wee hours of the morning. I had endured these in silence so that such words didn't seep out from behind the bedroom doors. I believed it would pass, someday. Day after day, night after night, the torments grew worse. *This is going to kill you*, I had warned myself, a year ago. This is why I had moved out. I thought it spared my life. I thought separation would give her the time and space to think about the marriage. My parents did not say anything. They kept Wani with them. I am the guilty party.'

For a moment, I feel that my body is becoming intense. My head is paining and my heart racing, an unexplained dizziness is cast over me. *Should I stop here, end this meeting?* I wonder.

'You don't know, Jeevs,' Kugesh continues, pushing away the empty cup of cappuccino. 'I think it is better to be completely insane or sane. Either is fine. It's torture when a man loses his health, his character. A few weeks have passed since I had moved out. Probably Wani has calmed down a bit. So mom has been asking me to go home. I went back last Saturday, as it was my father's birthday. You know how excited I get whenever my family members celebrate their birthdays. I bought a cake for him and went home. All of a sudden, my aunties came and the celebration started . . .' His voice breaks for a moment.

'What happened?' I ask a little impatiently. I can see some heads turning discreetly in our direction.

'The ceremony began. I was in my room. When the time came for the cake-cutting, not one soul, not even my mother came to ask me to come out to partake in the ceremony.' Kugesh is tearful.

'Oh dear me,' I exclaim, surprised at the sudden resentment building inside me against his parents.

'Why? Because I am sick, right?' he says. 'That's why I tell you, it's better to be completely mad, rather than hanging in limbo like this, between normality and malady.' He wipes his tears. 'I really hope I won't lose my job. I find it increasingly difficult to stay awake at school in the mornings. The principal has even suggested I take a one-term sick leave. What am I to do, go on unpaid leave? Who will stand by me if I don't even have a job? Even the children make fun of me, screaming out, teacher is sleeping . . . teacher is sleeping . . . when they catch me dozing off. I feel like strangling them at times.'

'I just had to do something to overcome the angst building up inside me. I got drunk. I tried singing an old MGR song. No . . . no . . . it was the one in which a very heartbroken Kamal

Hassan does a Bharatnatyam number on an extended pipe over a well. You remember that song?' he asks, waving his hands about. 'Earthly life is a dance,' he begins, but is still waving his fingers like a maestro conductor.

'Oh,' I finally realize that he's asking me to complete it. I start recollecting. 'Ah, I got it Kugesh,' I announce to him jubilantly. 'Life is an earthly dance, a journey we agreed to,' I sing out the lyrics confidently.

'See, see that. I agreed to all this misery, Jeevs,' he conceded.

I stare dumbfounded. Did I make a mistake?

'Every dog will have its day. I decided I was done. I was in a stupor. I jumped onto the railing of the old bridge in town and tried to cross over to the other side by walking on it. I gathered lots of spectators filming me on their mobile phones. Some shouted abuse while threatening to call the police, some cheered as I took each step forward, while some warned me of the swirling pool underneath. I had no fear. I didn't care what awaited me at the bottom of the bridge. It was too dark to notice, anyway. But I knew I will be a social media hero in no time. As I reached midway, the boisterous crowd became almost subdued. Only the flashes from their cameras flickered now and then. I was bewildered. I suppose I had come to the denouement. So my eyes began to close after all those weary nights. My vision blurred and I swayed like thin plywood against the cold breeze. I realized I was tilting. I was going to slip and fall into the sludge-filled waters of the Kinta River. In resignation, I cried out to my mother, lifting both hands in surrender. But as I took the plunge, my feet were clutched tightly by a few hands, which then pulled me on to the pavement. When I looked up, I found men dressed in such peculiarities. They took me to a nearby restaurant, bought me hot tea and fed me wanton mee. They did not ask me anything but discussed me among themselves, suggesting what to do with a desolate man like me. After clicking some selfies with me in the background, as I lay slumped and defeated on the white plastic chair, they called for a taxi, paid the fare and took me to Anna's house. I found myself in a little backroom in one of the shop houses in Brewster Lane, when I woke up today. I decided to take my life last night, Jeevs,' he said, breaking into muffled sobs. 'I wanted to die.'

I look around. I am baffled. This has become way too serious, I realize. What do I do now? I am speechless. I am relieved that he has survived this. But it worries me if this episode only strengthened his resolution. Probably I will call up some psychiatrist friends for advice. What else can a man do? How much can he hold on to? What would convince the world, his life? I should go to his house and speak to Wani, I decide. I will not stand aside and watch Kugesh dissipate away from existence. I will stand by him. I will advocate for him. Wani has to decide. She has to put a stop to her revenge-seeking schemes. I will speak to his parents. I am his friend.

'Aren't you attending your grad classes?' I ask to distract him from his present state of mind. The waiters, by now, are looking at us worriedly. Some of the other customers have stopped chatting. And I know that his sobs could easily escalate into wailing.

'I can't keep up with books,' he says, taking in a deep breath. 'I've put off my thesis by one semester. What about you? Any plans to get married?'

I shake my head.

'Don't let my mistakes haunt you,' he warns me. 'Find a good girl and make sure you have chemistry.'

I smile.

By now Kugesh is staring at the empty glass with his eyebrows edging close together.

'You want another round?' I ask.

'No, Jeevs,' he declines. 'I have to go back. Need to take the medicine or I will begin to feel very nervous,' he explains. 'Will you come and look me up at my rented place? You know I've moved out from my house and it gets pretty lonely.'

'Yes, I will,' I say earnestly, mindful that I would have to take time out from my heavy schedule at work. 'I really wish this had not happened,' I tell him wholeheartedly. 'But yes, we will meet again soon,' I promise before we take leave, and give him a long heartfelt hug.

Cikgu Ton

The low benches provided at the school canteen were intended for teenagers. Halimaton, affectionately known as Cikgu Ton in her school, sat down on one of them. She shifted about a little, balancing her buttocks to distribute her weight evenly on the plank. Then she opened her palms and recited the *bismillah*, watchful of a fly hovering above the glass of the tarik and nasi lemak she had bought for lunch.

Looking into the plate's contents, she shook her head. '*Takpe, pakcik engko yang bagi*,'[1] the words of the canteen operator's wife echoed in her mind.

When did he become my uncle? She wondered. *Should I eat his piece of chicken?*

Pak Mat, a man in his mid-sixties, had grinned suggestively as he dropped the meat into her plate while she was paying. '*Belanja, ambik pree*,'[2] he had said. 'Uncalled for,' smirked Halimaton unkindly at the stocky old man. Most of the female teachers avoided him. They unanimously echoed he was miang.

The canteen was abuzz with noisy students. *More like a holding pen for livestock*, thought Halimaton. They kept

---

[1] '*Takpe, pakcik engko yang bagi*': 'Its ok, your uncle gave you.'
[2] '*Belanja, ambik pree*': 'I spend, take it for free.'

pouring in from every corner, congregating under the cool shades of the canteen before assembling in the school field. She was about to take a bite of the nasi lemak but bit her tongue instead when she was nudged from behind. She turned angrily to reprimand the interrupter but was annoyed at finding Pak Mat. Holding a rag in one hand, and a worn plastic pail in the other, Pak Mat stood with a sheepish grin, exposing his large set of yellowed teeth, gums stained by nicotine, behind a pair of rubbery, thick lips.

'Uncouth,' Halimaton snarled at him, observing the dirt on his thin sweatshirt.

Pak Mat left the pail on the floor and the mop handle now leaned on his chest.

'Mintak maaf, Cikgu,' he apologized, adjusting his kopiah and pulling his long pants up to his knees.

'Tak sengaja, *Cikgu*,' he claimed innocence.

'Not on purpose?' Halimaton scoffed at him. 'You are old enough to be my father.' She turned to her lunch. Pak Mat still lingered, scratching his grey beard. This time, he circumvented the table and came to stand before her, pointing to her elbow. A splotch of chilli sauce had stained the three-quarter sleeves of her blouse. She shook her head and ignored him. But the old man pointed to her exposed wrists this time and asked, 'Tak tutup aurat ke?' before trotting away like a fat goose.

Halimaton was speechless. *Is this what it's all about?* She wondered angrily. *Did a few centimetres of uncovered female flesh warrant a free piece of chicken? Should I complain to his wife or inform the school principal?* Nauseated, she pushed away her plate. The children were running helter-skelter, engrossed in talk and play. The senior teachers had ganged up and occupied another corner and were engaged in conversation. *No one had noticed*, sighed Halimaton. *How much skin needs to be covered to be safe from this leech?*

* * *

It has been three months since she was transferred to the secondary school in Balakong. She was the coordinator for the 're-move' class sections for students moving into government secondary schools from primary vernacular schools. They received lessons in Malay and English, preliminary Mathematics and Moral Education. Most went through a year of culture shock, mingled with discipline problems and boredom.

She had hardly finished eating when a commotion broke out in the school field. From the cheers rising, she could make out that a feud had just started. Soon it would escalate into something serious. Almost at once, the children ran to see the spectacle, leaving their unfinished food and games. The crowd of white school uniforms was so thick that it was impossible to assess the situation. Two boys broke away and ran towards her.

'Teacher, teacher,' they called out as Halimaton watched the unfolding scene from the canteen. In between short breaths and beads of sweat trailing down their foreheads, they pointed to the cloud of dust. 'Ramu, it is Ramu . . . He is fighting.'

'Not again,' Halimaton sighed as she got up to wash her hands, leaving her exposed lunch to the feasting flies. When she appeared, the fighting subdued. The crowd thinned out. The prefects flanked two boys, relieved that somebody had come to their aid. The guilty boys stood with downcast eyes. Ramu, smaller and thinner, had his pockets torn, while Krishna, notorious for his roguish behaviour, stood with his elbow bleeding.

Mr Lim, the discipline teacher, arrived shortly. 'Take them to the staff room,' he told the prefects. The boys walked away. 'I'll take care of this, Cikgu Ton,' he told Halimaton. 'And Cikgu Ton,' he paused. 'Is it possible to borrow some students from your class afterwards?'

'Why?' she enquired.

'Oh, sports day is coming. We are drawing the grid lines on the school field for the event.'

'How many?'

'As many as possible, those who volunteer,' Mr Lim said, as they began to walk towards the canteen. Looking from the corner of his eyes, he waited for her response.

'Sure, no problem,' said Halimaton.

'Poor Ramu,' she thought sympathetically. The recent death of his twin sister had brought him to this. Otherwise, he was a well-mannered, reserved chap. He did his work and never bothered the others. Ever since the school's open day after the mid-year exams, she had noticed something awkward. The question had been troubling her like a mosquito buzzing at her ear. *Behind the aggressive behaviour of this boy, there is something else*, she was certain. She wondered if she should talk to him.

* * *

The bell rang, signalling the beginning of the afternoon session. The teachers around her picked up their bags and their piles of marked work and marched out of the staff room. Halimaton stood up, loosening the grip of her blouse on her skin. *And if biological contours are considered too revealing, I must get the head-scarf soon, a long, wide one*, she reminded herself.

The students had already filed into their classrooms by the time Halimaton reached her class. She planned to teach composition. Maybe she would ask them to write the popular essay on 'myself'. The students giggled as she entered. One of the students from the back bench had called out the nickname they had given her. Badak-a, rhinoceros. Though angry, Halimaton looked away. She knew that instead of walking, she galloped along the corridors. Students and teachers alike had told that her footsteps could be heard from miles away. The students were quiet, but this was the calm before the storm. They were waiting for her to react. The group of urchins would turn boisterous the minute she let go. That's why she was sent there, she supposed, to scare them with her size.

Asking the students to open their exercise books, she turned to write the topic of the essay on the blackboard. Badak, someone shouted again, this time loudly and clearly. The whole class ruptured into gleeful laughter. She smiled. She had resigned to the fact that the name had been circulating around the school for some time now, even among the teachers and the garrulous Pak Mat. But she turned around and caught out that voice. 'You, you, that big Indian boy behind the fourth desk, come here. Come here, at once,' she instructed.

Krishna sat in the last row of the class. He was famous for the jokes he played on teachers and students alike. He was the loudest and the vilest-looking kid she had ever seen. He was the tallest in class, stocky with uneven facial hair. He often walked about the school with a gang of followers and had been caught smoking and soliciting protection money for the thugs lingering outside the school. Krishna walked up to her amidst jeering classmates and made a sign for peace.

'What's your name?' she asked.

The boy, who was almost as tall as her, drew in his breath and said, 'My name is Rajinikanth,' referring to a Kollywood superstar. He raised his hands as if he were receiving accolades for his stint from his giggling classmates.

He cowered when Halimaton raised her hand unexpectedly. *Phlaaak*, her palm burned as it landed a sharp slap, packed with anger and energy on his flabby cheek. His naughty smile disappeared, and his eyes moistened. Pretending to be resilient, he turned around to go back to his seat.

'Go and stand outside,' said Halimaton. Krishna walked out. The class was reduced to silence.

'Now write this,' she told the class.

Sitting down, she fanned herself with a book she had carried to class. She caught Krishna's eyes, staring at her from outside the classroom. He puckered his chin and looked down. In a few seconds, he was standing sideways, leaning leisurely on the door panel. The man whom Ramu had introduced as his father on open day, had also enquired about Krishna. When asked, he said he was Krishna's new guardian. It was strange. What was even stranger was that he did not want to hear about Ramu's progress, which would have warranted some parental pride. *Ramu, who is more introvert and reclusive could do better in his studies with some encouragement,* she wanted to tell him.

* * *

'Why wouldn't they call you badak?' Her mother chuckled heartily. 'You are one hefty damsel. And how many times have I told you, your dressing has to change? You should be softer. Choose lighter tones. Go tame with that lipstick. No fierce, sleek, city girl looks. Talk softly, walk slowly. Why not sew a few

bland, long-sleeved, high-collared dresses, just for school wear?'
she suggested. 'Then the old man at school won't try to be itchy
with you.'

'But ma, everyone has boobs. Only mine?' Halimaton asked.

'Don't give him the pleasure of taunting you. For all you
know, he will blame you for tempting him,' her mother warned.

'Why should I be blamed?' Halimaton asked cautiously.

'Well, whether you are covered or not covered, they all think
alike. If they manage to lick one of your tits, they don't have to
ask for the other one. The downstairs door is then automatic,'
her mother cautioned.

'Ma, you are hilarious,' laughed Halimaton.

'The world is,' her mother sighed.

* * *

The children were hardly interested in the writing exercise.
They threw awkward glances at her, looking lost and displeased,
as if she had pronounced the death sentence on them. She
ignored them. 'If you don't hand in your work, you will go
and see the discipline teacher,' she threatened the rest of the
students.

She caught the reflection of herself in one of the bay
windows of the classroom. Her mother was right. Her shoulders
were hunched. They were broad and muscular, matched with
a protruding jawbone. She stood at five feet and a half and was
taller than the principal and the discipline master. Only the
tailored business suit fitted her flawlessly. No amount of exercise,
diet pills, regimented diet or even yoga had helped her. Protein
mass, fat mass can be reduced, but bone mass? Impossible!

The class was quiet.

A group of boys were making playful gestures at Krishna. He stood at the edge of the verandah, bathing in the afternoon sun. He was sweating profusely. Keeping an eye out for Halimaton, some of his classmates waved to ask if he wanted a drink or a chair to sit. Halimaton pretended to look away. *Let him stand a bit longer*, she decided. That will teach him a lesson for being rude.

Suddenly, she was distracted by some excitement that stirred the class. She found Mr. Lim standing at the door. He had Krishna's sideburns clutched between his thumb and finger. Krishna was grimacing in pain while his huge body tilted to one side. The class laughed at them. Halimaton laughed too, easing at once at the comical sight.

The girls grew quiet, burying their faces in their notebooks, their hands suddenly springing to life, crafting words into the blank lines. They knew exactly what business Mr. Lim had on his mind. They had no inclination to be at the school field at this hour. A few Indian boys put up their hands almost in unison. But Mr Lim needed more volunteers. 'If nobody wants to volunteer, I will have to choose some of you,' he said. The class laughed again. Krishna raised his hands, as if someone was pointing a gun at him, behind the discipline teacher. Four boys stood up and waited outside the classroom. Halimaton wondered if she should keep them inside the classroom. Another four Indian boys were selected, including Ramu. Halimaton asked Ramu to sit.

'Don't worry Cikgu,' Mr Lim retorted, a little displeased. 'They won't get any darker. And I don't think they want to be in class either.' Just to clear the doubt, he playfully asked the boys if they wanted to go back and sit in the classroom. 'A favour I would greatly appreciate,' he said. The boys remained quiet. Krishna being the empty can said, 'No.'

'I told you Cikgu,' said Mr Lim, 'they are champions.' He chuckled as he led them away. 'If you agree, I'll buy you a drink, Cikgu Ton,' he called out, winking at her.

'Miang,' Halimaton whispered quietly, biting her lips.

Maybe I could talk to Ramu, thought Halimaton. *Poor boy has lost his twin sister.* She understood how it was with twins. They were linked with an umbilical cord that bound them to the mystery of psychic attachment. 'Ramu,' she called out. The students stopped writing and looked up. 'Do your own work,' she chided them. He came and stood meekly in front of her, eyes lowered. She needed to know what had caused the fight with Krishna. 'Go and bring your chair,' she instructed him. He was hesitant at first. With some cajoling, he nervously brought his chair. Halimaton swiftly turned his chair to face her, so that he would not be distracted by the prying eyes of his classmates.

'I'm sorry about what happened to your sister,' Halimaton began. Ramu did not stir. *But would a child at this age understand social negotiations?* 'I'm really sad.' Ramu's eyes met hers. 'What was her name?'

'Geetha,' his voice rose timidly. 'Krishna said Geetha had turned into a ghost.'

She was correct. Krishna was the troublemaker. He had been taunting Ramu. She was aware that the children had also been 'bumping' into Geetha's apparition in the nooks and corners of the school hallway and library.

'What happened to your sister?' she asked.

He kept mum.

'Is Krishna your brother?'

Ramu shook his head.

'But your father came to me to collect his report card,' she went on.

Ramu acknowledged it, but he said, 'No.'

'Relative?'

'No.'

The answer bewildered Halimaton. 'What happened to your sister?' she asked again, intrigued.

Ramu pursed his lips, somewhat puzzled.

'How did she die?'

'She drank orange juice,' he said. 'Then she fainted. She died at the hospital.'

'How are your parents?' She wondered if orange juice could be as fatal as the boy claimed.

'Mother is sad,' he said. 'Very sad. She didn't eat for two days.'

'Your father?' *There is something very funny about that man*, she was sure. He was concerned about someone else's son and not his own.

'He is busy. He is always fighting with mother,' he said, drawing his arms together as if he were cold.

'Why?' asked Halimaton. 'Is it because of you and Geetha?'

'No,' said Ramu, his cheeks flushing. 'It's because of Krishna's mother.'

'Krishna's mother?'

'They fight because my father goes to Krishna's house. Sometimes he comes back late. Or he doesn't return at all.'

'Where is Krishna's father?' she asked carefully.

'Went off somewhere and never came back . . .'

'Went just like that? How long ago?'

'I don't know.'

'How does your father know Krishna's mother?'

Ramu almost smiled. 'Whatsapp!' he answered assuredly, pressing his thumbs on an invisible handphone. 'After that, my father fights with my mother every day. Make her cry all the time.'

Hmm . . . typical, thought Halimaton. *The man had taken advantage of the lonely woman.* 'I mean, who made the orange juice?'

'My mother. She makes orange juice every night to take to work. She leaves it in the fridge,' he explained. 'Geetha woke up at night and drank it because she was thirsty. Sometimes I drink too, but nothing ever happened.'

This is murder, cold-blooded murder, her thoughts raced. It was clear that someone had poisoned the juice. Someone had tried to kill Ramu's mother. Must be her husband! No one else would come between him and Krishna's mother.

'Where is your mother now?' she asked, confused.

'The police took her,' he said.

'And your father?'

'At Krishna's house.'

Bloody scoundrel, she almost slammed her wrist on the table. 'And you?'

'At my grandmother's house,' he said. 'I want to go home . . . I want my mother back from jail.'

Ramu began to sob, burying his head under his folded arms. The students stopped writing. They were becoming restless. One girl came up to offer him a pack of tissues. Two boys also approached him timidly. One patted Ramu's shoulders and the other stroked his back. The whole scene brought tears to Halimaton's eyes. Love of the innocents. *Well, justice needs to be served*, she decided. She had to console him. Then she would take him to the police station to meet the inspecting officer.

Next, she would call one of her lawyer friends in Shah Alam and post bail for Ramu's mother. She must set things right. *Justice must be served.*

She stood up. Asking the monitor to keep watch over the class and collect the exercise books, she led Ramu out. They walked to the canteen as quietly as possible. Pak Mat and his wife looked a little perturbed, seeing a sobbing child led by Cikgu Ton into the canteen at this hour. Once they were seated, Pak Mat's wife rushed off to offer them both a cold drink in her bid to be helpful.

'Cho . . . cho . . . cho . . .' Pak Mat chuckled the moment his wife left. Halimaton narrowed her eyes. *Now, where is this getting to?*

'Very nice, very nice,' Pak Mat began. 'So nice your teacher can console you,' he ruffled Ramu's hair. It must have had a soothing effect, for Ramu's sobs reduced to quiet sniffles. Pak Mat took a step back when his wife returned with two glasses of lime juice.

'Poor thing,' she said. 'I heard it from the other teachers in school, Cikgu Ton.' Then she left again to close her stall.

Pak Mat stayed back. He came closer and stood between Halimaton and Ramu.

'Poor thing,' he echoed his wife's statement. 'So young and so tender, yet so much burden. If only you understand and accept my will. You can be mine . . . if you agree, no more crying, only happiness,' he said. She could smell his breath and his sweat. He stroked Ramu's head again, smiling thoughtfully.

'So nice,' he said again, 'to have nice teacher like Cikgu Ton.' He caressed Ramu's shoulders.

'Can I kiss your hand?' he stuttered.

Kiss your hand? Halimaton wondered if she heard the words right. She could feel her fingers curling into her palms.

Krishna and the group of Indian boys had assembled at the canteen and stopped by a lone faucet by the side of the building, scrutinizing Ramu and Cikgu Ton as they waited for Mr. Lim to arrive with the marker tools to draw the grids.

Pak Mat edged closer to Halimaton's chair, and she could feel his trousers rubbing against her elbows. She was about to stand, when she felt three fingers, cold and wet, on the nape of her neck.

'Marry me,' he said.

That's it, she decided. 'Miang, miang,' she shouted. The chair toppled violently and rolled away as Halimaton got to her feet. The boys stood still in shock.

'Apa, apa, what do you want?' she asked, rolling up her sleeves. Her smooth fleshy biceps stood exposed. Ramu inched away from the table and walked towards the grid markers. Pak Mat stood his ground, his dark lips moving silently between laughter and fear. Without warning, Halimaton punched him straight in his face. He fell down, clutching the side of his face with his hands.

'Aduh . . . aduh . . .' he grimaced in pain.

Halimaton heard cheers booming from across the empty canteen.

Spitting on the crouching figure, she gave it two of her sturdiest kicks.

'Don't you dare come near me, you old, pathetic donkey,' she warned him.

Pak Mat's wife stood speechless, neither going near to help her husband, nor verbally defending him against the assault.

Pulling down her sleeves, Halimaton told Ramu, 'Let's go to the police station. I'm going to teach them all a lesson!' she shouted.

Sellama and the Curried Prawns

'Half blind, half limping and half dead,' Sellama mocked herself. Holding on to a lamp post, she climbed the pavement of the busy road and waited undecidedly at the zebra crossing in front of the local government clinic. The traffic whizzed by continuously, oblivious to the black-and-white stripes painted on the dark gravel. A few bolder pedestrians hurried across through the tight, narrow gaps between the vehicles. Chuckling at their manoeuvring, Sellama decided against the dare. 'Too old for that,' she cautioned herself, *especially when one foot is already in the grave.*

Instead, she walked down the road until she reached a huge intersection at the Old Klang Road. There she waited for the traffic lights to turn red. Taking a few seconds to make sure that the vehicles were really halted, she crossed the busy road. 'All praise to God,' she muttered.

A huge truck was climbing laboriously up the overhead ramp, drowning the noise of the heavy traffic below on the road. A cloud of exhaust smoke filled her lungs. Gathering the Triple 5 appointment booklet, her supply of medicines and the lunch packet, she bent slightly to cough. Using the ends of her sari, she covered her nose and continued to walk.

I should have taken a taxi, she chided herself. *But taxis*, she scoffed at the idea as an afterthought. *They wouldn't charge by the metre. They'll charge a flat fee for a three-minute drive. The money spent on a taxi could be spent on gifts for little Anju and Sham.* She had promised them both a Lego set for Deepavali. Gathering the phlegm at the tip of her tongue, she spat it out in a corner and wiped the corners of her mouth.

It's noon already, Sellama calculated the time, catching sight of her shadow. Fiddling about in her medicine bag, she realized she had forgotten to bring the umbrella. Looking up she found herself at pillar number fifty-five. There were nine more to go!

Her house was one among six other modern bungalow-turned-offices standing aloof, facing the underpass. These houses belonged to those who were too poor to turn their homes into business properties, or those who were reluctant to sell their land as prices were expected to appreciate. And some did not want to part with their homes, like Sellama, for they held memories. This was the house Sellama's husband had built. This was the house where Dorai had grown up. This was a place where she could be herself, living a full life.

After much effort, pillar number sixty-four stood before her like a welcoming arch. 'Ah, finally,' she smiled. A sense of calmness pervaded her taut leg muscles. The burning sensation on her hips lessened and her mind relaxed, as if she had just crossed the finishing line of a marathon. She reached for her purse secured in her petticoat and fished out a set of keys. *Now, some mooru for this hellish heat,* she told herself.

The rusty gate stood between the sidewalks that ran parallel to the main road. She unlocked a huge padlock, pulled the latch and walked in. A lone rambutan tree stood on one side. The remaining ground had been raided by bougainvillea and lalang shrubs. Dorai had cautioned her against snakes, scorpions and mosquitoes. But her hands had grown too weak to keep a tidy garden. The Bangladeshi gardener asked for thirty ringgit to clean such a small patch. But she would call him once the year-end rains started. If not for the current dry spell, she would probably have had the vines running up her walls and across the roof. She picked up the folded newspaper and dusted off the dried leaves clinging around its rubber band.

Sellama pushed her slippers under an old sofa in the verandah and opened the door. 'Phew.' She let out a breath of relief as her feet touched the cool tiles of the living room. She unloaded her supplies on the recliner. Moving to the bedroom, she unwound her sari and changed into a sarong and blouse. She hurriedly splashed cold water on her face, softening layers of powder, oil and sweat. She buried her face momentarily into a towel.

The midday heat was so consuming that Sellama decided to delay the household chores. She checked on the lunch she had meticulously prepared this morning. It was still warm. Filling herself a glass of mooru, she left the kitchen and slid onto the puffy cushions of her recliner. She smiled after taking the first sip, pleased that the fennel seeds had blended in and gave off a pleasant aroma in the buttermilk. She took more sips, twirled the copper tumbler gently while nibbling on the chopped onions and green chillies that got stuck between her teeth. She rested her legs on the coffee table nearby and glanced over the newspaper headlines. Bored, she put it away. Instead, she switched on the TV and realized she had missed one of her Tamil serials on ASTRO. 'They won't go far,' she comforted herself, anticipating the longer-than-life, dull, repeated plots. She reduced the volume and yawned at the all too familiar soliloquy.

Am I not lucky? But a little clever too, she complimented herself. *When children grow up, they need to be kicked out. When sons get married, they curl their tails between their legs.* She shook her head. 'Imagine sitting like this in the middle of your house with a daughter-in-law running around.' Massaging her temples, her thoughts turned sympathetically to Devi, one of the many ladies she knew at the clinic.

'Pity, pity,' the other ladies had expressed regret at hearing about the sudden demise of the woman. 'What a life she had had.'

Devi was sixty-eight, the wife of an ex-district police commissioner. Full of pleasantness, she came to the clinic with a modest pinch of lipstick, draped in newer cotton saris, a gold chain and bangles. She hardly resembled usual widows. She carried a leather handbag and brought pre-packed sandwiches and orange juice. Among the women, she complained the least and this nobility was well-liked. All her three children were successful professionals, two of whom were settled overseas. She lived with her share-remisier son who worked at the Kuala Lumpur Stock Exchange.

* * *

'Everyone dies, when their time comes,' sighed Indra, who sometimes hitched a ride home with Devi. 'You can't ask for a postponement, can you? But what's shocking is her real-life story, the constant nightmare she endured.'

Intrigued, everyone wanted to know what it was. *The story behind a polished lady can't be all that bad,* they thought.

'Wait at the dispensary,' Indra announced after her token appeared on the screen.

* * *

Sellama dragged the medicine box from underneath the coffee table and placed it on her lap. Opening it, she began to empty the medicines into their designated compartments. At sixty-five, she was independent, though her vision, clouded by cataract, had been deteriorating. She could cook, wash and find her way around town with no assistance. She gave credit to the long back-breaking days of working at the plantations, three decades ago. The rigorous work had kept her spirit robust and fit. *And those days people cycled or walked everywhere*, she reminisced. A motorized vehicle was a luxury. But now, her son Dorai, would drive even to the nearest shop. *Anyway, cycling is so dangerous in this kind of traffic*, she thought, *even walking. There is a high chance you would get mowed down like grass even when you're careful!*

Why have they given me aspirin for high blood pressure even when my pressure is normal? she wondered. The doctor had warned her that she would be put on insulin shots if she was not careful. 'Prevention, aunty, it's for prevention,' the young doctor had said. *What's happening?* she thought. *Consuming medicines has now become a way of life.*

Sellama hated medicines. At sixty-five, medicines didn't cure diseases, they didn't prevent sickness. *They just prolong your existence. You live on borrowed time. Unwelcome and unappreciated for overstaying*, sighed Sellama, dumping a whole packet of miniature white tablets on the floor to be swept away later. *We'll wait for high blood pressure to come knocking on our door first*, she told the strips of tablets before stashing them into a refashioned Nestle ice-cream tub. She pushed the box under the coffee table and reclined on the sofa.

She switched the channel to National Geographic. *Better to watch polar bears than the grief-stricken women of Indian drama on SUN TV.*

Her thoughts travelled back to Devi. Her funeral was the next day at 2 p.m. The women had deliberated on attending it.

Then it is straight to the funeral hall, Indra had informed them. *The final rites will be simple and quick. At the press of a button, off she goes into the furnace.* Sixty-eight years of living, snuffed out in twenty minutes.

'Why aren't the rites being performed at home?' the women had asked. 'It's the place where she had lived. Her soul would linger there for three days to see the faces she had cherished.'

'Didn't you hear? Didn't you hear?' Indra startled her friends. 'It's the daughter-in-law. The daughter-in-law.'

'What about her?' the women asked again. 'Was it a love marriage or arranged?'

'She was a disaster for Devi,' Indra said. 'She hand-picked the girl. She wanted someone who would stay at home and look after her family.'

'Then?'

'According to her maid, the moment her son left for work, Devi was locked out of the house until he returned.'

'Poor woman . . . but why?'

'How do I know?' Indra jerked her palms open.

'The maid said Devi would spend the long hours on the porch, reading papers, magazines or books. She had two square meals and took her medicines there, come rain or sunshine. She only entered the house when there were visitors or when the son returned after work, sometimes late at night. I heard all this with my own ears. Wait, there is more. Once, Devi fell asleep behind the kitchen. The daughter-in-law sneaked up to her through the back door and splashed cold water on the poor woman.'

'Shiva, Shiva,' the women chanted in horror.

'When the family lunched on meat and seafood, Devi was given rice, an omelette and ketchup. The leftovers were available only after dinner, if there were any.' Indra's voice began to break as she spoke.

'All this in full view of the grandchildren?' the women asked.

'Yes. And I think in full knowledge of her son, too.'

'Their maid related it to my maid, that's how I know. It's too late now,' sighed Indra. 'But the poor woman never said a word. Not even a word.'

* * *

It was half past one. *Dorai will be here any minute*, she thought. *My little mutt who's running with his tail between his legs. He even barks and yelps like Syamala.*

'You found the match, you got me married, and so whose fault is it, amma?' Dorai had said to her, when she had asked him to stick to his opinions and safeguard some of his family's interests, especially his mother's.

'But that was my duty. To find someone to look after you when I am gone,' she had explained.

'Am I not being taken care of?' asked Dorai, perplexed. 'I go to work, I earn the money. Syamala takes care of the house, the children, the finances. What more can I ask for? Maybe it's you who has a problem, not us, amma.'

My fault, my fault, murmured Sellama, closing her eyes momentarily. *I shouldn't have found someone equal to Dorai's status. If it was a simpler girl, from a simple family, with simpler needs, she would have been more obliging.*

The one I found turned out to be a maharani in her own right, Sellama began to grow regretful. *She had behaved her best.*

Dropping by twice a week, taking up chores around the house, cooking and washing. But the vixen had set her eyes on things I was careless with. How she enquired about the faded gold chokers and bangles, Sellama bit her lip. Syamala had also been busy. She had taken a look at the little property's land titles. She had information on its width, length and lease periods. She had weighed its prominence now that the place was developing. She had asked around for its value. She had set her will on selling it. Now that her one hand held Dorai, the other itched for the property.

Sellama closed her eyes and placed a hand on her chest. 'Only if I allow it,' she uttered.

The subtle halting of a car interrupted her thoughts. 'Hmmm . . .' she let out a sigh. Finishing her mooru, she got up from the recliner and moved towards the door.

'Amma,' the familiar voice greeted her. Dorai was smiling as he walked up. He turned abruptly and pressed the car's remote control. Two beeps were heard and the car responded with two blinks of the hazard lights.

Sellama smiled at the towering figure walking towards her with long, sturdy steps. *He resembles his father,* she thought.

'Here amma, this is for you,' said Dorai, handing her two plastic bags. He sat down on the old couch on the verandah to untie his leather shoes, his sunglasses hooked on the top shirt button. Sellama inspected the contents. There were grapes, two large pomegranates, a packet of Horlicks and a tin of Jacob's Cream Crackers, the word 'unsalted' etched upon it in bold letters.

'Adeh, this is unusual,' said Sellama, knowing very well that Dorai only dropped by twice a month. Once, to pass on her husband's pension and once to make sure she was still up and about (not dead).

'Syamala told me to pass it to you, amma,' he said, managing a smile. Dorai scratched his elbows and looked around.

'Adeh, this is more intriguing than unusual,' Sellama chuckled. 'My daughter-in-law sends me fruits whose seeds I cannot chew.'

'You won't choke on them amma, now don't get started,' Dorai warned her.

Two large mynahs had taken residence on the old rambutan tree. They perched on a leafless twig, chattering in high pitched sing-song voices.

'Those are new,' said Dorai, pointing to them.

'Oh yes, Dorai. They've just started roosting in the tree's cavity. Don't stand out here in this weather. Come inside, son.' Dorai took off his shoes and trailed behind his mother. Sellama left the plastic bags on the coffee table and waited for Dorai to sit.

'How are your wife and children?' she asked.

'At home and in school, amma,' answered Dorai, rather complacently. He began to yawn and look around the house uninterestedly.

His manner displeased Sellama. *Behaving like a stranger in one's own house*, she thought angrily. *You belong here, Dorai.* 'You want some mooru?' she offered, seeing him engulfed in his own thoughts.

'Ewwww,' Dorai replied in disgust. 'Not for me, amma.'

Of course, thought Sellama sadly. Gone were the days when he would ask her to prepare the mooru, her specialty. She would dilute yoghurt into three litres of water in an earthen pot, seasoning it with salt, curry leaves, shallots and green chillies stir fried with mustard seeds. How Dorai would down glass after glass of the tantalizing, rich liquid. He would tell his friends only his mother knew how to make mooru. *And now, he is twitching his nose at it?* Sellama sighed resignedly.

'Did the agent come today?' he asked. 'What about the evaluators from the bank?'

'No, they didn't,' Sellama answered curtly. *They won't take even one step into my property unless I allow it*, she vowed silently. 'Would you like to have lunch? I have cooked your favourite.'

'What, amma? Prawn and drumstick curry?' Dorai asked as he headed to the dining table.

Sellama poured out a tall tumbler of chilled mooru and put it in front of him at the dining table. Dorai picked up the tumbler and drank it with eagerness. She was glad when he sheepishly pushed it across the table and looked up at her. Then she served him a plate of warm rice, fried bitter gourd and a bowl of prawn curry. She uncovered a small saucer to reveal an omelette. From an old biscuit tin, she produced two crispy appalapoo.

Dorai sat fingering his rice. 'Some things never change, when you have your mother by your side,' she said, beaming. She would have to serve the dishes onto his plate.

However, she was beginning to be perturbed by the undercurrent of their conversation that lacked warmth. Instead, they both found themselves full of suspicion and strained camaraderie. Sellama understood Dorai was merely walking on a tightrope on one end of which was Syamala and on the other, she herself. He was in a difficult position, *but should he reach a solution at the expense of his own mother? Are old people so easily discarded to make way for the young?* She could not accept that from her only son.

'Amma,' he began with the unmistakable tone but stopped. He began to mix the rice with gravy before scooping up a mouthful.

'Here, have some murunggeka,' said Sellama. She ladled out more curry over his rice. 'How is it?'

'Why have you added so much masala?' Dorai chewed the fibrous pods of the drumstick.

Sellama scrutinized the gravy-coated ladle under Dorai's watchful eyes. She brought it to her nose and sniffed calmly. Her eyes smarted. The piercing scent of coriander tingled her nose and sinuses at once. She sneezed.

'How could I?' she pretended to be shocked. 'Did I get the measures wrong? Too much coriander?' she questioned herself doubtfully, observing that Dorai was now shaking his head. She knew exactly where this news would travel.

Dorai fished out a folded handkerchief from his pocket and shook it free from its folds.

'Are you not well, son? Do you have a runny nose?' she asked.

'Shoooh, yes amma. What happened to you today?' he chuckled, pushing away the extra gravy to the sides of his plate. He dabbed his forehead with the handkerchief.

'It's been the same; your father liked it this way,' Sellama answered, noticing the small beads of sweat on Dorai's cheeks and chin. 'Add more rice then,' she suggested, guiltily watching Dorai battling the curry.

'Why not sell the house?' Dorai proposed. 'And move into the Good Shepherd Home. You won't be so lonely, ma. Your meals and chores will be taken care of. Syamala says there are doctors who will check on you twice a day, nurses who will remind you to take your pills; no cooking, cleaning, or laundry.' He bit into a fat, juicy prawn.

'I know, I know,' said Sellama, gathering her loose hair and pinning them into a tiny bun. She wondered if there was anything she could do to stop this conversation. She poured herself a glass of mooru.

Silence ensued. She watched, nibbling on the onion and green chilli chunks from the mooru she was drinking.

Dorai was finishing the last piece of drumstick, sucking out the gravy from one end of the pod, before chewing the flesh and seeds. Spitting the dry fibre onto the plate, he belched loudly. Dorai puffed out softly. 'So spicy . . . hot, very hot.' He curled his tongue in and out of his mouth like an iguana.

'Here, take some more,' Sellama offered more prawn and drumstick in coriander gravy.

'No ma, it's too spicy,' Dorai protested, pushing away his plate.

'When are you taking me home?' she asked.

'Home?' Dorai seemed perturbed by the question.

'Your house,' said Sellama. 'That's where I belong. Isn't that home?'

'But amma, Syamala says you will have difficulty climbing up the stairs. It's dangerous to be home alone. Moreover, we won't be at home most of the time.'

Sellama chuckled. 'Syamala does not work, does she?'

Dorai coughed. 'Can I have some water, please? I'm done with mooru, and there are green chillies and spices inside.'

'Have you forgotten the taste of mooru, my son?' she smiled. 'And since when did your mother's curry stop agreeing with you?'

'This is not about food, amma. It's about you being in a secure place. Shhhoooo . . . sheeeshh . . . This house has turned into a ramshackle. It's not safe for you to be alone. What if you fall down in the middle of the night? Or thieves break in? Or the roof collapses? Foooooohhhhh . . . ' he sucked in cool air.

Sellama looked about the kitchen cabinet for a cup. When she found one, she left it on the table, empty, and took her time to fill the water jug.

'I want to stay with you and the children,' she insisted. 'That's what your father would have asked you to do.' She held the water jug to herself. 'I don't like the old folks' home. It reminds me of death. I need to be happy and contented. I need care and love and warmth from you and my grandchildren. I don't deserve to be left deserted in a place that reeks of urine and disease.'

'Amma, you don't get it,' said Dorai, as he wiped his forehead. His shirt was drenched in sweat. He unbuttoned his collar and cuffs.

'Here,' said Sellama, handing him a glass of water.

Dorai gulped down the water in a hurry, spilling some on his shirt pocket.

'You can keep this land or do whatever you want with it. In return, you will spare me a room in your house. Do you agree or not?' Sellama was adamant.

'We'll do the name transfers first. Then we'll decide if you can come and stay with us.'

Sellama was startled at Dorai's refusal to commit to filial duty. Here she was, running the last league of her life and pleading with her only son to accept her. And he was spelling out terms and conditions? On what grounds could she trust him? Could she part with her house? She drew in a long breath, full of disappointment and anger. She would not turn her life into a living nightmare like Devi's.

'It is best for me to stay where I am,' she told him firmly. 'I will continue to live here. I have made my decision. The house will go to my grandchildren. You may send me wherever you want the day I become oblivious to my own existence.'

Dorai's face turned pale with exasperation.

'Your amma can still read the signs, Dorai.' Sellama raised her voice. 'I took the LRT to Sentul, to see your father's old friend, Lal Singh. Remember him? They've expanded. Now, he is "Lal Singh and Sons, Advocates and Solicitors". He and his secretary stood witness to the will I drafted. It will be legitimate once the Commissioner of Oaths stamps it. I will pass a copy to you and your wife when I receive the original document.'

Dorai's face was flushed.

'Son, don't you have a place for your amma in your heart?' she asked desperately.

'Amma, Syamala and I think of only the best for you,' he replied almost absentmindedly, leaping to his feet. 'I'll see you on Saturday.'

Sellama smiled.

'I'll make chicken perattal for you then. And stir-fried cauliflower with mushrooms?' she offered. 'Bring Syamala along, too,' she said. She knew exactly how to corrupt the curry. *Ground dried chillies! That'll subdue her tongue and hold it still. I will teach her a thing or two for coveting my property.*

'No amma, don't trouble yourself,' Dorai shook his head. 'I think I need to use the toilet.' He rubbed his stomach.

When he emerged again she asked, 'What about the mortgagers? Are they coming?'

'No amma, right now I need to go back to office.' Dorai hurried to the comfort of his car. 'I can't stand this heat.'

She smiled benignly as she saw her son off. 'Now, for some lunch,' she said to herself, and walked into the kitchen to enjoy the pre-packed nasi kandar she had bought earlier.

The Sunday Assassin

Just look at the price of the bloody brinjals, Rishi almost stomped his foot in disbelief. *Are they made of gold?* He was tempted to ask the dishevelled fellow looking at him from the raised platform outside the wet market.

'Six ringgit,' the old man repeated, sitting on his hunches as he pulled out a plastic bag from under a heap of newspapers and leftover vegetable peels. He handed the packet to Rishi with a toothless grin.

'The price of everything has gone up,' the old man sighed. 'Four ringgit per kilo,' he gestured towards the heap of tomatoes. 'The farms in Cameron Highlands have been washed away by the floods. It's all over the newspapers.'

'There are no greens,' lamented Rishi. 'The whole market is devoid of leafy greens.' He thought of Lalitha's order for choi sum or pak choy. 'What is there left to eat?'

The old man laughed heartily at Rishi's concern, raising his hands. 'You better go and get some bean sprouts, I just saw the lorry coming in,' he informed Rishi. 'They'll go well with crab curry,' he suggested as he eyed one of Rishi's bags that had crawling mud crabs. Their hook-like claws had pierced through the bag revealing its contents. They also annoyed Rishi with the occasional scratch from the sharp claws that has turned his knee into a patch of red polka dots.

Bean sprouts and chives then, decided Rishi. He walked towards the huge cauldrons of spring water where the sprouts were being splashed and separated from their husks. He looked around while waiting for his turn.

A familiar face greeted Rishi at the beansprouts counter.

'Done with your shopping list, Robert Velayutham?' he asked formally. The man was younger to him at least by two dozen years.

Robert turned around and managed a smile. 'Yes saar, I have,' he answered. 'What about you?'

'Almost completed,' answered Rishi, looking up at the tall, hulking figure. 'How are your parents?'

'They are fine saar, thank you. I've completed the audit report you required, saar. Will pass it to your secretary tomorrow morning, saar.'

Rishi waved his hands as he walked away, 'It's Sunday, Robert. No work should be discussed outside of office.' He bade him goodbye, a smile forming a crescent on his face. 'Less work tomorrow,' he said, complimenting himself quietly.

'Saar,' Robert called out. Rishi stopped abruptly and found Robert walking towards him 'Taugeh saar, you forgot,' he grinned. Rishi accepted the small pack and fished his pocket for money. 'It's all right saar, I've paid for them,' said Robert as he hurried away.

A kilo of tomatoes later, Rishi decided he had had enough of the Buntong wet market. The restless movement in his plastic bag indicated that the crabs were very much alive and therefore, fresh. Thus, he decided there was ample time for breakfast before he headed home and prepared the crabs for the pot. The sweet smells of steaming loh mai kai, char siew pau and malai kuo stole out from the six-tiered bamboo wicker baskets, and filled the alley leading to the breakfast section of the market.

* * *

Belching after a bowl of curry mee, he looked about the clumps of shopping bags he had laid over another chair, and checked to see if he had missed anything from Lallu's list. Feeling accomplished, he sipped his coffee quietly, observing the hype of activities around him.

Rishi and Lallu lived alone. Rishi worked as a senior administrator of a private firm, a post-retirement job. It kept him occupied and wealthy, drawing a government pension (retired school teacher) with a private salary at the end of every month. He had finished settling his bank loans, paid for the house and was enjoying the fruits of his industrious years. Being a Chief Administration Officer, work at the private firm was not demanding. He had to organize schedules, assign workers their duties, audit paperwork, and supervise other administrative staff members. He had a personal secretary who did most of the paperwork. On an average, he worked not more than five hours in his office. And this had been the routine for the last three years he had been there. *I'm a glorified clerk,* he would chuckle, whenever asked about his job.

Though his contract had been renewed year after year, there seemed to be a problem this year. There was a contender. A new addition to his department, Robert, who was younger, more qualified and to his dismay, was going to be promoted to Head of Department. There had been nothing clearly stated about this, but his intuition was beginning to sound the alarm. Robert was going to take over his seat! There had been whispers among the management team that the GM was looking for someone more robust and proactive to work in the sales and promotional division, the very department Rishi had been in charge of for three long years.

He is gaining popularity with the other managers and senior staff, Rishi contemplated. *Is this it? Is the writing on the wall?* He had been losing sleep, neglecting his exercises, and becoming short-tempered with Lallu and avoiding their circle of friends, brooding over the resentment and anxiety that had begun to fill him.

'*Robert, Robert, Robert . . .*' The name poisoned his mind. It moistened his eyes with hot tears, filled his ears, clogged his nostrils and drummed his heart. He began to hear it in soft whispers. Sometimes he even misheard Lallu calling him 'Robert'. 'Why don't you stand up and tell him?' Lallu had burst out one day, 'rather than fretting about it?'

Rishi looked into his unfinished cup of coffee and pushed it away from him. Reclining on the chair, his hands clasped together, he stared, aware of the stress building within him. The little opening in the corrugated tin roof above him revealed an azure sky streaked with candyfloss clouds.

Transfer Robert out, secure the contract, he decided. He sat stoically, unfazed by the happenings around him. *The contract . . . the contract,* he mumbled silently. *The contract for holding onto the helm of the boat I have rowed and manoeuvred for three long years.*

The crabs were at it again. *Such clever crawlers, aren't you?* he chided them softly. The crabs, though their claws had been tied with raffia strings, had their pincers and legs mobile. With the basic instinct to survive, they had been working arduously to free themselves, looking for a way to escape.

'No, you don't,' Rishi said as he forced them back into the plastic bag.

The crabs had taken to climbing on top of each other, deliriously moving out of the plastic bag, through the loosely tied handles of the bag.

'You're not so clever,' said Rishi. Opening the loose ends of the plastic bag as wide as he could, he gave it a good shake and all the crabs tumbled onto each other into the bag's hollow belly.

'Be patient,' Rishi sniggered. 'Bliss is near.'

Deciding that he needed more time to sit and think, he signalled for the girl manning the char kui stall across the alley. Soon, two long deep-fried crullers arrived at his table.

Rishi ripped the twining char kui apart. He had been making plans for Robert. He would eliminate his competition, he decided. He will spread the news of Robert's transfer through the office grapevine first. Then, make an announcement during the staff meeting that Robert has been nominated by the GM, or hand-picked to be transferred, 'to shine in another department.' The management meetings were filled with storytellers, rumour mongers, and sensitive creatures. They would convey the message to Robert. They would take care of 'communication.'

The assassin is a two-faced cobra, he thought.

I should buy some horse hooves and ham chin peng for home, Rishi deliberated, as Lallu was fond of them. *Two ham chin pengs for tea*, he decided. Once microwaved, they bloomed into their crispy texture and were hot inside out. They went down well with a dollop of kaya, or a spread of margarine. But he would have to wait for the crowd to thin out first.

His nefarious thoughts returned. *Would Robert see the glinting knife of a backstabber?* He questioned his conscious self. *Would*

Robert sense what he was planning? No, he won't. Assassinations happened in extreme silences, in a vacuum of tranquility, Rishi assured himself. *Are people so dispensable? Am I so dispensable? Ungrateful all right, that's the way employers work these days. What about my age? Seniority? All that I am qualified to do? Dispensable? The fruits of my labor, enviable, but dispensable? Could I even tell this to Lallu? What would she think of me?*

He checked his watch. It showed half past ten. *I better get going,* he decided. 'Sau Loi,' he called out for the bill. A few heads turned in his direction. The noodle seller signalled to him to wait while making a mental calculation.

'Eight ringgit,' she shouted and her husband walked over to Rishi to collect the cash.

Rishi picked up his bag of vegetables, the bag of smothered crabs and walked over to the char kui stall. He found the large aluminium trays almost empty, except for two soggy char kui and three horse hooves. *Would two horse hooves suffice?* he wondered. But he had to wait as the lady behind the counter pushed the char kui to one side of the tray. The other workers were busy flipping a new batch of ham chin pengs which were sizzling on the surface of the hot oil.

He ruminated over his plans. *What should I do when Robert learns about his transfer? There must be questions on his mind. There is nothing stated in black and white. I have to make him feel unwelcome first. Make him feel that he does not belong.* And he knew exactly what he would do. There was going to be a staff meeting. He would simply, bluntly remove Robert's name from the department's attendance list. There would be confusion. Robert would be surprised. And he would come to him for an answer.

Poor Robert, Rishi feigned sympathy.

I will deny any knowledge of this, of having had any part in this. I will pretend this transfer was unwarranted. I will paint pain on my face. And tell him how hard I fought to retain him in my department. And despite everything I did, I was not able to convince them. Go, talk to the GM.

What if he does go and talk to the GM? Rishi wondered, exposing a hidden hazard.

Nah, he chuckled. *I know exactly what the GM will say to play safe.* Rishi took a breath of relief. *They all eat, walk and talk with an invisible catheter attached to their groins.* 'You are very good, Robert. You are good in everything. You can be here, there, north or south, east or west,' Rishi predicted an answer.

And when Robert returns, I will give him a pat on his back, like a father, and say that good things will come. One day, he will find out about this treacherous, contemptible act. But my pride is imperishable. No Robert, no Peter, no Tom, Dick or Harry can harm it.

Just then, a small boy appeared. He made his order in Chinese. Rishi could not make out what he wanted. The lady must have asked him to wait, for he stood subdued. He looked bright. He was spectacled, spiky-haired and thin. He was busy counting and recounting the coins he cupped in his hands.

Suddenly, Rishi fell back into despair. His face turned stoic and weary once more. He felt his muscles becoming taut.

'Robert,' Rishi called out to the little boy. The smoke from the wok warmed the sweat on his neck and hands. Rishi felt his heart beat picking up pace. *Must be the pressure kicking in,* he mumbled and felt his pockets for the spare CARDIPRIN 100 tablets. Picking one from a small pill wallet, he quickly gobbled it and waited for it to go down his throat.

'Don't panic, relax, breathe,' he pacified himself. He tried to think of all the good things he has amassed in his life. Lallu was waiting for him. There was the Sri Lankan crab curry for lunch. There was a movie he had recorded to watch on ASTRO after lunch. His mind raced, looped and coiled about in its convoluted plans. Soon, Rishi was suppressing an inexplicable anger, restraining himself from shouting at the woman who was taking forever to dish out the ham chin peng from the wok. *What's taking you so long?* he wanted to yell, but he caught the eyes of the little boy, examining him in a peculiar way.

'You want ham chin pengs, do you?' Rishi asked him.

The boy stared in bewilderment. He stood still.

'Do you think I will spare anything at all for you?' Rishi asked, pushing up his shoulders.

The boy tried to smile. He looked to the woman for assistance, but she was too busy wiping her oily hands on a rug.

'I'm a survivor. I run this race. I win. I came first,' Rishi announced sternly. 'Do you understand?'

Spreading the hot ham chin pengs to the centre of the tray, she finally deigned to take the orders, from Rishi first.

'Apa mau?' she asked.

'See, first come first served,' he told the boy who by now was avoiding eye contact.

'All,' said Rishi. 'I want all of them!'

Lifting a finger, he motioned a very large circle around the dozen ham chin pengs and waited for them to be picked up and shoved into the plastic bag.

He turned to the boy, who was eyeing the three remaining horse hooves.

'Over my dead body!' warned Rishi.

Just at the moment when the lady was about to ask the boy for his orders, Rishi pointed to the three remaining horse hooves for purchase, smiling maliciously at the boy, who now had lowered his head.

'You are young, you can wait,' Rishi parted with an advice. Proud of his haul, he left the market, forgetting for once, the crabs' painful pincers, scratching at the back of his knee and thigh.

Taxi Rescue

Raju's heart sank, hearing the whimpering noise coming from the back of his taxi. The road was almost deserted except for the row of scrawny rain trees, whose shadows spread out like angry witches under the bright street lights of Bangsar.

The noise grew louder. His heart began to beat nervously. He slowed down the taxi realizing he could have picked up a problem. *What if there is a police roadblock?* he wondered. *Or what if the rusted carburetor overheats and stalls?* He anxiously weighed the chances of things that could go wrong.

'Amma, amma,' he called out to his passenger. *So young,* he shook his head sadly. *Must be around nineteen. Could she be one of those college girls who have been infiltrating the night clubs on Ladies' Night? Should I call for help from the boys at the pub? No, they'll be up to no good. They'll take turns to finish her off and put their acts on WeChat video,* he shrugged distastefully. He weighed his options. *Shall I send her to the police station? Young as she is, she has a whole life ahead of her. No, no, not the police,* he decided. *I will have to make an official report and stand witness in this case. The world only believes in punishing. What if something like this befalls one's own children? All children are good. They come into this world, faultless and pure. It is the world that corrupts them.*

The girl moved about in the back seat, letting out loud moans. A few incoherent words could be heard between the coarse whining sounds. 'Aminu, you bad boy,' she said, pushing up her hands. 'Don't Aminu, don't do this.'

'Amma, don't kick against the door. It won't hold,' Raju warned her, but to no avail. The girl kept up her bouts of kicking against the loose door of the old Proton Saga. There was only one thing to do: park his taxi at the R&R on Federal Highway until she became sober enough—or take her to his house. He decided on the latter, fearing police patrols or tip-offs from the public.

'Who is Aminu, amma?' he tried to ask her.

'Aminu, Aminu,' the girl mumbled and threw up.

Raju stopped by the roadside, away from the street lights and stepped down to check on her. She was still lying on her stomach, stark naked, her buttocks rising like soft mounds of coffee buns under the quaint light. Exactly the way he had found her at the back alley junction of the infamous nightspot in Bandar Sunway. He had unloaded a passenger and was about to retire for the day just after midnight, when this nude Indian girl had staggered onto the little road. Nobody had followed her, and there was no one on the street.

She had tanned complexion, and long hair hid her face. A watch was strapped on her wrist and a thin gold anklet hung loose from her heels. Her bosom was full. The dark brown spots of her nipples stood out. Raju was transfixed at the sight, staring at the sensuous calves and the stubs of neatly cropped pubic hair. He was getting slightly dizzy. Now he was afraid of touching her.

'Wonder whose child this is,' he mumbled, finding that she had slumbered off on the back seat. *Wonder what the parents are up to. Leaving the poor girl to fend for herself. But children these days*, he suppressed a thought, coughing in the chill of the midnight breeze.

From his experience, most of these girls came from good families and from all working classes. Many came from outside Kuala Lumpur, and were instantly smitten by its lights and excitement. But most were tasting freedom for the first time. Free from the grips of a conservative family and the tight-knit community they had grown up in, they began to lose themselves in the world of delights and crossed over protective boundaries.

But why can't they have clean fun? Like the good old days? Or can't they even go clubbing with somebody they trust? Trust? That's the culprit, he deduced. Very often it was the circle of friends, or their boyfriends, who were the perpetrators. *And money*, he reckoned. Funds were so easily available these days, especially through education loans. *Makes everything so easy to obtain.*

'This way, this way, amma,' he instructed the girl, feeling his back hurt. He managed to turn her on her sides. His ears grew warm, as his palms ran over her smooth skin. He took in a few deep breaths. 'Shiva, Shiva,' he murmured. He unbuttoned his shirt and covered the exposed soft flesh. 'A child, a child,' he muttered to convince himself as he tied the long sleeves around her waist. 'Somebody's child is still my child.' Closing the doors hurriedly, he sat behind the wheel and began to drive towards his house in Puchong.

* * *

The neighbours' houses were covered in darkness and the lane leading to his house was empty. A few mongrels who had curled up conveniently on the pavements looked up and went back to sleep. A lone motorcyclist suddenly appeared from nowhere, throwing suspicious glances at Raju. *Must be an outsider*, he thought. He stopped the taxi and turned to look at the girl as he got out. She had curled up on the seat. He dreaded the next step as he opened the gates to his house. *Now, to wake up Sharada at this hour.*

Finally, he reversed his taxi into the small porch and got down again to close the gates behind him. The living room came alive with the flickering of fluorescent lights. *Sharada must not be fast asleep yet*, he thought. The doors opened and Sharada stood yawning before him. Running her fingers through her loose hair, she waited for Raju to go in before she closed the door. Raju did not enter. He stood by his taxi and waited.

'What have you got there?' Sharada asked, perplexed by his behaviour. Her face was taut with sleep as she stepped out clumsily to investigate. Sharada gave out a loud shriek, finding the sleeping girl, half-naked, and clad in Raju's shirt.

The first thing Raju did was to gesture for Sharada to remain quiet, in case she woke the neighbours.

'What have you brought this time?' she asked as she was about to retreat into the house with anger, when Raju caught hold of her hands.

'Please, Sharada, please, just this once,' he pleaded.

'Oh my God,' Sharada exclaimed, annoyed. 'Not again, not again!'

'Just look at this man!' Sharada began.

The children woke up and had come out to investigate the commotion.

'Can you be quiet?' he hushed her.

'Trust this man to go about driving a taxi to put food on the table for his family, and he picks up strays from the streets!' She raised her voice. 'And what did you bring this time? A half-naked girl, clad in your shirt. What will I do? What do I even make of this?' she lamented, burying her head in her hands.

'Can you just help me this once?' he pleaded again. 'She was helpless, standing in the alleyway. There was no one with her. She was waving frantically for a taxi, but nobody stopped. Just like that, and she's one of our own . . .'

'One of our own?' Sharada retorted. 'Charity begins at home, Raju. You can start with our daughters if you will.'

'Oh, Sharada, can you stop bickering? The neighbours might hear us. We'll let the girl sleep here on the couch till morning. Then I'll send her back. There won't be a problem,' Raju explained.

'Remember what happened the last time? You nearly got arrested for confining an individual at your house against her will! The parents of another girl you sent home refused to believe that you picked her up drunk. They told you their child never drank and nearly turned you in. Have you forgotten all that?' She snorted. 'What about that runaway maid? She scuttled away with my gold bangle. Have you forgotten that, too?'

'If we extend charity to other people's children in need, ours will be taken care of by someone else at their greatest time of need,' Raju philosophized. 'It's a terrible world out there, Sharada. One would never know what might befall her if she is left alone, Sharada,' Raju reasoned.

'Don't you dare equate this creature with my daughters!' Sharada pointed a finger at her husband. 'My girls would never end up on a road, naked, in the middle of the night like this damn whore,' Sharada shouted and hurried into the house. Raju followed her but stood at the doorstep, not knowing what to do next. A few moments passed in silence. A large beetle had stolen its way into the bright hall and took death-defying dives between the sharp blades of the ceiling fan. Raju entered the living room and sat beside her on the sofa and held her hand.

Sharada fidgeted, shook her head and moved away from the couch. She sat down on a lone chair and buried her face in her hands. 'I need to lock the door,' she said curtly.

Raju scurried out to the taxi and tried to wake the snoring girl. He brought a blanket out from his bedroom and tucked it under her. Then, with all his might, he carried her to the couch in the living room. The girl turned and the blanket dropped. To the baffled spectators she causally said, 'Switch off the lights, Aminu.'

'Aminu . . . why . . . of course. Now you know . . . her intestines might be full of cannabis. Raju, you just dragged a drug-mule home,' Sharada laughed wickedly. 'Here's your Aminu, right beside you,' she said bitterly to the girl and turned around. 'She could be dead in the morning if even one capsule bursts. Then what will you do, Raju? A dead mule, an invisible Aminu, the police and her parents! They will hold you accountable,' Sharada was convinced. She ordered her daughters to go back into their rooms.

'Kindness will never be remembered, Raju. She would not even remember your face after tomorrow,' Sharada slammed her bedroom door. Raju covered the sleeping body with a blanket and retired for the night. *Is she really pregnant with drug capsules? Is she really intoxicated? Ice? Syabu?* He began to sweat as he laid on the floor of his bedroom, wondering if police canines were capable of sniffing substances inside someone's belly. *Will they come knocking?*

* * *

A shuddering scream from Sharada awoke Raju from his slumber. He jumped up from the thin mattress and hurried out.

He found the girl he had brought home, sitting nonchalantly wrapped in their blanket on the porch. Sharada was standing a few metres away from her, asking the stoned creature to get into the house at once. Raju did not interfere. He stood at the door and observed the two women, hoping that the girl would open her mouth and say something.

'How did you get out?' Sharada kept asking. The girl stared at the sun rays stealing in through the awning.

'What happened to you? Who are your parents?' Sharada continued the interrogation.

Raju intervened at the moment when he thought Sharada was about to strike the girl. He stood between the two women, holding Sharada by her shoulders and pushing her away gently from the girl.

'If you don't come in, I'll throw you out into the street where you belong,' she threatened and went inside.

Raju stepped closer to the girl. Her face was pale and her eyes bloodshot. He bent down and tried to talk to her. 'Amma, amma,' he whispered. The girl remained as she was, like the granite structures of Easter Island, but there was a flicker of expression in her eyes. She had managed to pull the blanket under her armpits and tie a modest knot across her chest. Slowly, her face relaxed. She threw a look of disinterest at Raju. Pressing her lips together, she got up and walked lazily into the house.

'Don't ask her anything, she has a hangover,' Raju told Sharada, finding her in the kitchen. 'Let her collect herself. Give her some lime juice.' He avoided eye contact with his wife. 'If we have some lime.' The girl still did not budge. She looked around the living room, picked up the TV remote control and fiddled with it. The TV was switched off. Throwing the tool onto the table, she looked up at Raju as he came out from the kitchen.

Wonder what's she's looking for, thought Raju. *She doesn't seem to be too happy at being rescued and brought here.*

The lime juice never came. Asking again would invite Sharada's wrath, so Raju decided to leave both women alone. The girl needed time to recover from last night. She needed to wash out the toxins. *Alcohol or drugs?* He was not sure. He didn't want any of her drug capsules to burst, either. Leaving a large cup of cold water on the coffee table, he started to prepare his daughters for school and then went to drop them off. He returned home to find the girl seated on the same sofa in the hall where he had left her. He decided to take a bath and complete his morning ablutions. With a towel around his waist, he picked fresh flowers for the altar from his front yard. Then, he replenished the offerings of fruits and water before the array of smiling goddesses. He walked to every nook and corner of his house with sizzling frankincense. Poking a few incense sticks into the cracks of the door panels, he stood circling a tray of burning camphor over his doorstep.

'Do whatever you like,' said Sharada as she left for work. 'Bad luck doesn't have to come from outside our home; it's inside. Deal with it before I come back, or I will call the police right away. There is lime in the refrigerator. Make some juice for yourself, too.'

Raju ground his teeth. 'What a wretched world, Shiva . . . Shiva,' he hissed.

'Amma,' he called out to the girl. She turned grumpily towards him and folded her arms. *Ah*, he thought triumphantly. *The incense has livened up her senses at last.* 'Get ready. My wife has laid out some clothes for you in that room. You can bathe and get dressed. If you tell me where you live, I will send you back,' he said, pointing to the bathroom.

The aloof girl let out a yawn, got up from the chair, closed her eyes and scratched her cheeks. With no expression, she walked into the bathroom and locked the door behind her. Raju threw away his towel and quickly dressed in the dining area. Sharada had made some thosai and left a bowl of left over fish curry under the meal saver. He helped himself to the food and waited for the girl to come out.

Finally, she emerged, dripping from head to toe. She had gathered her hair and knotted it neatly like a silk tassel that hung over her shoulder. She looked fairer than last night, too. Tall and slim, she had oval eyes like those of a fish and a proportionate pair of cheekbones. Her earlobes were pierced, but nothing dangled from them. She limped across the living room, back onto the sofa without a word.

Raju was annoyed. There was only one thing on his mind, to return her to where she came from before the drug capsules burst and turned septic. *I won't be able to return a dead body anywhere*, he thought, growing cold at the possibility.

'You want some coffee?'

She did not answer.

'What about some breakfast?'

This time, she managed a smile. Raju moved away from the table. Gesturing for her to sit, he poured her a cup of coffee. The girl sat down and began to inspect the food as if she had not seen a thosai. She ate modestly, appreciating every morsel that she put into her mouth and chewing it slowly. It pleased Raju. The way she tore the sides of the thosai and carefully dipped its edges into the bowl, showed that she had been brought up well. Totally oblivious to Raju, she ate five of Sharada's thosais and drank two cups of black coffee.

Some colour returned to her face.

'Do you know what happened to you last night?' Raju began.

She lowered her eyes.

'What's your name? Where are you from?'

'Daksya,' she answered. 'Klang.'

Raju observed that her chin was puckered. 'Are you a student or a working woman?'

'Both,' she said. 'Both.'

'Where do you study?

There was silence.

'Are you local? Your parents live nearby?'

'Yes, Pandamaran,' she said, looking about the coffee table. 'Do you have a piece of paper, uncle?'

Raju was overjoyed with the sudden show of politeness. He ran into his daughters' room and returned with a pencil and a notebook. 'Here,' he said. The girl scribbled on a blank page. She tore it off and gave it to Raju.

'Finally, an address. I will send you there, amma, don't worry,' he promised.

'Who brought you to the pub?' he asked as an afterthought.

'A friend,' she said.

'What friend? Boyfriend? Was it Aminu?'

The girl lifted one hand and rested her cheeks on it. 'Aminu . . . Aminu Rasheed.'

What would a sweet, beautiful Hindu girl do with a *karuppan*? he thought, his earlobes warming slightly. No wonder the papers were full of such incidents. *This one is probably a future drug mule, or simply a comfort woman. A free smart phone, a laptop, weekly cash and the reputed big tools go a long way.* Raju shook his head.

'What's wrong with you? You have a whole life ahead of you, amma. You need to study, go to work, get married,' he started. 'What would people say? Your parents will be so heartbroken.'

At this juncture, the girl rolled her eyes and buried her entire face in her hands.

'Do you know, I found you loitering in the nude in the middle of the city? What would have happened if I hadn't bumped into you?' he asked angrily.

The girl laughed. Raju's words froze at the end of his tongue in shock.

Perhaps she knew what she was getting into, he began to realize. *Have I been so cut off from the ways of the world? Regret seems to be almost non-existent in some people's dictionary, and this mule deserves a lesson.*

'You don't care if your whole life is spoilt, do you?' he asked. 'Aren't you disappointing your parents? What if you got killed?'

The girl smiled curtly.

'You only live once, uncle,' she answered. 'Aminu and I were parting ways. He said it was good to have a drink. We went to have a drink. His friends came unannounced. I have no idea what happened next.'

Raju did not want anything more to do with her story. He would send her home. *She's probably possessed,* he thought. *Maybe she is not really Daksya. What she needs is a good bashing from a bushel of blessed neem leaves, or better still, Sharada's broom.* 'Get up, I'll take you home and have a word with your parents.'

The address led Raju to a huge house in a posh guarded community. The towering chrome gates stretched almost eighteen feet from one end to the other. Fancy wrought-iron grilles ran along a concrete wall and disappeared into a corner. There was a lush garden and two luxury cars parked in the porch. The girl opened a side gate and vanished into the house through its partially opened timber door, with a life-size carving of the elephant God, Ganesha.

'If this is what it means to be rich . . .' thought Raju.

He had told the girl that he would like to see her parents. He sat on one of the rattan chairs available on the tiled porch and waited. After almost ten minutes, the door was still ajar and no visible movement or audible noise indicated anyone coming out to see him. Raju looked for the doorbell, and pressed it twice, then thrice. A shadow moved towards him through the front door. He stood up in anticipation.

It was a maid, looking sullen and tired. She came up to him and handed three red notes.

'Where is the girl?' he asked her in Malay.

'Tidur,' she said, putting one of her cheeks on her palm.

'The parents?' he implored again.

'Sudah keluar, go out to town' the maid answered. This time, he could see that she was not very pleased to be out with him. 'Go away,' she said.

He twitched his nostrils. 'How can they be out when the cars are here?' he asked the maid.

'Miss say gip dis to you, sir,' she whispered shyly. 'I do work now, can you go?' she asked, smiling nervously. She pressed the three red notes into his hands and showed him to the gate. Once he was outside, the gate was latched and locked.

What has this world come to? Not even a slice of gratitude? He climbed into the taxi and rolled the crumpled notes in his hands. Looking about the house, he found a security camera turned in his direction. He wound down the window and threw away the money. While he waited to compose himself, he watched the notes fluttering about in the wind. One got stuck on the pavement leading up to the gates. Two notes rose high enough and vanished behind the wall.

To the Cheramah

Today, an excited Kamsiah had called upon Devi and Sui Kin to attend the 'Meet Your Local Representative' event, organized by the local municipality council. According to her there was free food, and also food hampers to be given away to those who attended from their housing area. They had been neighbours for almost ten years at the city's low-cost housing units and had agreed to walk together to attend the event arranged by the local town council. Kamsiah, especially, was looking forward to meeting the local MP who had dashing good looks and a complexion that was *putih melepak*.

Devi, a young mother of three, would have given it a pass. She was tired of the fanfare, having experienced it at wedding dinners and similar 'meet your politician' functions. The long wait usually exhausted her appetite, and the food would be cold and dull by the time it arrived. But the hampers had sounded promising. What her husband earns is enough to pay the house rent and bills. If she asks for more, he throws a tantrum. If she questions about his liquor spending, he beats her up, sometimes in front of the children. If only she could save some money from the grocery list, she could take her son to consult a specialist in a private hospital. *Any extra provisions are a welcome too. Why waste them?* She had thought. Thankfully, a friend had agreed to swap shifts with her at the battery chicken farm where she worked.

Devi got dressed and powdered her face for the second time. She made sure her pottu stuck properly between her eyebrows. Dressed in a wide, pastel-coloured skirt and blouse with flower prints, she wondered if she looked too flamboyant for the event. *A sari would be a nightmare in this heat*, she shook her head. In her hands she squeezed a neatly folded handkerchief that she had grown so accustomed to carrying from her school years. Only a few more things to check before she goes on her way to the event.

'Devi, come faster,' a voice called to her.

She consciously confirmed to herself that she had passed the spare key to her eldest son, who would be back from school with his siblings in an hour. She then inspected the small square table in the kitchen where she had left the lunch of fried mee hoon kosong for the children. She also remembered warning them not to play on the wet sand in their compound or suffer a caning. She took her purse, made sure her identity card and money left from her salary were inside, and shuffled it into her skirt's side pocket. She made sure her only gold chain and two bangles were safely secured in a pouch, hidden in one of her husband's old trouser pockets. Finally, she drew all the curtains close, switched off the electrical appliances and went out to close the door behind her. She did not have an iron grille protecting her door, but put all her trust in a padlock, and left the house to divine protection.

Sui Kin, her immediate neighbour, had arrived. They would meet Kamsiah at the end of the block of houses on their street. Sui Kin wore a navy blue skirt and blouse, a jade bangle, and carried a large velvet purse. *She looks a tad too elegant for an event in her own backyard,* thought Devi.

'How is your son?' Sui Kin asked, concerned as they began to walk. 'He started to go to school or not?'

'Yes, aunty, but his health is still not good,' replied Devi sadly. 'He is still vomiting from time to time, aunty, although the stomach cramps have reduced. The medicine from the clinic is not very effective. Yesterday, I pulled out another worm from his eye.'

Sui Kin gave Devi a stare down.

'Haiya, what's wrong with you people?' Sui Kin snorted. 'How many times have I asked you to go and see the specialist? One time see specialist can solve the problem. If worm coming from eye, serious one. Can die, you know. You still want to wait ah? Haiya . . . haiya . . . just spend a few hundred only.'

'Yes, my husband said need to wait for a few more days. He said he has asked his friend to borrow us some money. The money I have saved is not enough. I am trying very hard to make ends meet, and I have no one who can help me also aunty,' said Devi, almost resigned.

Sui Kin shook her head. A large figure in a bright orange baju kurung with a matching tudung, brooch and black shoes stood scrutinizing the buntings tied to the poles of the street lights.

'There she is,' Sui Kin pointed to Kamsiah as they walked up to meet her.

'Let's go,' said Kamsiah, without wasting time.

The narrow road leading to the hall was exceptionally clean and livened with rows of banners and more buntings. They displayed portraits of the VIP, party logos and captions. A chrome arch had also been erected at the entrance of the otherwise dull houses lining the street. The roads had been resurfaced; the street lights fixed and brand new sign boards stood proudly in the place of the pale, dented ones. Their neighbourhood had been spruced up beyond recognition, observed the three ladies, and they were satisfied.

'All for the VIP, lah,' exclaimed Sui Kin. 'Then the reporters can say nice-nice things in the paper tomorrow.'

The sun shone right on top of their heads. The three ladies were sweating as they trudged up the road that led to the hall. The street was already crowded with cars and people.

'Why are you not dressed properly?' Sui Kin asked Devi. 'VIP coming one, haiyo, must look good one, lah.' Devi looked about in search of an answer. *Now, what is this Chinese aunty thinking?* She thought, annoyed. *I'm already at my wit's end each month, money dissolving faster than water and she's concerned over my attire. She thinks I can afford pretty clothes and go gallivanting? What does she know about my problems, with each day being a struggle? School fee and pocket money for the children is a struggle; shopping, even during Deepavali, is an unthinkable feat; or a KFC treat that is random lunch for some is something I deliberate upon for weeks, at least. On top of that, I am putting up with that crook of a husband who could not spare his drinking money for his sick child.* Kamsiah, who was a step ahead of them, sensed the tension building up in Devi and intervened in time. She reassured Devi that she looked just fine and urged them to hurry up.

'What did you cook today?' asked Kamsiah.

'Eat outside, loh,' Sui Kin replied.

'Fried mee-hoon Kak,' Devi said. 'I'm on leave today.'

'Good lah, good, good. We had late breakfast today and teh'o,' Kamsiah said from in front. 'Devi, your son okay now?' she asked. Without waiting for an answer, she suggested to Devi to cement the compound of her house. 'You know, children like to play on the sand. That's how the eggs enter the body, through the fingernails and toenails.'

'Now, I don't let them play outside,' Devi replied. 'But it is my mother-in-law who is minding the children when I'm away at work at her house. I think she is careless.'

'I know, I know. Even if they play with sand, make sure they come inside and wash their hands and feet with soap, correct or not?' said Kamsiah.

'Correct, correct,' Sui Kin answered. 'Maybe you could ask your landlord to tile your compound or cover it with cement. Safer and cleaner.'

Devi gave out a short laugh. 'My landlord is stingy,' she said. 'Won't even repair the leaking water tank or extend a wire. Scared we would ask him to turn his house into a castle. Wants to forfeit our deposit at the slightest of repairs. Nothing like you owning your own house. But we won't demand anything from him. He is kind enough not to harass us over delayed rent payments.'

'One day, you will buy a house, Devi, when your children grow up, just be patient,' said Kamsiah, giving her a little pat on her shoulder.

Sui Kin sighed.

The deafening beats of a dozen kompang drowned the voices of Kamsiah, Sui Kin and Devi, as they approached the local community centre. Men in various uniforms were running about with walkie-talkies in their hands to ensure that the VIP's arrival was smooth. The police had already cordoned off the main entrance to the hall and guests had to use the side doors. Traffic policemen wearing white gloves were directing traffic out of the crowded car-park. The organizers were dressed elegantly and dazzled in shiny *batik* outfits with programme booklets in their hands. People from the housing area continued to fill the hall. At the entrance, younger men in traditional attire stood sweating profusely with bunga manggar, while two pretty ladies in elaborate costumes waited under the shade of the canopy with a large scissor on a tray.

'Waaah, already full house,' said Sui Kin, looking at the crowd.

'Don't worry, aunty, I have already booked the seats for us with my friend's help, so that we can get a cool spot under the fan,' Kamsiah replied proudly. 'We just need to look for her now.'

The hall was packed with familiar faces. People were exchanging greetings and the place was abuzz with their conversations. There were about forty tables and each had ten chairs cramped tightly around it. The plates and cutlery were in place with plastic wine glasses, serviettes and a large silver chafing dish covering two-thirds of the table space. It looked like an elaborate affair with the sides of the hall decorated with balloons and ribbons, and the stage adorned with more plastic flowers. The backdrop had large pink words carved out from Styrofoam to match the tables and chairs covered in smooth pink linen skirting. The VIPs sat in the middle of the hall, at the larger table with a grander chafing dish, so big that it gleamed like a flying saucer. The smell of sweet syrup and pungent spices wafted throughout the hall.

Kamsiah looked around and found her friend. They waved to each other. She had picked the most elusive spot. Their seat gave a perfect forty-five degree angle view of the VIP table. The ladies exchanged pleasantries with those already seated at the table. Devi and Sui Kin sat down first. Frowning, Sui Kin bent down to massage her knees and aching muscles. The other ladies who seemed to be Kamsiah's acquaintances got up, gathered around her and took a group photo. Then, they retreated to their chairs and sat listening to her as she narrated stories about her home, her husband who worked at the National Electricity Board, her three children (the eldest studying on a state-funded scholarship at a foreign university, her two younger sons studying at a religious, full-boarding school, two states away) and people who were absent from the function.

The noise from the kompang troop sounded like a boom box as they began to march into the hall and the audience rose from their seats, a sure sign that the VIP had arrived and was making his entrance. Kamsiah quickly looked about in her handbag and produced a small digital camera. A clicking race ensued between her and the other guests and the official photographers. Being too shy to move closer to the podium, she started taking pictures from where she stood. She raised her hands, careened her neck, and moved sideways to get her shots. The camera buzzed as its shutters opened and closed, auto-adjusted or zoomed in and out for a perfect view. Two ladies standing behind her, jerked their heads at her relic and laughed with their mouths cupped. One even tapped softly on Kamsiah's shoulder to say that it was enough. At one point, they jokingly suggested that she was short and should climb on a chair. Kamsiah couldn't care less. She continued until the VIP and the guests were invited to take their seats and the official protocols of the majlis began. Satisfied, Kamsiah began to inspect the pictures. They sat down again after the VIP took his seat.

'How many children?' an older lady sitting beside Sui Kin enquired.

'Two,' Sui Kin replied, short and curt.

'How many for you?' the same lady asked Devi.

'Five,' she said. Her voice was jittery, worried that her eldest son might start playing with his siblings on the wet sandy compound again since she was away.

'How old is your eldest?'

'Eleven,' said Devi, wondering if the children would eat their lunch on time.

'All still small,' the lady gauged the rest of the children's ages. 'Where does your husband work?'

'Public Works Department. Contract labourer,' she answered the nodding lady. 'What about your children?' the lady asked Sui Kin who pretended to look away. 'Busybody,' she whispered into Devi's ears.

Sui Kin on the other hand had two sons, who she usually dismissed as useless, lazy and tidak peduli. One had dropped out of school after his O-Level exams and was helping out at his father's car workshop, while doing a part-time Automobile Diploma at a nearby college. The other boy had finished his A-levels. Unable to secure a medical seat at the public university, he was waiting for a scholarship that would fund his studies in Taiwan. Sui Kin's house was one of the best renovated on the street, making Devi's rented property an eyesore. Their backdoors shared Kamsiah's.

'How is your son, the one overseas?' Kamsiah's friend enquired.

'Oh, he is in Bristol,' Kamsiah replied. 'Very cold country. Very expensive. He already is planning to come back.'

'Why?' the ladies chorused.

'He got offered to do dentistry. He doesn't want that course. Maybe he wants to finish his Foundation studies only. Then come back here and do sports science.'

'But expensive to live there and do nothing lah,' another one said.

'He got scholarship money. His girlfriend also gets allowance, they share lah. He will stay there and travel also. Waste you know, you go so far and never travel.'

'Yes, yes.'

'Lagipun,' Kamsiah added fervently. 'Their English is a little slanting a bit. Difficult to catch up what they say, he complained. That's why cannot study.'

The women shook their heads sympathetically.

'When we get something for free, why not take it?' Sui Kin butted in.

'Like today's makan also free, so why not,' Kamsiah blurted with a laugh, patting Sui Kin on her elbow.

Devi's eyes were fixed, not on the VIP, the government officials or the buffet, but on the little hamper everyone would get. Kamsiah's husband was a member in the working committee for the event, and he had informed her of the hamper's contents. A sack of rice, cooking oil, two packets of sugar, two tins of sardines, baked beans and peas, a tin of biscuits, and a carton of condensed milk.

That should keep me going for a month, she thought, motivated. *That money could be used to consult the specialist. He has lost so much weight. At least four kilos,* she thought worriedly. *He has no appetite, even if I bought him his favourite Zinger burger.* Her eyes began to grow moist. Now she was tremendously worried. The worms, according to the doctor at the neighbourhood public clinic, would have infested his internal organs, like his heart. He needed urgent medical attention. But at government hospitals, appointments came late. Devi had hardly slept ever since. She did not wear a watch. So she depended on Sui Kin, mindful that it was irritating her each time she asked the time.

Kamsiah was intoxicated by the all the views, smell and sounds, and had been rendered breathless by the time the VIP had taken his seat. She kept pressing her cheeks from time to time and muttered words like 'lawa lah dia', to the women around her who were busy decoding where he lived, what car he owned and whether he was married.

The VIP was tall and athletic, exceptionally white (Javanese, the women deduced), and had defined features (Indian or Arab, the women were fickle). He was smartly dressed and intellectual-looking (must have studied, lived or worked in Europe) and had a stately aura (royal blood) about him. He smiled and was very obliging to the organizers.

'In front of the cameras, sure like that lah,' Sui Kin snorted.

The rest looked bewildered at her condescending remark.

Noticing their displeasure, Sui Kin retorted jokingly. 'I am very hungry, where is the food,' she asked, as she tapped on her watch and looked away.

Devi and Kamsiah too felt a little pinch in their stomachs. Some of the women at the table were already taking sheepish peeks into the chafing dish and making wild guesses at the menu. The aroma was inviting and did not help in keeping hunger at bay. Sui Kin and Devi deduced that there was good food awaiting them.

'But, it will be long before we can have the food,' warned one of the ladies, sighing.

'Nasib baik, I had something earlier at home,' said yet another.

Another lady, probably used to such events, produced small packets of peanuts, dates and raisins and passed them around the table. 'This should hold,' she said.

The majlis started with a prayer. Kamsiah and the rest opened their palms and sat still. Then, the national anthem was played. They stood still. First, there was entertainment. It was called the tarian muhibbah, an integrated multi-racial dance number. Men and women from the same dance troop performed a medley of traditional dances—Malay, Chinese, Indian, Portuguese and Indigenous. They looked funny, mismatched, when they presented the short spurts of the Indian and Chinese numbers, both in their costumes and dance movements. And Sui Kin was appalled.

'Chinese got dance like that, ah?' she asked Devi who now was smirking, her mind still fixed on her children at home. Kamsiah was again busy clicking on her camera, not wanting to miss anything.

'Eh Kamsiah, you snap pictures of dancers or the smiling VIP?' chuckled Sui Kin. The ladies laughed sheepishly too.

Then, the speeches began. By now, it was already 2 p.m. The crowd was becoming restless. Most of them were elderly and probably diabetic, or had kidney problems and hyper-tension—common illnesses that were a shared legacy among Malaysians. There was worry on their faces. If their sugar levels dropped, they could go into a state of hypoglycaemia, and this would not augur well. But this, the organizers did not take into consideration. There were strict protocols that could not be breached. The first speech was given by the chairperson of the Housing Committee, somewhat long and over-courteous. Then it was the mayor, whose speech was longer, infused with free-flow Arabic. Finally, it was the VIP's speech, the most important, so it was longer but business-like. Nonetheless, all the speeches were uniform in information about the government's effort in improving lives with the people at its core. Halfway through the speech, the hall came alive with whispers, people fanning themselves and simply nodding off.

The thick layer of foundation on Kamsiah's face melted like lava-cake. Now, her face, neck and hands were of different shades. Bored and exhausted, she too had resigned herself to the situation and sat resting her arms on the table, picking at the table cloth, interrupted now and then by the other ladies. At intervals, she remembered to pacify Sui Kin and Devi by telling them that food would arrive shortly. Sui Kin settled herself on the plastic chair that she didn't quite fit in. She fanned herself with her handkerchief and folded her arms. Her face blushed red, lips pursed with annoyance and she swayed her head left and right.

Devi, on the other hand, sat detached from her surroundings. Nervously, she asked Sui Kin if she could see the time on her watch. Sui Kin jutted out her wrist across Devi's face, almost brushing her nose. Thin lines crossed her forehead. She wondered loudly if her children had arrived home from school safely, if they had helped themselves to lunch or if some unforeseen calamity had visited them in her absence. She was hushed by Sui Kin, who was clearly irritated.

It was now 2.30 p.m. and another prayer was recited over lunch. Servers came and opened the chafing dishes as silently as possible and revealed an assortment of preparations arranged side-by-side in octagonal bowls. There was chicken curry, beef rendang, vegetables, pineapple sambal, pickles and dhall.

'But where is the rice?' murmured everyone. Soon, they realized that rice was kept for the last, as servers began to carry it on platter loads and place it on the tables. However, the servers started from the VIP table first.

Soon, the speeches forgotten, clanking sounds of china, forks and spoons echoed in the hall. Here and there, people stood at tables and helped to pass the food to each other. At Kamsiah's table, everyone filled their plates with the dishes first, while waiting for the rice to arrive, some taking their bites beforehand.

'Food presentation,' Kamsiah scoffed at the server, and the other ladies nodded.

'This is beef,' Kamsiah warned Devi and pointed to the darkest dish on the bowl. She pointed to a few more. The vegetables had been fried with strips of cow liver, and after tasting the dhall, she confirmed that it was cooked with beef, too. One by one the ladies sympathized with Devi.

Oh, you're Hindu?

Hindus cannot consume beef, right?

Can you push away the meat and take only the vegetables or just the gravy?

They had all tried to help, but could do nothing. 'That's three out of five, Devi,' Sui Kin cackled. 'And look out for the ladles, too, they've been dipped into every other bowl.'

'Never mind, never mind. You can eat this,' the ladies offered, and pushed the bowl of chicken curry towards Devi.

Sui Kin giggled. When Devi had taken a piece, she moved the bowl to the centre of the table. 'We can all share. Devi cannot finish eating all of it.'

The rice finally arrived and was passed around the table. Silence fell as everyone began to eat to the beats of Chinese and Tamil songs, interspersed with patriotic and Siti Nurhaliza songs aired on speakers around the hall. The syrup was gone in a few minutes and the dishes, too. Kamsiah asked the servers if food could be replenished, but her request was turned down.

The lady sitting beside her told her that everyone should go home if they are still hungry. Kamsiah scowled at her.

Then the announcements were made. It was time for the hampers to be given away. Kamsiah wiped her face and the corner of her lips with serviettes and applied another layer of powder. She adjusted her tudung and asked her friend to click another picture of her on her camera, tilting her neck and smiling seductively for the pose. The VIP walked up to the stage and was joined by the organizers. The MC had a long list in his hands and he began to read out names from the list in alphabetical order. An hour had passed, but there was no Devi under the 'D' section or Sui Kin under the 'S'.

Devi was hopeful, though, at the sight of extra hampers left on the stage. However, the list came to an end after a long row of people had ascended and descended from the stage. The hamper presentation ended. No more names were called thereafter. The organizers were cheerily shaking hands with the VIP and with each other on the stage. The VIP was asked to wait and a huge token in a glass casing was given to him, with two paper bags bursting with extra hampers. Then, he too descended from the stage and walked to his table, with his assistant carrying the souvenir and hampers.

They were left without hampers.

Devi felt a pang in her heart. The guilt of eating the good food without her children broke her heart. On top of that, there was nothing for her to carry back home. At least she could have afforded to buy a bottle of Horlicks for her son if she got the groceries. She knew it could rejuvenate his strength momentarily while awaiting money to buy good medicines. She felt angry being left out. She had done nothing to deserve this. She felt she should walk up to the politician and tell him off. Why not feed her, too? It is she who's battling a tapeworm infestation, not them!

Sui Kin looked down, tired, green-eyed and embarrassed.

Kamsiah managed a few smiles. The rest of the ladies smiled, too. The problem was diagnosed after a little while.

'Did you register?' one of the women asked.

Sui Kin said, 'No. Nobody asked.'

'Where are you from?' another asked. 'Do you live here?'

'Lived here all my life,' said Sui Kin.

'Takpe la, never mind,' the same lady butted in. 'The lunch was good.'

The rest nodded.

Kamsiah remained quiet and looked away.

The majlis ended at teatime, with the VIP escorted out first. Everyone stood up after he was out of sight and got ready to leave. Kamsiah was not excited anymore, nor did she click any photos. Then the guests slowly trickled out of the hall, tired and sleepy, bidding goodbyes while lugging their hampers.

As they left the hall, Kamsiah began to undo the ribbon on top of her hamper and rummaged through its contents.

'All inside lah, don't worry,' Sui Kin assured her.

Kamsiah held the hamper packet under one elbow and took out the condensed milk tins and shoved them towards Devi and Sui Kin.

'Take,' she offered, 'we don't really use these.'

Devi and Sui Kin declined, an unexplained heaviness marking their tone.

Then after thinking for a few seconds, Kamsiah rummaged through her package again, managed to take out the tin of biscuits and pushed it into Devi's hands, smiling.

'Give this to your children,' she said.

Devi accepted. *Better a tin of biscuits,* she thought gratefully, her mind still coveting the huge bag of rice and cooking oil she had seen earlier.

Shaking her head, Sui Kin pushed the condensed milk tins again towards Devi, who took them.

'Got condensed milk, no tea dust, how to make tea?' she asked Kamsiah playfully.

'Owh,' Kamsiah tapped her fingers on a large BOH tea packet. 'We use this also,' she said. 'But never mind.' She stacked it on top of the condensed milk and biscuit tin on Devi's hands.

'What about you, Sui Kin? I cannot let you go home empty-handed,' she said.

'Don't worry about me,' she replied. 'We keep everything in stock. If not, we drink sugar water,' declared Sui Kin as she gave a big, hearty laugh and walked on, her velvet purse tucked tightly under her armpit.

Flesh

'Get up, faster, faster,' a familiar voice cajoled Syamu.

'The rubbish men come, move away,' Big Sister shouted, her nose clamped between two fingers. She tried to open her eyes, but they were held shut by sticky rheum. She could hear the whining noise of the dumpster's mechanical slurping of the rubbish getting louder.

Big Sister picked a cardboard to slap Syamu. 'Wait lah, you fucking bitch,' Syamu cursed as she laboured to get up, just in time for the municipality workers to push out the large-wheel bin from the garbage chamber she called home. Like a blind, she felt her way to the concrete steps that went up the brothel's back door where she used to work. There, she groggily scraped out the muck from her eyes and squinted at daylight. She caught attention of something lying on the drain cover and stopped.

'Now what's this?' she murmured as her fingers crept up a packet that had rolled out from the trash bin. 'Waaah,' she yelped, discovering a half-eaten bun.

Big Sister, clad in a pair of denim hot pants and singlet, stood at the door, noisily drawing iced Milo from a large packet through a straw. Her wooden clogs tick-tocked as she shifted her weight from one leg to another. The buckle on her belt shimmered. The empty wheel bin was pushed back into the trash vent and the dumpster rolled off to the next street. Losing interest, Big Sister handed the half-finished drink to Syamu and vanished behind the blinds of her establishment.

'Look, we have breakfast,' Syamu whispered, examining a small bump surfacing around her belly button.

Straining, she squatted slowly. Lifting her skirt, she pulled her knees towards her chin and closed her eyes. Her pelvis convulsed with pain and almost numbed her bladder. 'Sheesh, sheesh, sheesh,' she murmured. A burning liquid oozed between her legs, sloshing her calves and the concrete slab where she squatted. The ordeal over, she dropped her skirt and moved away from the pool of thick green liquid, sighing with relief.

Rearranging some cardboard sheets, she planned to resume her sleep before going out to beg. *Trash bins smell worst after they have been cleared*, she thought, perturbed by the trash that tumbled down the garbage chute and scattered on the floor. Tearing off a piece of newspaper, she brushed away cooked vegetables and a soiled diaper into the gutter behind her.

Noise from the rickety dumpster seemed to have woken up the residents of the notorious Jalan Thambipillay that hosted the red light district's love holes. Prostitutes and transsexuals began to fill up the small lane, sashaying down the emergency staircase from the rear of their brothels, sleep-stricken and moody.

Syamu retreated into the garbage chamber and peeped from her corner at the monorail's elevated tracks that formed a welcoming arch. The back alleys provided a discreet entrance to the brothels for office workers, college students and migrant workers who wanted to indulge in short and quick fixes of ganja or sex. By late afternoon, the traders came to set up their stalls and the back alley became crowded with shoppers and pedestrians, alike. There were food hawkers, fruit sellers, florists who sold colourful chrysanthemums in buckets, garment and textile traders, Malay exhibits of glossy religious books, coils of tasbih and perfumes and the occasional evangelists who negotiated everlasting, contented lives in heaven with competing porn VCD peddlers.

Syamu must have dozed off, when again she was jabbed gently in her ribs. She looked up. A gaunt woman whose face had thick lines of age had stopped by. A pony tail hung from the end of her bald scalp with hair clips holding the thin strands together. Pulling the sides of her mini skirt, she made a guttural sound and squatted before Syamu. It was Atiqah, grinning like a cat. Her heavy make-up against the grey eye-bags made her look like an emaciated corpse. Atiqah's transparent amulet broke into a rainbow in the bright sunlight as she placed a lunch box by Syamu's side. Sliding her hand underneath Syamu's dress she rubbed the full belly and closed her eyes. Then she left quietly.

Syamu brushed away a lone maggot that was inching up her elbow. The cramps in her belly and spine were becoming unbearable. Sitting up, she leaned against the moss-covered wall of the garbage chamber, her nose filled with the mustiness around her.

Syamu opened the lunch box and inspected its contents. Her baby almost kicked in revolt, sending a bout of nausea. She shook her head, looking at the fried salted fish and oily sawi, swimming in a sea of bright yellow coconut and turmeric gravy. She secured the lid of the Styrofoam box and put it aside. She would leave it for later, if the collection for the day was bad. *Begging, these days,* she thought, *was not promising.* The Myanmar syndicates put her through harrowing shifts. Sometimes, she had to carry a toddler. They took a large cut. Other syndicates beat her for trespassing into areas controlled by them. In the worst case scenario, beggars were rounded up by the city council, never to be seen again.

Syamu pondered on a garlic naan with butter chicken gravy. She salivated at the thought. Her baby kicked again. *I will look for Ghulam today*, she decided.

The muezzin's call for prayer gave music to the smog-filled atmosphere of Brickfields. Soon, men clad in cheap lungis, rubber slippers and drenched in attar oils would fill the brothel. Within the remaining time from the long Friday lunch breaks, they hurriedly humped the prostitutes, smothering their painted faces with their bristly facial hairs. Syamu hated the smell of the attar oil. Their strong odour poisoned her sinuses. But all that changed after a peculiar customer walked in one day.

* * *

Syamu did not understand his peculiarity at first. She was only accustomed to the thirty-sixty-ninety packages—blowjob, sex with or without condoms.

'Take care of him, good, good,' Big Sister had instructed Syamu. At the door, stood the handsomest of men she had ever seen. He was well-dressed with refined features of the princes depicted on murals that graced the walls of north Indian restaurants. His height, athletic shoulders, facial hair, puffy elbows and sturdy knees looked proportionate in his long, white *shalwar*. Syamu gasped, taken in by the perfection. She had heard of such beauty in women, *but a man?* she wondered.

He entered the cubicle and sat meekly at the edge of the bed, his back to Syamu. 'Thirty, sixty or ninety?' asked Syamu to get down to business.

'Thirty,' he said.

Once a man unzipped, everything alike. Her role became arbitrary and all else was irrelevant. Syamu touched his broad shoulders and got down to work. Once it was over, he pulled up his pants, knotted the waist string of his trousers and left abruptly. But, his perfume lingered.

The following Friday, Big Sister put her hand over Syamu's shoulders. 'One customer like you so much, he wants two hours today night,' she blinked. Syamu raised her eyebrows. *Is she teasing?* 'You good girl, so I gip you 50 per cent,' Big Sister promised. *Then it must be a big amount, bigger than ninety,* Syamu concurred. 'He gip you this,' said Big Sister, passing a white plastic bag. Inside was a new kurti, made of cheap cotton.

That evening, the pimps threw curious looks at Syamu. The other prostitutes sniggered playfully as they started their shifts. Atiqah said she smelt a rat, but advised Syamu not to think too much.

'Maybe you now become Cinderella,' she laughed mockingly. 'Can I see your shoes?'

'Too much of Disney up your asshole,' Syamu scoffed.

Syamu put on the pale kurti, wore a plastic necklace and adorned her hair with jasmines. She waited, like a bride on her nuptial night, giggling at the new arrangement. Soon, she heard the unmistakable thumps of Big Sister's clogs on the wooden flooring. The door creaked open, and a whiff of rose-scented perfume assailed the cubicle. *It is the same man,* reckoned Syamu, *but his gait is more confident and sturdy; he dresses fashionably but is not rich,* she observed. Standing before the mirror on the old rustic dressing table, he loosened the cuffs of his sleeves. He took off his brass rings, his watch and arranged them neatly on the table. Syamu caught a glimpse of him in the mirror. He turned around and smiled.

'Ghulam,' he said in a husky voice, as he came to lie beside her. She found his congeniality slightly obnoxious and cocky.

For some reason, Syamu was embarrassed by his etiquette. Men came and did what they did. Nobody told or asked anything.

She felt a gentle touch, firm yet pleasing, pulling her towards the pillow. Ghulam laid on one elbow rubbing his beard with the back of his fingers. *This is the nearest I've got to someone I like*, she thought nervously. She looked into his deep eyes, wavy eyelashes rimmed by kohl. She wondered if she could run her fingers over the thick eyebrows. Her eyes seem to close under Ghulam's intense stare. She swallowed a few gulps of the rose-scented air. *Am I drowning?* she asked herself.

He touched her forehead. Syamu turned her attention to the soggy walls of the room they were in. The pretty flowers on the peeling wallpaper were blushing. A warm, ticklish feeling enveloped her as Ghulam began to run his fingers over her cheekbones, shoulders, arms and cleavage.

'You are beautiful,' he said blandly, his hot breath warming her earlobes. He untied the waist string of his trousers. *Unlike others, he is composed*, Syamu realized. He touched her lips, but would not kiss them. He touched her flesh, but would not grope or kiss or nibble. *Is he without experience?* she deliberated. He was now tilted on her side, slowly shifting his weight on her. With one leg he parted her thighs. Syamu let out a little laughter.

'What is funny?' he asked. He climbed on top of her and without warning, slapped her. Shocked, she tried to apologize. *What if he leaves and complains to Big Sister?* she panicked. Another slap and she surrendered. Ghulam tore Syamu's blouse like a hungry lion. With one hand, he pulled down her trousers. He penetrated her, making her squirm. He snorted as he went up and down. The bedding and floor were littered with the petals of jasmines from Syamu's hair.

He spat on her face when he pulled out from her. She gasped for air. She got up and limped to the adjoining bathroom. While checking on the shambled make-up and disheveled hair, a strange satisfaction crept up her legs. She felt released from an unknown yoke. She felt lighter as she nursed the wound on her lips. She splattered water on her face, liking the burning tinge. She heard the door open and shut. The bedroom was empty. The rose scent of the attar oil was fulfilling. She slept at once.

'He was happy-happy yesterday night,' Big Sister chirped the next morning.

'He was annoyed.'

'Haiya, some men like annoyed one lah, you donno meh?' she asked. 'Make them strong-strong lah.'

The anticipated Friday came with another package. 'You very-very lucky, horrr,' Big Sister snorted. In a surprising move, she paid Syamu a 50 per cent commission in cash. Inside was an old skirt. It was so heavily starched that it hardly moved around her hips and thighs. 'Lampshade,' Atiqah laughed. She had found out where Ghulam worked. He manned the tandoor at Mujibhur, one of the makeshift eateries along the sidewalks in Brickfields. 'The place is full of them, all scratching their crotches and beard together at once.' She giggled. 'No wonder he has such soft hands,' Syamu said. 'He is a flour sifter.'

Rose-scented attar oil announced Ghulam's presence as Syamu entered her cubicle. He raised his eyebrows and pressed his lips, a sly shadow cast on his smile. He stared at her skirt and the pink sleeveless top she was wearing. Syamu found his jeans and shirt hanging on the hook behind the door and he was sitting languidly cross-legged in a sweatshirt and boxers. His brass rings and watch sat like obedient children on the dressing table. Syamu grew nervous, like a doe being stalked. She began to perspire; the lone rickety fan being of no help. The smell of the attar oil intensified, mixed with the ammonic sweat residues of the stale brothel air.

She recounted what Atiqah had told her that morning. 'Flour sifter?' she had sneered. 'He was fighting his government, I heard. He sifted gun powder into empty tubes,' Atiqah explained with pomposity. 'What is he doing in Brickfields?' Syamu wanted to know. 'How do I know? Holiday, maybe,' Atiqah laughed heartily. 'One day, after running his supplies, he went back home to find his work shed blown to pieces. Slabs of human meat hung to every rock and brick. They belonged to his wife and daughter. That's when he decided he would sift flour instead.'

In a few minutes, he was upon her. He raised the skirt to her waist, held her head between his palms and pressed it. His fingers ran through her hair, making a mess of it. He pulled off her top and paused, throwing a look of disdain at her exposed breasts. Gripping and scratching and bruising her with his nails, he muttered, 'Whore.' Syamu looked into his blank stare, as he raced up and down in heightened ecstasy. He let out a short grunt, collapsed on top of her and remained there.

The pain of the fresh blisters underscored her mounting sympathy. She felt her heart beating in tandem with his. The wallpaper before her sprang to life. Birds were singing. Flowers bloomed and tress swayed in the cool breeze. The warmth of their bodies enveloped her thoughts, calming her. There was an urge to caress his wet locks of hair. She wondered if he would relent. She wrapped her hands over his back. Flouting brothel etiquette, she moved and rested her cheek softly against the nape of his neck, only to be pushed away. 'Get over it,' Ghulam hissed. Wiping himself with his sweatshirt and rolling it into a small bundle, he got dressed and left.

The following week passed slowly. Syamu waited on customers, almost lethargically. She irritated Atiqah with silly questions, paranoid that customers changed hands at the brothel. She lost appetite. She became aloof. Her heart tugged hopelessly at romance. She wondered if she should go to the naan joint. She took in his smells, applying rose-scented attar oil she bought. She grew restless with the customer—prostitute mechanism. Much to Big Sister's chagrin, she began to withdraw into herself.

'You're wilting in love,' Atiqah told her.

Fridays came and went. Syamu had stopped entertaining customers and lost Big Sister's favour. The warts that appeared on her private parts were the last straw. One day, Big Sister forced her down and inspected her after a customer's complaint. The blisters—black and ugly—had spread. Immediately, she was kicked out from the brothel, the only world she had known. Syamu lingered nearby, taking up residence in the trash vent at the corner of the block.

To survive, she serviced the homeless drug addicts and drunkards, who also called the back alley home. She sniffed glue to keep hunger at bay. One day, when the weather changed for worse and Syamu had to stay in the enclosures of the garbage chamber, Ghulam appeared. He was talking to Big Sister, holding the unmistakable package. Syamu hid her face when Big Sister pointed in her direction. After a few minutes, the package was handed to her by Big Sister. Upon inspection, Syamu found that it had a clumsy-looking dress with bright floral designs and two warm naans wrapped in sugar paper. She sighed. The glue had turned her lifeless. No excitement stirred within her. She remembered the old bottle of attar oil from her clothes bundle that she hid behind a cluster of cardboards. She unscrewed the lid and let a fresh whiff of rose escape into the putrid air.

There was a thunderstorm when Ghulam returned, later that night. He looked fidgety and a little lost. He ascended the concrete steps, but stopped. He caught sight of Syamu by the garbage chamber, walked towards her and stood scrutinizing the brothel door and her. Then, he dithered about, a coy smile appearing on his face. Syamu crawled back into a dark hollowed space in the trash bin and laid on her back. Ghulam keeled over her, unwinding the waist-string of his trousers. He took deep breaths. In the fading pink hues thrown by the brothel's lights, he grasped Syamu's chin and turned it this way and that.

She could feel his body heat intensifying. His lips were full, blood shot. He tore the satin gown, and stared at her sunken breasts and dirt-caked skin. He entered her, like a ravaging disease. He spat on her face. He slapped her and held her hair in his fist. Syamu did not close her eyes. She smiled smugly when he called her a whore. She could only look into his eyes. Ghulam's cream complexion bathed under a full moon. A faint scent of the rose attar oil arose from his armpit and neck. Syamu closed her eyes. She was back in a garden. Fireflies flew between her elbows and calves. Jasmines, roses and lavender perfumed the air. Her belly felt warm and full.

When her sweat began to absorb the cold air that stole into the trash bin, her stomach churned and her pelvis burnt, as if someone had thrown ambers into it and opened her eyes. She saw the dull pink lights of the brothel breaking into fragments of blue, green and crimson. She pulled herself up, clutched the sides of his head, dragged it close to her face and kissed him. Disgusted, Ghulam freed himself and slapped her hard. The smell of rusted iron crept up her nose. He wiped his lips. He pulled up his trousers and knotted its waist string, infuriated. Syamu did not move, exhausted and wasted, fully aware of a few shadows closing upon her naked body.

* * *

She finished eating the rice bought by Atiqah.

'We go and look for Ghulam,' Syamu whispered to her baby. It wriggled slightly. She lifted herself with effort and began to stagger down the alley. People threw awkward stares. *But they do that all the time, don't they?* She thought. Fear came upon her as she passed the monorail ramp. *I have not done this for a very long time*, she realized. Atiqah did not want to be responsible for her possessions in case something went missing, so Syamu had to carry her bundle. She also had a little present for Ghulam, a bottle of the attar oil that she had purchased to fill his absence.

Following Atiqah's directions, she walked along the cozy mall, past luxurious skyscraper dwellings, away from the Monorail station along Jalan Tun Sambanthan. She stood out like a sore thumb amid the well-dressed pedestrians. Dazed, she took haughty steps, aware of the old rag she was wearing. All the faces on the street were unfamiliar. She clutched her old bundle tightly and cautiously turned her eyes away from the glass panels of the air-conditioned restaurants.

Syamu was putting down her bundle when she caught a familiar figure at the entrance of a narrow stall, squeezed between two blocks. Atiqah was right. Men in off-white kurtas and ghulabs stood about. One burly man scratched his groin and beard, as he stood before a huge, pumpkin-shaped kiln. He held a long iron rod. And beside him, Ghulam was rolling and flapping a piece of dough which he deftly stuck to the sides of the earthen oven.

Keeping an eye on Ghulam, Syamu quickly prodded the depths of her dirty bundle and found the bottle. She approached the shop warily. Nobody seemed to notice her. Before she could make her presence known, Ghulam lifted a huge plastic tub and vanished into the restaurant, behind the thick crowd. Syamu thought she heard a whimper from her baby. 'Patience,' she said, 'don't be hasty.' The restaurant was crowded. Men in long sleeves and neckties and women with painted faces sat amicably, as if untouched by the searing heat, drawing water from glasses with ice. Syamu walked in to discover that the crowd, the chairs and tables, were chaotic. She found herself in a maze, unsure where to turn. A few waiters threw angry glances.

A shout echoed from the entrance. It was the fat groin scratcher. His voice was threatening. He pointed his finger towards her. The rough edge of a mop stick struck her shoulder. The same knob jabbed painfully at her hip bone, forcing her out of the restaurant. A partially eaten naan was thrown towards her. It brushed against her cheek and fell onto the dirty pavement. She did not pick it up. The fat man grumbled loudly. Ghulam came out, threw a furtive glance at her, meekly sweeping the naan into a dustpan. Her blood curlded in shock. She raised her limp hands, but he looked away.

She needed to pee badly, so she inched her way to a spot where a mongrel was resting. It wagged its tail. She chuckled. Her throat was parched, so dry that she could not feel her breath. She opened her mouth and realized that she had dropped her bottle of attar oil when she was nudged out from the shop. She paused. She was too afraid to retrieve it. Her eyes moved towards the stall, wondering if Ghulam remembered her or heard his baby cry. The fat groin scratcher was shaking his head. A small crowd has gathered. Someone tossed a coin towards her. Among them, stood Ghulam, watching.

She could hear the breeze whispering to the palm fronds above her. She sat on the hard pavement and leaned on her bundle, the shade of the palm tree less defined under the gathering dark clouds. Her feet were swollen, her belly was full. Her baby had grown quiet; there was no movement when she rubbed her taut belly button. Picking up a familiar scent, she forgot her pain, and lost sight of the crowd. The broken bottle of attar oil had spilled its contents on the pavement. It evaporated and the fragrance of rose lifted and filled her nose. Pleased, she closed her eyes.

Tropic Quest

Anjali turned her head left and right, up and down to loosen her neck muscles. Straining her eyes, she concentrated again. First, the small numbers on the notepad seemed to float around her. She blinked. Now, the thin fonts appeared smudged. She pinched her forehead and tossed the pencil she was holding into the air. She was sure she would start crying. How she wished she could simply curl up and hide inside a shell like a tortoise. *Isn't it convenient to be able to carry a roof over one's head?* She thought in desperation. She was only two days short of being evicted by Prema.

There was cacophony in the office—the droning of overworked photocopier machines, the wheezing of the incoming faxes and the constant tapping of keyboards. An acrid smell caused Anjali to cough. *Change the machine or change the toner*, she pleaded silently. Heads bobbed here and there above the red and blue cubicles. A few people walked down the aisle. The tea woman appeared outside her cubicle, and emptied a sachet of the usual 3-in-1 Nescafe into her mug of hot water.

'I want Milo,' Anjali blurted out, though she knew it was a bit too late. The old woman twitched her lips, disapprovingly.

'Why didn't you tell me earlier?' she accosted Anjali, resting one hand on her hips. 'What about this one! Who is going to drink it? I now have to walk to the pantry for Madam. Wash this cup all over again.'

Anjali ignored her and turned to the stack of papers before her. She smiled as the smell of chocolate entered her nostrils and calmed her senses. The old Indian woman grumbled while stepping into the tiny cubicle and placed the porcelain mug of Milo on her table. She looked about the table, her reddened lips looking quite noticeable against her pale yellow face, thanks to the years of fresh turmeric paste facials. Anjali fished out a coaster from under a file and handed it to her. The old woman shrugged her shoulders and placed the steaming mug on it, spilling some of the drink. Then she left. Anjali sighed and pulled out some tissue papers from her drawer and dabbed them on the spilt drink.

She heard a subdued greeting from the adjacent cubicle. 'What would you like to drink?' The old vixen politely enquired of the occupant. The glasses did not rattle against each other. Even the sound of the spoon was muffled. *Idiot*, Anjali murmured under her breath. *Since when did administrative officers have to listen to tea ladies?*

One side of her cubicle rattled, giving her a rude shock. A pale face appeared over the partition.

'Kenny, how many times have I told you . . .' she began.

'Not to scare you, right?' Kenny replied, a naughty smirk rising on his face. He rested his arms on the partition. Anjali shook her head disapprovingly, examining the documents laid before her.

'Lunch at 1 p.m.?' he asked.

She looked up again. Kenny was waiting for an answer, his eyes scanning the office space. Anjali noticed the short but thick strands of hair peeping out from his nostrils and turned away. 'Don't you people trim your nose hair?' she asked.

'No need. We don't grow beard and moustache. So, we hardly notice. Quick,' he hissed, 'I think Ms Lee is around the corner.' Before Anjali could offer consent, he had already ducked his head and vanished into his cubicle.

'All right, 1 p.m. then,' she replied, quite assured that he heard her.

'What's happening at 1 p.m.?' a nasal voice enquired after her. A large woman stood before the entrance of her cubicle. Anjali remained quiet and smiled pleasantly. 'Good morning, Ms Lee,' she greeted her. *There is no need to explain my business to you, is there?* She wondered.

It was a wonder among the office staff how Ms Lee could walk undetected, despite her size. Must be her shoes, or black magic, or she could have been a ballerina or trained as a geisha. Ms Lee, the manager of the logistics centre Anjali had joined two weeks ago, surprised everyone by stealing upon her staff unexpectedly. She could appear and reappear when she was least expected and many knew that her favourite haunt was the pantry. 'Walls have ears,' Kenny had warned Anjali, so they only spoke when they were outside the walls of the company, during lunch.

Ms Lee walked in and began to inspect the nooks and corners of Anjali's cubicle, tipping her glasses from her cheek from time to time. Unable to extract an answer from Anjali, she turned to leave. *Thank God*, Anjali sighed. *Ms Lee did not see of the long list of numbers on the table.* As if remembering the purpose why she swept down the aisle, she told Anjali that she wanted to see her before 1 p.m. 'Exactly at 12.30 p.m., in my room,' she emphasized. Anjali heard soft giggles around her cubicle.

'What a sleazy bugger,' a male voice muttered. Ms Lee stopped in her tracks and looked up, trying to find the source. Giving up, she walked away quickly.

Anjali shook her head. Her attention reverted to the list of numbers on her table. She glimpsed through them tiredly. *Twenty-three*, she counted. Number seventeen had been struck out with uneven lines, she noticed. Some were in bold. There were a few crosses in thick red ink. A skull in black ink and a middle finger stood out among the numbers, too. And a hole appeared at number sixteen. She closed her eyes and breathed deeply. She was on the fourth list of numbers she had procured from the long walks in the residential areas of PJ and Kelana Jaya.

All she needed was a room for rent. And getting a room in this part of town seemed a challenge. Prema, her aunty, had cleared the second bedroom for Anjali's temporary stay in her three-bedroom terrace house. Though she lived in an upmarket residential area and owned the most expensive property among her relatives, her house was merely a covered open space, subdivided with beaded blinds and clever interior design. The living room and the dining area shared the same space. The kitchen was so narrow that it only accommodated two persons at most, at one time. The third bedroom was only good for storage. And the house rules only applied to Anjali, to restrain her from meddling with Prema's private space. *No cooking. No cleaning. No guests.*

And there was the cat, Naveen. Oh, how deplorable he was. The tabby was a nuisance and he was constantly at war with her. Like Prema, his owner, he did not take very kindly to trespassing females. He hid in corners and lunged at Anjali. And in the mornings, before she left for work, he crept up behind her and clawed her heels. When she came back from work, he would lounge comfortably on the bed or on top of the closet in her bedroom. His entries and exits were a mystery and the corners of the room often reeked of urine. He left his scent everywhere, defending his territory against countless intruders who sometimes came and lounged with Prema on Friday nights. He would make much noise in the middle of the night, running up the roof and meowing wildly, like he was getting ready for a battle. Anjali was definitely losing the battle with him.

Anjali pinched her temples and browsed through the list of numbers again. She dialled another one.

'*Wei*,' the voice answered.

'Hello, I saw your ad . . . I'm Anjali.'

'*Wei. Wei . . . An-chaaa-li?*'

'Hello, yes, room for rental . . . room, on rent?'

'*Wei . . . wei . . .*' and the line went dead.

When did Malaysians stop speaking English? Bloody retard, she yelled angrily in her head.

She crossed the number with a pencil. There were two more contacts left to dial. She massaged her cheekbones. They were hurting. She had spent the entire weekend combing the streets of Petaling Jaya. Wearing rubber shoes, a cap and carrying a notepad in hand, she had been scrutinizing advertisements hung on rickety gates and windows. Some of these were handwritten on old tattered cardboards and calendar sheets and had decayed under rain and sunshine. The better but expensive ones were advertised on plastic boards or buntings. They also bleated out a common criterion:

Chinese Speaking! Chinese Female! Chinese only!

Anjali wondered if the non préféré did not need rooms to live in. One placard even said that minding one's own business was the key to harmonious living. After her legs could carry her no more, she had gathered almost twenty plus telephone numbers, though a fraction of these contacts were either unreachable or did not exist. She had just completed her Bachelor's in Business Administration. She can be counted lucky for securing employment, three months after completion of her degree. Many of her Indian peers were still struggling, partly because employment opportunities were tight, or their employability skills were low, or got caught up in the sinister job requirements of having mastered neither Mandarin nor having the skin colour that fit the GLCs. On top of that, her mother had been a constant pain, reminding her of thieves, kidnappers, flashers and rapists who were forever lurking around since her childhood. What amuses Anjali is that her mother never needed to get a job, so she won't know that it's pretty difficult to find the ideal place where you could travel to work and back without getting wet in the rain.

The next number belonged to a property agent. It was answered by a polite woman, chirpy and congenial. After explaining the required deposits and utility payments, the woman's voice stopped momentarily. *Maybe she has realized that we only spoke in English*, Anjali thought.

'Are you Chinese?' she asked.

'I just need a roof over my head. I'm a very good tenant,' Anjali tried to press on her. 'I work in a Logistics company. I have a stable income. I can afford the rent.' After a short silence, the woman said unsurely, 'I have a house.'

'A house!' Anjali exclaimed. She knew it was impossible to afford. She was sure the number had advertised a room. 'No, no, I'm only looking for a room.'

Another short pause followed. The agent cleared her voice, 'Oh, I'm sorry,' she sounded apologetic yet firm. 'I'm afraid it has been let out.'

Anjali's eyes clouded with tears. 'Let out, within the duration of the telephone conversation?' Anjali ground her teeth. She held the receiver until the line went dead. She was sweating despite the air conditioning. She felt claustrophobic inside her cubicle, as if the four walls were moving towards her. She lifted her mug and found that her drink had gone cold. She walked to the pantry to calm herself. *Prejudice has taken over human compassion*, she was dismayed. *I need a place, no matter how humble, just to go back to after work.* She emptied her drink into the sink and filled it with water. She pushed her hands under the flowing water and closed her eyes.

She was also getting fed up of Prema's impatience in this matter, her only relative around. She seemed to be bent upon kicking her out from her property to be able to indulge in her sexual escapades. She brought back men to the house, mostly migrants—Arabs, Indians and Bangladeshis. Worse, she left them at home when she went to work. Two nights ago, she had found a stranger coming through the attached bathroom into her room, clad in his underwear. And these men helped themselves to the refrigerator and the cash and gifts she gave them. Other relatives were aware of this, but what could they do? They could only blame her! It was Prema who had turned her life upside down after her recent divorce. She had developed bizarre mood swings and was temperamental, rude and messy. Anjali had to be careful so as not to step on her toes.

Anjali came back from the pantry and slumped on her seat, fixing her vacant eyes on new mail plopping into her inbox folder. 'Any luck?' Kenny popped his head over the partition again. As was his habit, he rested his chin on his palms on the thin edge. A spot of light reflected on his spectacles and hid his left eye. Anjali laughed. Kenny smacked his lips.

'Nothing, Soon Siong, nothing yet,' she sighed, flapping her hands to fan her face.

'Call me Kenny,' he said curtly.

'I won't. You know I won't' she replied, realizing that she had known him long enough to call him by his given name and not his English name. They had been to university together. Still, she refused to acknowledge him as Kenny, for it was artificial, she thought. Now, having found him at her workplace, the bond had grown stronger, much to Ms Lee's suspicious chagrin, who assumed they were in an interracial relationship and disapproved of it.

'I'm down to the last two numbers, Soon Siong.'

'Call me Kenny,' he repeated, feigning irritation. 'Try again, don't give up. Worst come to worst, you can move in with me,' he tried to encourage her.

'Excuse me, you know I won't,' she scoffed at him. 'I'm a nice Indian girl, not into cohabiting' she said, 'and with a Chinaman, on top of that!' she sniggered.

'Move in with my family lah, eating too much curry is turning you into a garrulous woman,' Kenny sounded displeased.

'Awww, that's really sweet of you, but no thanks,' Anjali rejected the offer. 'Too much of you will make me sick.'

'Quite an old-fashioned Indian except for the dressing, I guess, not even opportunistic, I'm only wasting my time with this old aunty,' Kenny sighed. 'Continue dreaming lah, get down from LRT, is your house door. Step out from the gate, already the restaurants. Open the back door, already the workplace. Why not ask your mother to find a house for you, or maybe conjure up a spell?' Kenny gave out a hearty laugh. Anjali threw an eraser at him, hitting him on his left cheek. 'Ouch,' he let out a sharp shriek.

'Ha ha,' Anjali started. 'Serves you right. You talking too much there. One can never stand up against Indian mothers. You'll know one day, Kenny. Haishhh, how I wish things were a bit different,' she sighed.

'Wish what?' asked Kenny, perturbed. 'This time what are you wishing for?'

'That my father had bought a property in KL, all those years ago,' Anjali sighed. 'Then I wouldn't have to put up with all this selfishness.'

'Ah, how is your father connected now? Should I laugh or cry?' Kenny scratched his pimple-ridden forehead. 'Now, try dialling those numbers again. You need accommodation.' Kenny vanished again.

Anjali picked up her phone.

'*Wei,*' a voice greeted.

'Hello,' said Anjali. 'Hello, I am . . .'

'*Wei, ni shuei shenma?*' the voice enquired.

'Anjali. Anjali . . . I am looking for a room. You advertised . . .'

'*Haiya, wei, wei . . .*'

'How come you cannot speak English?'

The line went dead. The rest of the responses were in unison with the ones she's grown accustomed to.

The house is full oredi.

No speak English, only Chinese.

No advertise, where got?

I now in JB, how to see you?

Kenny emerged again without knocking, this time standing by her cubicle entrance, beaming. Anjali felt she could twist his big ears until they became bloodshot.

'Can I take a seat?' he asked, fully aware of Anjali's futile search.

Anjali nodded, realizing that it wasn't time for lunch yet. She needed to be alone. But she could not stop or even want to stop Kenny from walking in and sitting down before her. He looked apologetic and smiled kindly at her. That was all she needed.

'Where is the list of numbers?' he asked, wiping his spectacles with the end of his necktie. She passed it to him. 'Which is the one you want?' he asked, scrutinizing the list.

'There, this one, number four,' she replied.

'Four? You sure you want number four?'

'Are you joking? Do you think this is a joke?' Anjali was miffed.

'He he, cool, cool,' he said, and signalled to her to pass the phone to him. 'Number four,' he began philosophically. 'Number four in Cantonese is sei. Sei also means die . . . either you go die or you die already, he he he . . . that's why I asked. Must double-check with you mah. Maybe you should learn some Chinese after this,' he winked at her.

'I should,' Anjali agreed solemnly, half-laughing at his gimmicks. 'And do more lunches with you, I guess?'

'Clever girl, that's why I like you,' he grinned broadly.

'No wonder,' Anjali laughed, slouching on the executive chair. 'Ms Lee has been going around asking why you are following me everywhere.'

'She is jealous lah.' Kenny raised an eyebrow.

They both laughed. Anjali relaxed. She handed him the phone. 'Why do you like this particular room? It seems to be pricey.'

'It's the master bedroom, with an attached bathroom,' she said. 'More space. Better privacy.'

'Okay,' he said. 'Then are you fine with mixed-gender occupants?'

'Fine,' said Anjali. 'As long as they are Chinese men.' She sipped her cold drink. 'And it's near the LRT station, sparing my mother's paranoia.'

'Aiyo, now your mother is involved, again.' He shook his head.

'From the beginning, actually,' she said.

'The price seems to be steep.' said Kenny, still wondering if he should dial the number. 'But, yes, I know this area. Not so safe at night. Snatch thieves abound. However, there is the LRT and lots of convenient shops and eateries.' He smiled. 'You have a driving license, don't you? Get a small car soon,' he advised.

He dialled the number and spoke in Chinese. The conversation was curt and businesslike. From his tone, Anjali could make out that he was negotiating. Before he hung up he uttered only one comprehensible word that Anjali recognized. Krenti.

'It's done. I just secured number four for you,' he announced triumphantly.

'How?' asked Anjali, unbelieving.

'Simple lah, I gained the chief tenant's trust and recommended you.'

'Recommended? Like what? Did you tell we are dating?' She wanted to know. 'It's just a room.'

'No, no, it's not like that,' Kenny explained. 'Many landlords here have suffered bad tenants who have delayed rent payments and bill settlements. Some did not even honour the one month notice in their contract, so there is a lot of distrust.'

'All of them were named Anjali?' she fumed.

'Ha ha ha, what to do? Not all Anjalis are sweet like you, what,' he said, trying to be charming. 'This particular landlady even had her furniture and electronic appliances go missing, and her walls were riddled with nails when the tenants moved out. So, it's all money lost in repair work, etcetera.'

'So, you are not capable of all that?' she asked, biting her lips, wondering if she should turn it down.

'Not like that lah,' he hesitated. 'After I recommended you, she was okay.'

'What did you say?'

'I said you are an educated woman. And you work as a logistics officer with me. And with a good job, you can afford to pay the rent, and you won't steal the water heater.' He laughed. 'Simple as that . . . and I also said she can come looking for me if she is not happy. Don't worry, I can handle her. Just be thick-skinned a bit lah. You can move in end of the week. It's a universal problem, not an Anjali problem. Your meeting starts in ten minutes,' he reminded her as he got up and left her cubicle.

'Thank you so much,' she whispered, almost in tears. A feeling of calm prevailed over her. For the first time in two weeks, she allowed herself to smile and closed her eyes momentarily to let relief take over. Life would be better away from the clutches of Rani's gloom. Above all, she would be away from the prying eyes of Rani's visitors. Snatch thieves would be a lesser danger than a territorial cat, too, she reckoned.

Kenny knocked the partition from his side. 'Aren't you running late?' he reminded.

'Yes, yes, I'm going now,' Anjali replied, getting up.

'I'll still wait to go lunch with you,' he promised.

'Okay.'

The Elephant Trophy

Exhausted, we reach the vast house built by my grandfather in the 1960s. Made from solid timber, the structure is a grand sight with its whitewashed courtyards, winding steps, wide verandah and the four carved teak wood columns that gave the house its grandeur. The doorway is in the middle and one can see the backdoor from the entrance, built according to vashtu requirements to ensure an easy passage for the wind in and out of the house.

As we pull up in the driveway, a number of people I assume are the villagers stare for a moment, before vanishing into the house. A bald man and two women descend from the house and walk hurriedly towards us. They are my uncle and aunts, looking serious and pale. Uncle is the first to approach my father and slowly stutter a few words. He says Paati's condition isn't encouraging. My aunts stand close by and break into sobs, while my father consoles them. My mother joins the adults, leaving me with my younger brother and sister by the car. By now, a small crowd has gathered again, some of them familiar. Nobody bids us welcome, as it is taboo.

We climb up the house on flat concrete steps that led up to a large wooden door. The living room is quiet and almost empty, contrary to the indication given by the number of cars parked outside. Paati lies in the middle of the hall on a metal-framed bed with two unknown women who are fanning her and massaging her feet and temples. Medicated oils, a huge packet of adult pampers, wet wipes, talcum powder, towels and an ice-cream box filled with medicines are arranged on a small shelf beside the bed. There was a jug of black coffee left on the side table, a copper funnel covering its mouth. The women look up and move away from the bed as we approach.

Paati seems to be asleep. The windows are shut and the room is filled with the smell of camphor and incense sticks. Uncle bends close to her ear and calls, encouraging her to see who has come to visit. Paati stirs a little and opens her eyes slowly. She looks at father, me and my sister and then back towards father and gestures to ask if he has eaten. Father kneels by the bedside and murmurs something, holding back his tears. 'Has she eaten?' he asks one of the women standing behind him.

'Nothing, only a bit of coffee,' she murmurs quietly.

Soon, we are ushered to the back of the kampung house, where the cemented courtyard is. In this space between the rest of the house and the kitchen, a long banquet table has been placed, filled with jugs of coffee and tea, trays of idli, bowls of coconut and tomato chutneys and saambar. A soft breeze airs the place, making it pleasant and cool. The atmosphere contradicts the sombre mood of the hall where Paati has been left in the silence that she must learn to endure soon. The car owners, cousins and uncles and aunts from near and far, are all here exchanging greetings and pleasantries, catching up on old stories and discussing the length of our stay at Paati's house.

For almost a week before we were called to Teluk Intan, Paati had been slipping in and out of consciousness. At the height of senility, she was speaking and laughing like a baby or sleeping for hours at a stretch. She would suddenly wake up, fully conscious. It was at these moments that she asked for food and drink or asked after her husband, parents, children and siblings. At times, she made unintelligible signs in thin air, much to the amusement of the household. These strange actions had increased now.

The news of sudden breathing complication travels throughout the house and we adjourn into the hall, blocking the much-needed air from the doorway and windows. Paati sucks in air and appears to struggle to release it. She keeps gesturing, or trying to clear something from her mouth though she has not had solid food for some time now. Probably it's her mind that keeps her everyday thoughts and habits alive. At times, she raises both her hands and moves them as though she is cooking, stirring, frying, or feeding someone. Or she pushes open invisible windows and doors. Nobody has any explanation for this, so they stand helplessly and watch.

Night falls, bringing to life the nocturnal crickets and moths. Dark green mosquito coils burn at the corners of the house. A river terrapin strays into the kitchen compound, signalling worse things to come. After a short commotion, it is swiftly caught by Uncle and released into the canal that runs behind the house.

'We just have to wait.' Everyone is sure that these are Paati's final moments and keep vigil lest she finds herself all alone when Yama comes for her, riding on his buffalo. The two unknown women have left, gone back to their homes and families; the final task is now reserved for close family members. The adults discuss. The rituals have to start. Children, grandchildren and great grandchildren are now gathered at the hall to pour spoonfuls of milk down her protesting throat after whispering their names. By midnight after gulping down almost four litres of milk, and having had her diapers changed by Aunty, Paati falls asleep to the sounds of frogs playing under the hedges.

The lights are turned on and at the porch the men sit in circles, indulging themselves in card games, smoking and talking about important things, especially the preparations a funeral involves and informing distant family friends and acquaintances. The women walk about the house, tending to the children and other relatives, making sleeping arrangements, and exchanging gossip with each other. My mom, sister and brother are nowhere to be seen; they are probably sleeping in one of the many square rooms. I sit with the older boys, slumped against the wall and try to steal some sleep between answering their questions about my life in the States.

A few hours must have gone by, when the chiming old clock stirs me awake at three in the morning. The chilly draft is almost unbearable. I get up and move into the warmer living room and sit on the rattan bench. The men have dozed off on their chairs, smoke from some of their unfinished cigarettes rising up in pretty curves. A small pile of firewood is still glowing; the embers keep the mosquitoes at bay. Dead termites litter the stairs leading up to the first floor where some cousins have taken up the old benches and sofas.

A loud gurgling noise makes me jump. Paati groans a little and says something just in time when an aunt comes out from her room, yawning. In her weak voice Paati asks for kopi-o, her favourite drink. I sit up from the bench. Aunty tells me to sleep and goes into the kitchen. Within minutes she is back with a small cup and spoon and feeds Paati. Paati gurgles about and starts drifting into her monotonous babbling thereafter. Aunty props up a pillow behind Paati's shoulders and turns her to lie on her side, leaving a towel under her chin. She sighs heavily and leaves the hall. With the caffeine boost, Paati's babbling becomes intense and incessant. I had probably dozed off again, for when I wake up I am shocked to find Paati staring right into my eyes.

'Kumudha is coming to fetch me,' she says, taking a deep breath.

Who is Kumudha, I wonder. *Could it be one of the female relatives?* I take a moment to recollect the names of all my aunties. *There is no Kumudha*, I realize. *Should I go and fetch one of them?* I keep playing these thoughts in mind. Her eyes soft and her face lit up like an excited child's, Patti signals that I move closer to the bed.

'Kumudha is coming,' she whispers again, 'and we are going to see her at the temple.' There is glee between the wrinkles that run deep across her face, in the hollows of her cheeks and chin.

'Yes,' I agree with her, trying to play along. *Probably she wants to see someone. And I need to know who it is. I cannot deny her last wishes, can I?*

Paati reaches out her hands and runs her stiff palms over my face. 'You look like someone I know,' she says. 'But I have become very forgetful these days. Have your wife and children arrived?' She seems confused and wonders whether she is asking the right person the right question to.

'No Paati,' I try to explain, 'I'm not married. I came with your son, Balaraman.'

She exhales, then rests her hand on her chest, turns and stares at the ceiling.

'Aiya,' she calls me, 'is it Vinayakar Chakurthi?' It is a question about the popular feast of the elephant-headed god that Hindus celebrate. *But it's still June*, I calculate. It has to be the tenth day in August. What month in the Tamil calendar, I cannot tell.

'No Paati,' I inform her. 'Two more months to go.'

'Oh, really?' She is surprised.

At this point, I am relieved that she has understood. But just when I am about to bring up the name Kumudha again, she raises her voice. The lines on her face seem to point to her eyebrows, and in an instant her mood has changed. There is a strange energy in her voice.

'Where is your mother? What's happening to these women?' she demands. 'It's Vinayakar Chakurthi and nobody is doing anything. I need to get started, need to prepare the modagam, grind the lentils, grate the coconuts, and sift the flour.' She raises both hands in an effort to get up. Before I can lift myself from the floor and catch her, she falls on the soft mattress. She is panting even though it was such a simple feat. She closes both her eyes and concentrates on taking in air.

Modagam. Paati made the best ones in town, I remember. Thick hot palm sugar mixed with mashed lentils and grated coconut stuffed into snow white flour dumplings; they were the talk of the town. And they were made only for the festival or on one of those rare occasions when she felt charitable enough to bend her back and toil.

'Oh Kumudha,' Paati begins reminiscing, her voice calmer but weak. 'She was the most gracious thing, had the most benevolent of eyes, flapping ears, was huge as a bus but slow and plodded gracefully throughout the streets, our Kumudha. But she had a temper too.' Paati points her index finger at me, 'She had long magnificent tusks.'

'Wait a minute,' I deduce. 'So, Kumudha is not a woman, it's an elephant. Oh, what had I been thinking all this while?' I slap my thigh in disbelief.

In south India, particularly where Paati came from, Vinayakar Chakurthi is celebrated on a grand scale. Temple elephants, often decorated with gilt caparisons, have coloured *rangoli* patterned on their bodies and silk parasols for headdress. They are used to carry the idol of Ganesha for the parade. Often seen chained at certain corners on the temple grounds, the elephants have to work and they make money for their keepers. People throng to these sections to receive blessings from the elephants, revered as sacred animals. Upon paying a small token, one can make offerings of food to the elephants; fruits, sugar cane, sweets etcetera, that the creatures often roll and pop into their mouth and then place the tip of their trunk on the devotees' head as an act of blessing.

'Let me tell you something,' Paati cautions me. 'Elephants do not forget.' Her face turns gaunt and foreboding. Her eyelids are still closed, but I can see the pupils moving about. She continues to speak in a low whisper.

'Remember Achutan? The coconut seller?'

'Who?' Where? But she is not waiting for me to provide answers.

'Appa has tied up the sugar cane bundles, and there are also other kinds of fruits and inner stems of the banana tree to be given to her when she arrives. All of us are happy. Kumudha is coming to our street today. We are all dressed in our best clothes. Amma is wearing her jewels. The pooja tray has to be offered when the chariot bearing Ganesha goes past our shop. Oh yes. This year Kumudha will walk in front of the chariot and bestow blessings on the devotees. Probably we will get to touch her as she marches, caressing everything with her trunk on her way. This is the best time to go close enough to touch the loose folds of skin between her hind legs and enjoy watching mischievous children trying to catch hold of her swaying tail that moves like a pendulum, much to the chagrin of the elephant keepers,' Paati smiles.

Elephants are an integral part of Hinduism, and for devotees of Ganesha, the elephant represented him. Legend has it that when Brahma, the Creator, first breathed life into the cosmos, the universe took the form of an egg without a hard shell. As Brahma continued to blow life-giving winds, the egg became volatile and began to wobble dangerously, unable to bear the turbulence. On Earth there were earthquakes, firestorms, thunder and lightning, and the sea began to rise and move inland. Unable to bear the pain and worried that she might be thrown off course, Mother Earth summoned the great sages from the Himalayas for relief. The *rishis* descended from Kailash and recited prayers. After days of rigorous fasting and observing impossible *saganas*, the *rishis* were answered by Indra himself. From the Ganges emerged Indravata—Indra's riding elephant—followed by Kumudha, Vamana and Anchana, who then took up their positions to hold the earth's four cosmic epicentres with their tusks until the universe stabilized.

Some minutes pass before Paati wakes up again. She looks about the room and nods at me a few times. She laughs quietly and closes her eyes, still smiling.

Perturbed, I call out to her, 'Paati,' to which she waves her hand, asking me to be quiet.

'Do you hear them?' she asks. 'The *nadaswaram* troop is nearing. I can hear the drum beats, accompanied by the blaring of trumpets. It's coming from the Brahmin quarters. We are ready. Kumudha will arrive at our street anytime now. The coconut merchants live in the next street. As the street is full of people, Appa has agreed to pick me up and seat me on his shoulders. The entourage has appeared! The golden parasol shielding the deity on top of the decorated chariot is followed by Kumudha, looking resplendent in her decorations!'

The men shouted excitedly, while the women got ready with their silver trays laden with offerings and the children stopped what they were doing to see what all the commotion was about. The music grew louder and as Kumudha approached, I could hear the tinkling of the huge bell round her neck. She looked benign, munching away on the sweets and fruits, sometimes shaking her head. The mahout sat right on top of her flat head and moved his heels into her ears. While the adults offered prayers at the chariot, the children lined up to be blessed by Kumudha.

Soon the poojas ended, and the priest signalled to the mahout to move. It was then that Kumudha refused to obey orders and began to shake her head violently. She groaned and trumpeted loudly, interrupting the *nadaswaram*. The musicians paused, distracted by her sudden change in behaviour. The large crowd gathered on the opposite block was equally puzzled at the turn of events. The priest was agitated and began to scold the mahout, who in turn began to shout and kick and poke Kumudha on her head. Kumudha took a few steps back and then complied, but suddenly, as she reached the opposite bazaar, she became restless and all hell broke loose.

Nothing could stop her. She trundled back and forth aimlessly, kicking and smashing anything that blocked her way. Her deep trumpeting was furious and deafening. Her mahout shouted orders, kicked her ears hard and poked her flat skull with his iron hook. With one strong shake, she threw him off her back and he slid down. He got away just before she turned. Once he fell off, she was free.

People ran helter-skelter, climbing trees, walls and roofs and the footpaths of the shops were crammed. More and more keepers ran up the street with policemen, one even carrying a shot gun. Everyone rescued anyone they could find—the elderly, the women, and the children—and pulled them to safety. A huge cloud of dust enveloped the whole street. Kumudha kept kicking up more dust. The mahout, gathering his lungi and his strength, ran boldly towards her, collided head-on with her trunk, in a bid to restrain her. But her will had been decided. She knocked him away with ease. In the unfurling chaos, many had failed to read that she had something in mind.

She dashed forward and for a moment stayed on the street of the coconut merchants. She found what she was looking for and barged into one of the shops, and out came Achutan. She ran after him. She seemed to have singled out Achutan from the throng of spectators and soon, the brave youths were trying to distract her. She chased him down the street, entered an alley and cornered him. More and more people ran towards them, shouting and setting off firecrackers or throwing stones and objects at the beast. We could only hear Achutan's terrified screams, the frantic shouting of the elephant keepers and the panicked shouts of men and women in the crowd and the helpless policemen.

Then a policeman fired a bullet into the air. The panicked crowd suddenly cleared the entrance of the alley and ran out into the clearing. Kumudha moved out and using her trunk, she tripped Achutan who was trying to get away from her. She pounced on him, pushing him into the dirt with her forehead and trunk and rubbed him fiercely onto the gravel. She picked him up, as if showing him off to the crowd and threw him down. By this time, Achutan was lifeless; even his clothes had been ripped off.

Just as soon as it started, it ended. Kumudha was pacified, and her front legs were chained tightly. She looked weak as she was made to take small steps. We could hear her heaving as she passed our shop. As if she had forgotten something, she turned and looked around. She put her trunk into the corners of her mouth and took out a round white, yellow and pinkish substance that looked like a rubber ball. With her trunk raised, she threw it into the street and walked away. Upon closer examination, the men reported that it was a partially ingested coconut, its cavity filled with chalk, pus and blood.

'Achutan,' everyone wondered, 'what evil drove him to commit such atrocity? All that chalk would have burnt the lips, tongue and inner cheeks of the poor helpless creature. And judging the content's state, Kumudha could have carried it in her mouth for almost a week!'

'Why did Achutan resort to such treacherous behaviour?' people wanted to know, but it was too late. By the time he was picked up, his legs and arms were all mangled.

'An elephant never forgets,' Paati sighs as she begins to drift into sleep.

I rest my forehead against the cold frame of the bed and am transported to the world Paati described.

Dawn comes silently. I wake up to the screeching of perhaps a hundred cockerels.

Paati is conscious, but she is not saying anything. At sunlight, she asks for her younger sister and has her fill of kopi-o. Her breathing is coarse and difficult. The little feeding hole punctured at her throat is now closed, bandaged with plaster and a cotton ball. I cannot sleep, so I walk around the house like a zombie, my mind fixated on Kumudha. Already my uncles and cousins have been asking me to rest, to prepare for the journey home after the final rites.

But like me, Paati's mind is also wide awake, for she has started babbling again, calling upon Kumudha. The two attendants have returned and changed Paati into a cleaner blouse and sarong. My aunts must have changed the diapers this morning and cleaned her, for she smells fresh with talcum powder.

Having nothing much to do in an unfamiliar household in an unfamiliar town, having freshened up and having had my belly filled with homemade pancakes, I come back and sit down at the same spot where I spent the night, at the front door, wide ajar, watching the two women doing whatever they can find to do.

The sun is higher; more visitors pour in and try to shake Paati out of her perpetual slumber. Nothing happens. Its noon and Paati has started to make the same gurgling sounds, breathing in and trapping air in her mouth. She is making different gestures, but I can decipher them. First, she pushes up both her hands vertically and clasps her palms, like a diver on a springboard. Sometimes, it even induces a clap. Then, she opens her palms again and moves them in circles. Then, she lowers her hands and again pushes them out as though she is rowing. She looks upwards and smiles. Suddenly, she cups her hands as if she is trying to feed someone. Then, she looks up again and smiles. She uses her hands to open imaginary windows and doors. She does it repeatedly amidst her squeaks of worry and wonder. And she becomes very still thereafter. In between sobs, father tries to pour milk into her mouth, but it does not go through.

'A sure sign,' everyone has agreed. 'It is done; turn the bed to face east.' I just shake my head and smile.

Would anybody understand that Paati has just met Kumudha? Or would anyone take seriously the story she was trying to tell me? One thing I do know is that Paati is visiting her past. She has reunited with her favourite people. It is a memory she has probably held onto. And I think I know this for sure; she was not with us from the very beginning, but far away from home, in paradise.

Annama's Treaty

'*A-haik . . . A-haik!*'

The woodcutter puffed out a slight shriek of air each time his axe fell thumping on the chopping board with each split. The chopped dry rubber wood were then stacked orderly against a wall on one side of the wooden house under a flat zinc cover. A cockerel stood in watch from the top of the pile, supervising his cackle of hens that littered the sandy compound. The glimmering lake across the lane from Annama's house shone like polished emerald and disturbed her eyes. She sat at the entrance of her simple cement floored house, observing the woodcutter, edged by fine sand that drew the borders between house and the sandy compound.

Muruga must be drunk, she surmised, *or he would not be able to chop a tonne of wood for the market tomorrow.* The pre-ordered sticks laid in bundles secured by raffia strings on the verandah, which would be delivered by her to the familiar families and businesses in town. Though wood stoves have been replaced by gas stoves, they were still popular among the poor, restaurateurs and those who preferred to save on gas. *Cooking with firewood produced tastier food too*, some attested to it. Scared of a fiery mishap, Annama had avoided gas stoves, so she did not know. She got up and straightened her back, letting out a soft groan. Singling out a sturdy filament from a bunch of lidi, she brushed out sand and peeled out the dry cakes of chicken shit that covered the jute rag used for a door mat. It was midday and her father had not come in for his meal.

The droning noise from heavy vehicles distracted them. A few lorries had kicked up dust so large they hid a portion of the lake from Annama's view. Muruga stopped chopping to look up and shook his head. Already, their tiny village is being swallowed by urbanization. Many developers had come to seek the land that Annama and a dozen other neighbor's had squatted on illegally for many years now, in dingy-looking houses, without water and electricity. But the state government had intervened, and divided this narrow strip of land by the lake's edge into twenty-four lots, and had given the settlers ownership for a small under-market price. However, the land value had soared the moment the reclaiming projects started on the opposite side of the lake where modern housing projects were slowly taking shape. Many had sold their plots for handsome prices and moved to the town. Some had stayed back and rebuilt their homes, with tiles and concrete. Muruga could only afford to build a wood and brick house.

Must be still angry, she retorted, *for diluting his liquor with water to reduce the wild effects of its intoxication*. She stood watching him with the lidi bunch in her hand, observing the sun-beaten, shining black mass of Muruga's back, bending and straightening, working the round tree trunks into manageable slices. A few chicken were roaming about the open porch of her hut and had started a clownish fight over a dead caterpillar. Red ants were marching in a single file from a crack in the outer wall and vanished into an invisible vortex under her house. A large black-and-white TV stood alone at the centre of the cemented hall, serving its main purpose airing the much-awaited weekly Tamil movies on Saturday afternoons. She would also not give a miss watching English movies that Muruga forbade her from. Though she did not understand the language, she understood other things that taught her about adult pleasures, bubble baths and the sensual kissing scenes from *Dallas* and the rare preludes to shirtless *Chips* police officers.

'Nobody is going to marry you,' her father screeched unkindly, as he raised his axe and landed it precisely on a split point. It sent a splinter of bark flying into the sky. 'Just look at you,' he lamented, his voice shrill with judgment. 'Your mother must be very happy, having left you with me to fend,' he decreed, spitting out sharply. 'No man will marry you,' he said again, 'too ripe, flat-nosed, hipped like a cow.'

'If you talk again, I won't give you lunch,' Annama shouted from where she sat. The chicken stopped picking and looked up, bewildered.

'Say what you like,' she shouted at the old man, his testicles dangling loose against the thin worn towel he wore each time he bent down to hack the wood. It caught Annama's eyes and she sat helplessly containing a gaggle of laughter.

'Say what you like,' she shouted again at his childlike annoyance. The hall was rife with the smell of fried anchovies in onions and green chilies that she made for side dish. Turning away from the tall and muscular silhouette, she rolled up a newspaper and started whacking the flies that had sought the cool cement floor to escape from the scorching heat.

Losing her interest at the flies, she looked down and examined her palms. They were toughened and sturdy from the years of tying up firewood bundles for the market. If Muruga was sick, she did the chopping, bundling and delivering.

'One day when I get married, I will leave you,' she shouted as she twisted and thumped the knob of the lidi broom against her palm before leaving it behind the door. 'I will do exactly that. Let's see what becomes of you then.'

'Aiyo Kadavuleh,' Muruga looked up to the sky and slapped his face.

'If there is a God, he would have remembered to pull my nose,' she protested at her father's prayerful pretence.

'Just make sure you have a roof over your head wherever you go,' Muruga chuckled, his mood disappearing as suddenly as a midday sun behind a rain cloud.

* * *

All gods are ONE, her father had assured her throughout his curse-laden life on earth. Annama had arrived at the church for her life's biggest bargain.

She sat at the furthest end of the airy wide church; her gaze hankered onto the large wooden cross that hung behind the large carved altar. Unseen butterflies took random flights in her stomach with each entry of a church member. The women walked in like dazzling movie stars, in cotton and silk saris, numerous colours that outmatched the flowers on the altar. Annama was dressed in a sandalwood-coloured sari, which someone said could help tone down her complexion. On her side, the pews were filled by veiled women and children. She wondered if she should also do likewise, pulling the ends of her sari and covering her head. Neither the girls nor the younger women covered their heads. Only the old ones did. Annama pulled her *mundanai* and wrapped it modestly around her shoulders like a shawl, trusting that God is only interested on the intent.

She averted her attention to the ceiling where busy chirping of birds began to interrupt the sound of the organ. Brown common house sparrows were emerging from the small crevasses of the ceilings and beams of the church, flying in zigzag diversions to avoid the ceiling fans and free themselves into the world through the ventilation shafts. From the transparent naves on top of the side doors, she observed a gloomy sky. The church bells rang, signalling the call for worship.

Pray, pray, she told herself. The bells stopped chiming and the congregation rose to sing the adoration.

* * *

'Nobody will marry you,' she thought she heard an echo. It sounded like Muruga, who had succumbed to liver cirrhosis some years ago. Though Annama's firewood peddling days had been replaced by a job as a factory operator, Muruga's voice remained sturdy in her head. *A familiar voice, thin but shrill in the blessed air*, she reckoned, *distant and untruthful*, she assured herself, and chuckled slightly as she felt comforted by the fond thoughts of her demised father. Annama craned her neck, looking out for the man whose very purpose she was here to fulfil; the only man who had wanted a part of her heart and filled her feelings of void, when she nearly abandoned the idea of being loved and being wanted, in her mid-forties.

And the object of her affection entered through the mahogany doors, hurriedly in the middle of the singing. Resplendent in a white silk veshti, a white shirt with a pressed and folded towel draped around his shoulders, George Amirtham entered. Smiling benignly, carrying a Bible in his right hand and holding onto the mid-split of his veshti with his left hand, he marched up the aisle. Complementing his sagely looks was his curly white hair, cotton white moustache that nearly tipped at both his ear lobes and a grand Seiko gold wrist watch that hung stately on his left hand.

Annama swallowed a glob of saliva and closed her eyes, relieved by his presence. However, there was a bargain. She had fallen in love and maintained a rather conspicuous relationship that bordered on the needs of a man whose wife had retired from his sensual pleasures, undergoing *men-o'-pause*. Annama, on the other hand, engulfed by loneliness and dreading a virgin death, grabbed at the chance to be loved. The English movies became too surreal to be given a pass. They were inside her, mind, body and soul. Fair in complexion, with thick eyebrows; standing at almost six feet, and athletic for his age of sixty-eight; made most attractive by the rarest luminous eye-pigmentation for a South Indian, he was her Eric Estrada from *Chips*.

'I like you,' he had said at the plastics and hardware factory where they worked. He, manning the security department and she, an operator working on cancer-causing melted sulphur moulds for daily wages.

'But,' she had said, raising a finger to touch her nose.

'You're lively, funny, full of zest and honest,' he said as he pushed away the finger from her face, 'sometimes being too honest to save yourself.'

'But here, look here,' Annama pointed to the smacking tinge of flesh that rested on her round chubby face and hips.

'I don't see anything,' he retorted.

'Not even this?' asked a cautious Annama, pulling out the scarce sprigs of hair amassed at the edge of her forehead, springing happily like wild flowers.

George Amirtham laughed, hysterically at first, then gently, his teeth arranging themselves suavely along his thick lips.

'And no more betel leaves for you,' he had said.

Aware that George Amirtham was called a pomble poriki by the factory women, usually behind his back, Annama was drunk with the elixir of life. Here she was bathing in sunbeams of the unexpected magical showers of life. She had prepared herself for a life of absolute detachment from belonging, surviving for the sake of living, like an empty vessel drifting about tethered to an empty shore. And now, she is released, paddling towards the beautiful indigo horizon that she often saw in her ocean of dreams with someone at last.

* * *

Losing her mother at twelve was never easy for Annama. Distressed, Muruga consumed alcohol for curing the thinning solace against his deprivation. He was absolutely clueless about child rearing, in turn, hardening Annama into a boy child. It was a common sight in the village to see father and daughter peddling firewood in the market corners and streets. Thankfully, some concerned neighbours came to his rescue and re-gendered Annama by schooling her in the home sciences. Muruga and Annama were too distraught to include God in their lives, taking life one day at a time and eventually isolating themselves from religion and their relatives. The One was only summoned or recalled on three occasions, Ponggal and Deepavali, or when Muruga ran short of his samsu, the latter contending a rant or curse.

There must be a God, Annama assured herself, fixing her eyes on the huge wooden cross at the centre of the church, illuminated by a golden hue from its back. For there is a promise of marriage . . . or an arrangement of sorts that could keep her and George Amirtham convulsed in an affair enveloped in a by-consent from his wife of forty-two years, Rebekah.

Rebekah was a petite-looking woman, whose thinning curls dropped daintily on dark, slender shoulders, her gait rotating on proportionate slabs of fat that sandwiched her midriff. She had a composed stature about her, a focused stare in her eyes, a crescent dimple appearing on her none too cheerful face. She walked into church flanked by her eldest son, daughter in law and grandchildren. Annama noted the rich silk on her sari, and the jewels that gleamed from her wrists and neck. She greeted the priest and the laymen in long robes with reverently clasped palms, collected the hymn book and the Order of Service, pulled the loose end of her sari over her head and herded everyone to the front pew where George Amirtham was waiting.

The symphonic vibration of the organ filled the church. People bowed, stood, knelt and sat at numerous intervals. Peace was shared. The offertory taken, the weekly announcements were made. The choir and the singing were resplendent. The priest's sermon, however, was a moral chastening against premeditated sin, and the punishments that rained down from heaven. Annama gulped down blobs of guilt filled air into her lungs. It was sinful for man to even look at another woman with lust and covetous intentions, especially married ones. These were punishable, and hell awaited them.

'Intimidation' Annama heard a middle aged man whispering to his wife from the back pew, 'this early in the morning,' he lamented.

'Quiet,' the woman rebutted.

And so the service continued, with children running wild with tested patience, the young tapping disinterestedly on their mobile phones, the adults dozing and yawning in pretentious prayer while the old piously rallied against bloated stomachs or farting, grumpily.

I must cross over, Annama conditioned her being, filling her eyes with moist hope and warming her heart with the transcendent light that shone from behind the wooden cross.

Two hours had passed, when the women around her began to fill their handbags with their Bibles and those with children tidied their dresses, rolled up mini comforters and bundled their babies while the men straightened themselves with ease, waking up refreshed. The sight made Annama nervous, as it signalled the end of the church service and she would need to meet Rebekah to be rightfully admonished.

George Amirtham had been caught red-handed in this affair by his own carelessness despite his eagerness to maintain the relationship as discreet as possible. Too much publicity had given rise to suspicion and Rebekah had launched a personal investigation herself. She knew probing her husband about the news that was carried to her by outsiders would not help. She had to investigate and she knew exactly what to do. She had filched his mobile phone, sending him on a wild goose chase that lasted a week. Having scrolled through the exchanged messages, having tracked down the registration details, she finally appeared at Annama's workplace, in time to witness the product of her labour, sacrifice and commitment about to be shared with a contender over the canteen table. She walked over, stood calmly in front of her bewitched husband, a confused Annama and a mass of intrigued eyes, obtained an extra plate and began to serve the packed food she had parcelled for her husband in her tiffin carrier.

'Did you like my cooking?' she asked a startled Annama, and pushed her down to her seat when she tried to get up. Mission accomplished, Rebekah let out a sigh, stacked the empty tiffin carrier that George Amirtham had ceremoniously laid out. 'I will talk to you when you get home,' she sneered at him. 'My brothers will be waiting,' she announced.

* * *

'Join us for breakfast, aunty,' the same lady from the back pew invited.

Annama smiled.

'Are you new to our church,' she asked. 'Christian?'

Annama smiled coyly. *If only she knew what brought me here*, she cautioned herself.

'No, I'm a Hindu. First time I am coming here,' Annama answered, for she knew that she still had to find her way to the kitchen where breakfast was served.

'Oh, come with me, come with me,' the lady prodded her, clutching on to her thick arms. 'Where do you live?' she asked.

Two huge pots sat on a flat, narrow banquet table. A few women stood behind it, passing plates and serving food. Annama collected the food—two steamed idlis topped with coconut chutney and chicken curry, and a paper cup full of hot coffee. Then, she stood, staring like a lost pilgrim. The woman who had led her to the breakfast area was nowhere to be seen. The tables were fully occupied, and she was shy to take the vacant seats, too uncomfortable to eat with strangers.

* * *

Rebekah had summoned most of her male relatives by the time George Amirtham had shaken himself off from the matinee shock. A struggle had ensued between him and her marauding brother. Men from the local caste council had to intervene. Unable to fend off the humiliation, abuse and the unruly behaviours of his in-laws, George Amirtham had no choice but turn to Rebekah, pleading for forgiveness, to escape from the hands of the small mob from dicing him into a bloody mesh.

'A compromise,' she said.

'Compromise?' George Amirtham repeated unsurely.

* * *

Spotting George Amirtham, Annama walked over to Rebekah's table and stood silently, slightly repulsed at the sight of food on Rebekah's plate. The steamed rice cakes had been mashed up with the chutney and curry, which by now looked like a child's loose motion. Rebekah was seated in the middle of the large round table, dropping lumps of the mashed up food mechanically into the mouths of her grandchildren. George Amirtham sat with his shoulders hunched, fingering his rice cakes and staring at the plate of sliced watermelons in the middle of the table. Rebekah's son whispered into her ears. She looked up and smiled and bid Annama to sit at their table.

'A new member?' asked a parishioner as he was passing by.

Rebekah's son and his wife looked stressed. Even their children seem to have been listening with all the attention that one's mind and spirit could afford. Even the church members, who took friendly steps to the table and tried to linger around to quench their curiosity, walked away, sensing the atmosphere.

'Yes, she is,' answered Rebekah exchanging a courteous smile with those passing by the table.

As if on cue, the other adults at the table arose and left, ushering the children along with them. George Amirtham remained silent with his head bowed. He gurgled as he tried to gulp down hot Nescafe. Annama took her seat, neither too close nor too far from Rebekah. The people at the other tables have begun to throw ubiquitous looks observing the newly formed triad.

'I have no use for my husband,' Rebekah started, in a slow dial. 'It's been forty years of married life, now I feel I have no use for him,' she said, pushing away her plate. Using a fork to pick a slice of watermelon left on another adjacent saucer, she sighed. 'Thirty-five years of letting him into me, all that washing, cooking, caring and looking after his children,' she pursed her lips tightly. 'All that to no good, no reward,' she puckered her lips and glared at George Amirtham.

'So, what do you propose?' Rebekah asked, biting into a sliced watermelon.

'Propose?' asked Annama, bewildered, getting more apprehensive.

'I'll let you have him,' Rebekah answered, spitting out the watermelon seeds into her cupped hands. 'But there are some conditions,' she answered, in a disdained manner.

Annama eyed George Amirtham nervously. She was this near. She didn't expect Rebekah to be so easy.

'I have not been paid in full, nor compensated, for all the years of my labour,' she began. 'And it's not fair for you to expect a bite of the life I had built with this man,' she presented her case. 'I have good children; they take good care of me. I have a house, cars, money and lived long enough to see my grandchildren. I have a home. I own a home,' she corrected.

'And because I oversee everything my family owns, I will also oversee what my husband owns. In pain, in life, in sickness and in death, we are still equal. I believe in the Word, I will do His will. I will uphold justice. This man has committed adultery. And you wretchedly took his bait. Do I blame you? I blame him? I only have myself to blame. I have failed as a wife. I have fallen short of my duties,' Rebekah spoke animatedly, wiping the corners of her eyes, her throat choking with dissent.

The cluttering laughter and the high pitched, disarrayed quality of singsongs of the children from Sunday school broke the intensity of the conversation.

'What profits you? Nothing . . . it has to be nothing. I have decided to lease him to your needs.' Rebekah's mouth was wry and sharp, her voice curt and focused. Her eyes were peaceful and calm, but welled up in their corners were droplets of her sorrow. Taking a deep breath, she laid out the rules, one by one.

'You will neither interfere in my family affairs, nor my husband's.

'You will not lay any claim to anything from my household.

'You will not live out this affair in the open.

'You surrender all your earnings to me at the end of each month. I will see to your needs on behalf of my husband, food, clothes and medicine.

'You will name my husband as sole beneficiary to your savings from the Employment Provident Fund. To secure care for your old age.

'I will rebuild your father's house if you transfer the land title to my name, and will be occupied by my younger son and his wife, and in which you will be given a room to stay. What you do there is your own business.

'Your other needs will be taken care of solely on the ability and discretion of my husband. If you behave, I will see that he gives you a proper burial; I would not promise that it will be a noble one though. There is nothing further to discuss.'

Rebekah got up and left.

George Amirtham smiled sheepishly. The treaty being sealed, he too got up. He nodded towards Annama, picked up the empty plates and cups and followed Rebekah into the thinning crowd, without a word.

The quietness was strange. Not a soul lingered in the vicinity. The wind blew in a soft breeze.

'No man will marry you,' her father's voice echoed.

Still holding her untouched plate of breakfast Annama looked into her cup of coffee. The fluffy rice cakes were too soggy to be eaten, and the coffee had grown cold in her warm hands, forming a pale layer of cream on top.

Is a man worth everything? She wondered shortly, a whiff of a thought swirling in her heavy head.

When she peered close enough into the concoction of her cup, she spotted the unmistakable shine of the blue and green fluorescent flecks of a dead bluebottle, belly up!

The Truth about Mo

All truth passes through three stages, a subtle thought vibrates in Rukku's head. It is a line she had read on Facebook and memorized. Sighing at the sight of black moss mapped across her kitchen walls, Rukku wipes the counter with a dry rag. She then ladles a spoonful of coffee into her mug and stirs it slowly. All around the village, motorbikes have sprung to life and fill the streets noisily like an army on a march. She looks out from the window of her rented home, the extended back portion of a large house, and notices that Ramesh has not returned from the temple. The modest porch is strewn with dry mango leaves brought in by the hot air that swept down from greater Kuala Lumpur. *All truth passes through three stages*, she repeats, the bitter, hot coffee searing her taste buds.

First, it is ridiculed.

Dragging a chair toward the kitchen window, she leans her elbows on the counter and cups her narrow chin. The allamandas that Ramesh planted are in full bloom. They extended from the tree to the kitchen wall and formed a hedge that separated the main house from their portion. She often teases him for his liking of flowers as being effeminate. But how she wishes she hadn't said such things now. She should have listened to him, especially on the day Mo turned sixteen and declared that he wanted a motorbike and nothing less.

Ramesh did not buy the idea. He was reluctant. He said only he knew what boys did on the back of their motorbikes. The days that followed were the most unfriendly ones, with both father and son sulking around each other. Blinded by affection, I took Mo's side. I should not have scoffed at Ramesh, putting akin his fear for the fast and dangerous to the liking of his effeminate hobby—horticulture. I downplayed his opinions, disregarding his experiences as an office boy who moved around town on a motorbike himself. I failed to realize that his fatherly concerns for the safety of his son came from his awareness of the devilry that was stirring Mo's hormones.

'The first two weeks, that's all,' Ramesh pointed out over tea one evening. 'The first two weeks they'd be fine. After that, once they get used to the machine, they will surrender themselves to it. They will hardly notice the time as it passed by. Their adrenaline will be shooting through the roof. They think they are invulnerable. It's total ecstasy, I say,' I thought I heard Ramesh choking as he spoke. 'And he would not be left alone. They'd come, in gangs and in pairs. They'd whisper secret initiations into his ears. They would block his ears and cloud his mind. I've seen it happen. Too many times, Rukku. Will you please listen to me?' he pleaded.

'But Pa, our son has come of age,' I chirped inconsiderately. 'He should be doing what all sixteen year olds do. He needs to move into the world. Absorb the universe. Become a man. Unless he is given the motorbike, he will not earn his freedom. He will not be at liberty to make decisions. He will not be able to solve problems. Or take ownership of his life and learn responsibility,' I debated while Ramesh lit a cigarette.

'On the road, there are dangers he must learn to look out for. We cannot keep protecting him, Ramesh. Our boy must grow up. On top of that, he could send me to work. I'm tired of waiting for the feeder buses. Mo could drop me off at the LRT station on his way to school. Stop laughing. Ramesh! I could go to the market on the weekends while you're off on your part-time work. I do not want to depend on you all the time. There are millions of boys out there and even girls of Mo's age who already have a motorbike. I think you are being paranoid, simply paranoid, Ramesh. Let go, Pa. He will be fine. And we can afford to buy a motorbike, can't we?'

There was no reply from Ramesh. Pushing the cigarette butt into the ashtray, he got up to leave. I got agitated. 'I just don't want you to turn Mo into one of your flowers,' I shouted angrily at him.

'Are you mocking me?' Ramesh asked. 'I am talking about my only son,' he retorted. 'I'm concerned for his safety. I want him to remain as Mo. To hold my hand when my legs give way and my vision frays. He has to light my pyre when my time is up. He is my only hope. And who will see to your needs when I am gone? There are hundreds, thousands, no doubt millions riding around town on motorbikes, but we've got only one son,' Ramesh growled in a stupor. 'Don't you dare mock me!' he warned.

All truth passes through three stages. First, it is ridiculed. Rukku closes her eyes. It has been two weeks since Ramesh had spoken to her.

Then, it is violently opposed.

She closes her eyes again and strains her neck against the chair's headrest. She feels a minute's relief from her stiff shoulders and neck. She sips more coffee. She catches sight of the allamanda again and smiles ruefully. Their bright yellow hues that used to warm her heart now remain bland and neglected. She notices that they've grown so wild that they've climbed to the top of the mango tree. This huge shrub overtaking the garden grew from tiny saplings that Mo brought home from school one day. It was a class project designed to inculcate in children a sense of dutiful love to all living things. When the saplings outgrew their soil bags, Ramesh replanted them along the hedges that separated the big house from their compound. Small birds nested on the bushels, house sparrows and humming birds. There were a dozen or so new nests hidden in the bushes, Rukku remembers. Soon the compound will be filled with the fluttering noise of the birds tending to their new hatchlings.

Ramesh was right all along . . .

The motorbike arrived one Friday evening. Mo was delighted. He ran in circles and hugged us silly. Such is the sweetness of a child's gratitude. We took it in, mindful that danger awaited Mo in dark hidden corners. Ramesh began to teach Mo a thing or two about road safety, motorbike etiquette and maintenance. In the evenings he took Mo to show him the simple routes he should be taking—from home to school, from home to my workplace and from home to the market. Ramesh applied holy ash on the polished chrome fenders every morning. It tickles me though, when I think of it, for it annoyed Mo. But Mo had other things on his mind.

In no time, he threw away his books and set his heart on the machine. First, a large sticker of a hissing cobra appeared on the front flaps of his motorbike. Then he started pestering for more money to spend on his modifications. Ramesh refused. Mo turned down what I offered, saying it was insignificant. 'It's a new motorbike, why does it need modifications?' I kept repeating. But it fell on deaf ears. Mo grew remorseful. He snapped angrily at his father. All he could talk to me about was modifications to add swiftness to his motorbike. *Ma*, he called out from the front of his motorbike one Sunday, *if only I could add field coils to the chain and callipers*, though I could not envision his words, *we would reach the market in no time*. 'But there is no hurry. You have ample time,' I told him. 'The market is not going anywhere,' I joked.

The late nights out with his new friends estranged Mo from us. He hardly touches his dinner anymore. He is curled too tightly in his blankets to be shaken awake for the Sunday markets. On weekdays he leaves for school at half past seven in school uniform and arrives home in the late evening in casual attire, none that I remember paying for. And he has stopped asking us for money. On one particular night, after three months of Mo acquiring his motorbike, I began to grow worried when I didn't hear his usual revving on the porch by midnight. I lost touch with his arrivals and departures. Police summons arrived in the mails too. Ramesh had to settle them.

Neighbours informed Ramesh that they had seen Mo riding his motorcycle during school hours in the quiet residential areas. Sometimes they'd seen him parked along the roads or junctions, waiting for others to show up on their motorbikes. They left after discreet exchanges of small packets and notes during pretentious conversations. A visit to the school confirmed that Mo had been playing truant. Ramesh flew into a rage when Mo admitted that he planned to drop out. He stood defiantly against Ramesh, chest to chest, father to son. Ramesh unbuckled his belt and started striking Mo with all his might. Mo stood like a stubborn ass, staring. I tried to intervene but knew the better to stay out of this.

The beating subsided and Mo left the living room without a word. I followed him. Much to my dismay, Mo took out a pack of cigarettes and lit one. He stood by the window in his room taking out rolls of money from his pockets. I gulped a few times and approached him quietly. A new sense of fear clouded my mind at the realization of Mo's changes. Sensing my dread, Mo laughed, threw the rolls of money on his bed and said, 'Ma, this is everything. Life is useless without money.' He took off his T-shirt and opened the windows. He shrugged and pushed away my hands when I wanted to touch him. Amid the rising pink and purple welts, I noticed how much my skinny boy had put on weight. The welts stood atop his muscles like stamp marks. It was then I realized that the motorbike had taken away my boy and given me a brazen young man. Ramesh was wrong to have struck him. But I also knew I was losing Mo.

Mo left school the following year—when he was only seventeen—much to Ramesh's disappointment. Ramesh became more of a recluse from then on. He would turn down Mo's gifts and would take no part in Mo's revelries or invitations to eat out together. He would lower his head when walking and rarely spoke to anyone. His voice had become heavy with a worried undertone. He abandoned his garden. His allamandas grew beyond reach.

All truth passes through three stages. First, it is ridiculed. Then it is violently opposed. Lastly, you surrender to it. Truth is accepted as self-evident.

The last fifteen days have been terrible. Grief arrives, unannounced on swift winds, like a huge storm that unfurls its contents—hail, thunder and rain—at once. It uproots and damages everything in its path. It is blind to everything. It has no mercy on whoever it crosses paths with. It pelts the soul mercilessly and leaves everlasting pain. Rukku pulls out some tissues from a box on the kitchen counter and sneezes into them. She closes her eyes again and shakes her head. She looks at the clock and rolls her eyes at it. 'What's the hurry?' She mumbles. She lifts a finger and makes a counterclockwise twirling movement and giggles. She opens an overhead kitchen cabinet and takes out a square plastic container. She uncovers the lid and adds some sugar to her lukewarm coffee. After taking a sip, she cups her mouth and brings a hand up to her chest, stroking it. The tears break free like opened floodgates and blur her vision.

It was Deepavali. Mo stayed at home for the longest period of time since the motorbike had arrived two years earlier. 'Let's celebrate,' he announced. I filled a whole tin full of achu murukku and atharasam, which puffed up on the surface of the hot oil like lucky stars from the deep wok. A canopy was erected on our little compound, its peripheries bordered by chasing lights. With Ramesh's consent, Mo had invited his new friends over. These were a total contradiction to the neat, timid boys in pressed uniforms and plain hairstyles I was accustomed to. These were stylish men who arrived in polished cars, heavily tinted windshields, wore excessive jewellery, dressed fashionably and sported identical tattoos of a hissing cobra. Ramesh pulled me aside and lamented that Mo had certainly learned a thing or two about feasting. Fireworks lit up the village sky, cartons of beer cans floated in a plastic tub filled with ice and lots of curried and barbecued meat were served. His friends joked about Mo's interest in a girl I had never met. I smiled politely, knowing that Mo was only eighteen and still loved the dangerous life he had chosen.

I was perturbed when one of the boys suddenly ran out to his car and produced a roll of fire crackers. A few others joined him. They tied one end of the coil to a branch of the mango tree and lined it in a zigzag manner across the road outside the gate. When it went off, it was loud enough to shove all evil into Hell. From within the thick, sulphuric fog appeared a buff, middle-aged Chinese man, bedecked in a thick, gold chain carrying a large hamper. He was followed by his wife and two young children. Unlike the others, he was modestly dressed in khaki shorts, a pair of sandals and a white sweatshirt. A long serpentine beast was tattooed on his right arm. Mo received him as if a great sage had arrived at our home, while the other boys stood by reverently. When he left, I found a thick wad of hundred ringgit notes in the hamper.

Mo was his normal self throughout the party. He was not even drunk. He helped me clean up the compound and ate his dinner last. I served his food. He left home to visit his friends thereafter. In a funny way he asked if I would be awake when he returned home that night. But I was too tired. I woke up when I heard Mo calling for me. It was 4 a.m. I had overslept. I quickly got up and checked his room. It was empty. So was the porch. We waited for three nights for Mo. There was no sign of him. His friends were silent. Ramesh was silent. The neighbours grew silent. Three nights later, a policeman knocked on our door and asked if we were Mo's parents. The stocky policeman looked uncomfortable and distressed, having had to convey the unpleasant news. For the first few minutes we were distracted, probably saved from a cardiac arrest by trying to discern his words. 'Pasensspiss, pasensspiss,' he blurted. Ramesh had to repeat the words after him, 'patience please'. The revolving blue lights from the strobe of the patrol car were bright enough to stir the neighbours awake and fill our porch. Maybe they too knew that Mo's revving of the motorbike was never to be heard again.

At the mortuary the mouth-full-of-tongue officer kept asking us to remain calm as we were ushered to the cold chambers to identify Mo's body. From a file of papers he flashed a picture of a tattooed cobra. It annoyed me, as he kept pushing the picture onto our faces, even to the hospital staff at the mortuary. 'Don't you have anything else to show?' I shouted at him angrily. It stunned him for a moment. He quickly put the picture into the file that he was carrying while searching for words. 'A finger, a toe, or a mole and scar, a face,' my voice broke. 'Why don't you show everyone a face? Show me a face, damn you!' I screeched and kicked the medicine dispenser down the corridor. 'Pasensspiss, Pasensspiss, madam,' he pleaded. I calmed down. 'He is my son,' I informed him.

Ramesh stared me down as he signed the release forms at the mortuary.

With the help of Mo's friends, we brought his body home, wrapped in hospital sheets. Ramesh was too distraught to oversee the funeral arrangements. Thus, I took over the responsibility. I hardened my soul. By the time our relatives had arrived to console me, my tears were gone. Though everyone protested, I braved up and offered to bathe him myself. I instructed his friends to carry him into the bathroom. It was large enough to lay him there with four of us. I turned on the shower. I folded my legs and sat on the cold tiles, absorbing the water that ran down from his body. In the midst of grief, I found lesions, swelling and clumsily stitched punctures on his body. The boys who helped me bathe him whispered about beatings and assassinations. I closed my ears. I rubbed soap on his cold body and sprinkled warm water over him, feeling every inch of my only son. His skin was rough with hair, and his muscles were hard. When they turned him, the birth mark on his buttocks remained a dark splotch of green. Everyone who visited me when Mo was born claimed it was a good sign. 'You are lucky,' they had told me. As they patted him with dry towels, I laid his head on my lap and gazed at his face one last time before I combed his hair. I could hardly recognize him anymore. All I could do was dress his bare body in sandalwood paste and perfumed rose water, like marinated chicken prepped for the frying pan.

People talked. People talked a lot about Mo. Was he the perfect bait, a victim of his allegiance to the triad boss who he served chicken and mutton curry during Deepavali? The rumours were thick, and it wafted around the funeral tent. What took them three days to return him to his family? Did he really die in an accident? Wasn't he the one who would rev his motorbike in the middle of the night and disrupt everyone's peace and quiet? He did not listen to his parents. Wasn't he a drug pusher, greedy and selfish? Imagine how many parents lost their children to his business? How many wives would have lost their husbands? Children their fathers? He chose his path and karma returned its wages. All he gave his parents was nothing but grief. Blame the mother. She spoiled him. She gifted him the motorbike, and it took him to his untimely grave!

I knew something was amiss. The rumours were not true. There were roadblocks all over town that night on Deepavali. Maybe Mo was not carrying an illegal substance. Maybe he was arrested on suspicion. Was he tipped off by those he trusted? There was no proof he was carrying drugs. And the reports mentioned sudden death caused by an accident. It bewildered Ramesh, our relatives and Mo's friends. Mo's possessions had all gone missing. Nothing was returned except for Mo's motorbike a week later. His gold chain and rings, handphones, his leather sling bag and even his bloodied clothes had vanished.

But I knew his soul was not at peace. Mo kept appearing in my dreams, standing at the front of the village police station and calling out to me. Sometimes I heard the revving of a lone motorcycle at the porch. I even saw Mo from the corner of my eyes, polishing his motorbike. I remembered riding pillion to work, Mo's strong shoulders blocking the wind. I had weird intuitions that Mo had asked me to cook his favourite food in the mornings. My son is not dead. Not dead yet. His spirit is restless. *Mo, if you had only listened to Pa. If only I had listened to Pa.*

I buried my face in my palms and cried so much that my breasts cramped.

All that milk you suckled, Mo, is now wasted blood.

On the date commemorating the sixteenth day since Mo's death, Ramesh busied himself preparing for the prayers. But Rukku visited the police station first. She told the officer-in-charge that Mo had been held in the lock up. The puncture marks on his body were bullet holes and there had been no accident. She told them that she needed to do the prayers at the spot where he died to liberate his soul.

The officer was bewildered. He almost convinced her that her claims were fraudulent with grief before showing her the door. She protested. More officers crowded around her, confused by the event unfolding before them. They told her to stop. They called her a nuisance. They said she was up to no good, a troublemaker like Mo. They said they would arrest her.

Much to their chagrin, Rukku marched out of the station to the corner that housed the lock-up cells. Amid the jeers and mocking, the stocky, mouth-full-of-tongue policeman appeared again. At the top of his voice he shouted, 'lezzisbe, lezzisbe.' The officer stopped between Rukku and the other frenzied officers, gathered his breath and said, 'Let it be.' Flustered, Rukku taped Mo's picture on a tree standing adjacent to the building that housed the cells and hung a string of jasmines across it. She spread a banana leaf on the ground. Burning three incense sticks, she laid a bunch of bananas and poked them into one banana. From her bag she produced a coconut, raised a machete and halved it in front of the shocked officers and split it open. She scrutinized its split edges and noticed that it was jagged and not smooth as she had feared. Leaving the halved coconut on the banana leaf, she reluctantly conceded that Mo's passing was fated. She clasped he palms reverently and uttered her prayers. Then, she left for home.

How dare they tell me that Mo is bad, she listened to the voice in her head. *How dare they label him useless? How dare they call him a menace? This society, did they not shorten his life with their assumptions? I've seen the money. But illegal substances?* The punctures on his chest and sides remained in her mind, as big as the pottu on her forehead, crusted like dried blood. But her protests were muffled. Her hands were twisted and her mouth shut. Ramesh would not come to her aid. The neighbours smirked behind her back. Her relatives blamed her. The policeman asked her to accept the death and let it be.

Rukku wipes her eyes and looks into the cup to find it empty. She catches sight of Mo's motorbike on the side of the porch, covered in a grey tarpaulin sheet. Resentment arises from her guts, creeping up to her head like the allamanda wines. She should have listened to Ramesh. She had laughed at him. Ramesh knew it would take Mo away from them. She gets up and walks toward the motorbike. Ramesh has arrived with the priest and is helping with the arrangements. Mo is smiling down from the wall where his black-and-white portrait is hanging. A thick garland of roses is hung across his picture, with a smudge of vermillion powder splotched on his forehead.

Rukku quietly pulls off the tarpaulin and pushes the motorbike toward the allamanda bush. She fetches kerosene from the kitchen and pours it all over Mo's motorbike. 'It's all because of you,' she stutters in anger. A few neighbours have stopped to watch from over their walls. She hurls the empty kerosene container into the thick bush and drives away the roosting birds from their nests. A bystander from the roadside comes to ask what she is up to and calls out to Ramesh. Rukku snubs him angrily and lights a match. In no time, a huge fire engulfs the entire motorbike and the overgrown allamanda.

Ramesh hurries out and pulls Rukku away from the flames. No one tries to extinguish the fire. They stand and watch the motorbike burn, thick black smoke rising toward the sky.

Interview Blues

The thick curtains failed to filter the stealing rays of the morning sun from creeping up Ben's pillows, tickling his closed eyelids with their feathery touch. Ben forced open one eye to trigger himself awake, wondering whether the alarm clock had set off. He turned on his back and tried to steal a few more minutes of slumber, but could not stop his subconscious mind from reminding him that *it is an important day*. He managed a few stretches, turning this way and that, kicking aside the blanket and dislodging a pair of boxer briefs that had clumsily tucked at his side. He tried to ascertain the strength of the light that appeared through the ventilation shaft above his windows and deduced that it is still too early for his appointment at Kelana Jaya.

He turned on his sides, hugging pleasurably onto his huge bolster, mindful of the cool air and the slow twirling of the ceiling fan. He checked the time, it was half past seven, and he had two hours to go before the walk-in interview started at 10:30 am. The cold began to seep up his bare skin, and proved to become uncomfortable. It had rained last night, making sleep welcome, but not now. He took a deep breath, and looked through the window for the short glimpses of daylight offered by the narrow flapping of the curtains.

He scratched his arms and chests, pushed back his hair and then proceeded to rub his cheeks and chin to check for signs of stubbles that he needs to shave afterwards. He sighed. He needed to change his life. He was determined to travel the world and work in a world class cabin, as promoted by the Malaysian Airlines System's recruitment ad. He was bored, taking up jobs and salaries that were measured by his Higher Diploma. He was tired of cajoling two jobs at a time and the random melancholy it offered. After thirty-two applications, twenty-two failed interviews, and ten KIVs, he was getting ready for the thirty-third, which he has promised himself to be the last attempt. Working as a sales clerk at the Kuala Lumpur International Airport's duty free shops had not helped him to kill the dream of working in an airliner, being swathed by the presence of the numerous pilots, stewards and stewardesses who walk in and out from the terminals. He secretly harboured and coveted their bearings, as they straddled out from the arrival hall, pushing their trolley bags in their work uniforms, elegant and glamorous.

He got up from his bed with a slight heaviness in his head, despairing at the thought that he might fail again. He had consulted almost every availing trickster in town from fortune tellers to palm readers; even recommendations from airport authorities, but none of them could assure him the position he had hankered after for so long. On top of that, his persistence had been ridiculed by his circle of friends and criticized by his mother. Only his father had stood by him, all the twenty-six times that he had to get a ride in his taxi to the Malaysian Airlines Academy in Kelana Jaya where the walk-in interviews were held.

He massaged his temples, did a quick push-up, reached for his towel and hung it on his shoulders and stood in front of the mirror. He combed back his hair with his fingers, parting them sideways and pushing them upwards into the middle. Turning his chin and cheeks with his thumb and index finger, he pulled and squeezed to check on his facial hair again. He stretched lethargically and gave a wide lazy yawn, at once noticing his smarting eyes and relieving his muscles. He stood sideways, and then in front, moved closer and farther from the mirror, flexing his muscles, in case he could not detect anomalies that only the interviewers might notice. He mentally filled up the requirements outlined in the advertisement. He stood at 1.76 metres. He had sharp features, large ears. He fulfilled the age range (twenty-eight), fluent in both English and Bahasa Melayu and had no problems communicating with the general public. He pushed back his shoulders and observed the lump of pectoral muscles bulging on his biceps and mane and the perfectly formed 'wings' on his back. He was pleased, better looking after months of toning sessions at the gym. He also couldn't help noticing the veins running up his neck, forming turquoise lines on his smooth and tanned complexion. *All the veins were of colour*, he noticed, bluish and greenish, under his armpits, on his forehead, arms and hips.

But what could have gone wrong, he couldn't help musing. That in turn made his shoulders heavy, reminiscing on the past failed interviews and bad lucks that resulted in bouts of indecipherable anxiety. But he had to try. He could not switch off the world and pretend to be happy working at its backyard.

'Your time has not come,' his father had explained calmly. 'Therefore you must wait and not give up.'

Ben let out another huge sigh, uncertain of the outcomes of this day. Outside, it had started drizzling slightly but there were birds chirping about on his window panes. The smell of coffee assailed into his room accompanied by the bustling noise that his family members made as they went about preparing themselves for the day.

He turned off the heater, and opted to test his valour under the cold shower. Satisfied with the shave, and the sweet smell of shower gel, he emerged from the bathroom, clad in his towel and began to prep himself up. Everything was ready, he just needed to dress. While waiting for the aftershave to vaporize he checked the contents of a brown envelop lying on his table. Emptying it, he found the application form, neatly filled up in capital letters and bold, black ink. His name, Parthiban Chan, surfaced out from the square blocks on the paper, like a statement, assuring and sturdy. He checked the other particulars and made sure that every column was filled with the correct details. A spare form was tagged with it with a paper clip, just in case there was a mistake. Two coloured passport sized photographs were also attached with a completed C.V. He pushed back the papers as delicately as he could and folded the ears of the envelope inwards.

He dashed himself with a thin layer of talcum powder. He greased his dark hair, and gingered it to a low but trendy spike in the middle. His sideburns were both short enough to expose the white scalp of his head. He massaged his ear lobes, so that the punctures would not be too obvious during the interview and lifted his head high enough to inspect if any hair showed through his nose. Then, he proceeded to check for stain on his teeth and gums, and finally his fingernails. All these were prepped up a day earlier, but he had to be sure, and before another self-grooming test he would subject himself to at the gents' at the academy. His wardrobe was ready. They were hanging importantly on hangers, all pressed and smoothened, free from wrinkles, complete with a necktie draped around the buttoned collar. He wore his singlet, and took to scrutinizing the navy blue-and-white striped shirt that he had bought a month ago, especially for this interview, as instructed by the temple priest.

Prayer, he had come to agree, *is the last resort of the disbelief.* That's when his friend Ravi had introduced him to a temple that had long existed on the same stretch of road that Ben travelled for work but had gone almost unnoticed for years. He did not belief in the divine, probably because both his parents, a Taoist and a Hindu, ditched religion at the point of their marriage and pretty much had learnt to live without it throughout their married years. A win-win formula, they emphasized for a conflict free marriage. Their children however, were given the freedom to choose. And it turned out to become a choice that had never occurred as an obligation to Ben.

Ravi had brought news, (rather a reminder) of this particular deity of this temple that bestowed great favours and answered any vows taken by its devotees, sans race, creed or calling. Ben had agreed as to consult the deity as last resort, as he had exhausted all attempts for job opportunities at the airlines. The meeting was arranged on a Friday three months ago with Ravi agreeing to be his mediator, conducting consultations on Ben's behalf. The priest was known to inherit powers bestowed by Datuk Hitam, some believed to be the sacred spirit of an ancient warrior who lived in the early sixteenth century. This was because when the priest got into a trance, his other personality often depicted someone walking with a hunchback, needing a staff, and constantly pulled down an invisible long beard as well as twining the visible moustache in both ways. Ben was astonished when he was first seated in front of the priest, and the medium had spoken in very old Malay, 'What has brought this grandchild of mine here?', and laughed sinisterly at the disbelieving Ben who was both awestruck and afraid.

Ravi spoke. The Datuk listened benignly from where he sat, glancing up at Ravi and Ben and those who have gathered. In front of him were placed trays of offerings—glutinous rice cooked in turmeric; boiled quail eggs; local fruits; betel leaves and nuts; five types of flowers apart from the throat-wrenching smoke of incense on live coals; and freshly lit cigars. The first meeting was short. Datuk had empathised with Ben's situation. First he had asked Ben to move forward, placed his right arm on Ben's shoulders and recited something. Ben was to observe some ceremonial sacraments. He had to mandi-bunga, soaking five types of flowers and bathing in its water before sunrise. Then, turning to Ravi, the second instruction was given for Ben to encircle the resident sacred snake nine times for nine consecutive Saturdays and to leave milk and eggs at the base of the cobra's nest thereafter. With much hesitation, Ben followed the instructions, accompanied by his friend's assurances and warnings of worst luck that could follow any disobedience. The nine weeks had paced quietly though Ben had been pessimistic about the presence of the resident cobra. Though the anticipated creature was absent, its home, made of mounds of laterite clay, drew visitors day and night with queues stretching up to a hundred at a time. The only consolations were the free meals provided by the temple kitchen, platter loads of curried goat, fresh from the morning sacrifices served by very accommodating volunteers.

The final Saturday arrived, and it was the highlight signifying the completion of the undertaken pledge and an offering had to be made. A verdict was given, if the divine was merciful. Sometimes people cried or fainted, if the predictions were unfavourable or if they had brought the wrong offerings. But Ben's request was simple, and he had soldiered on patiently and dutifully, as assured by Ravi. After the bhajans, the priest had taken the centre stage and started conversing in Malay, the beat of the drums and cymbals stopped, and the devotees formed a line. When Ben's turn came, Datuk made a gesture to ask him to come forward and sit in front of him.

'Did cucu bring what Datuk has requested?' the medium asked, with such calmness that Ben felt an enormous yearning for love. His eyes blurred, tears welling up, unexplained to him.

Ben put forward the requested items. The main item was wrapped tightly, for only Ben was supposed to know its contents, accompanied by jasmines, a bunch of banana, betel leaves and nuts. '*Ya*, Datuk,' he uttered politely and placed the items before the medium.

Datuk sat still. A few minutes passed and he dictated, or rather managed two sentences, while an interpreter knelt beside him, in case Datuk spoke in imageries and symbols. Two things he had said.

One, 'If you believe, you could find God in even a slab of concrete, He is there.'

Two, but this time raising one eyebrow and smiling coquettishly, he instructed, 'Dress yourself in blue.'

With that, the medium looked down and remained that way. The interpreter gestured for Ben to get up and leave. Ben's eyes widened in disbelief. He opened his mouth? *That's all?* He wanted to question.

Excuse me, he said, trembling, in fear and dismay, disappointed that his nine weeks of religious adherence had resulted in the simplest form of terms as benefits. *Divine grace?* He scoffed at the idea, having had expected a prophecy from

God Himself. *If the supernatural had a funny bone, this was it.* 'Wait a minute,' he said. He wanted to shout, raise his voice, *where are your snakes*, he wanted to question. *Didn't they report about the milk and eggs?* he wanted to query. The medium, still in a trance, stirred from his current position, looked up to him, and stared. By now, Ravi was already on his feet, pulling up Ben by his shoulders, as the interpreter was getting very annoyed. The curious onlookers had begun to susurrate excitedly, like a strong wind brushing against dry tree branches.

They left.

But that was the very last thing Ben could trust; *a blue shirt*! *What could a blue shirt do?* He had contended. He had even disputed on the meaninglessness of colours, reprimanding Ravi for committing him to such a fallacious act. He could not bring himself to fathom that his entire future, all that he had hoped for, was going to be dictated by a blue shirt! *It does not even augur well with my tanned complexion,* he fumed. However, having gathered his senses, he concurred that there was no need to disobey divine orders. And he too had begun to believe in the untoward repercussions if such things were ignored.

He walked to the corner of the room, where the cloth hanger was. The neatly-ironed navy blue shirt with very thin white stripes *is perky*, he observed optimistically. Bounding the collars loosely was a shining silk necktie, the colour of oxford blue. And, attached to them was a pair of black long pants that he was going to wear for his interview. They hung on the corner of the rack, like being suspended on an invisible mannequin.

Blue, he remembered as he traced his fingers along the contours of the soft material. He sprayed 'Bleu de Chanel' that he had bought last week. He waited for the crisp tinge of perfume to linger. He proceeded to draw open the curtains and rested his eyes on the blue hues of his room, reflected by the scant sunlight that fell on the walls. He took a deep breath and dressed up. He felt a little cheerful. *Let it be*, he sighed. Dressed, he picked up his files and the brown envelope and took one last look at himself in the full mirror before stepping out.

His father was already outside, wiping the side mirrors of his taxi off the morning dew. Ben forgo the coffee, afraid of staining his teeth and avoiding any form of carelessness that he could not afford.

His father smiled when Ben got out and stepped into his shoes. He looked pleased. 'Ready to go?' he asked.

As per ritual, Ben took his seat in the front and adjusted himself, careful not to crumple his shirt and trousers. The files and the envelope were left on the back seat.

The car started, and before it rumbled off, his mother waved to stop them.

'What did she forget to tell me now,' murmured his father, complainingly under his breath. She came out and stood at Ben's side and tapped on the window screen.

Ben lowered the window, half-sulking.

'Keep this in your pocket,' his mother said. And from her wrinkled fists, she produced one of her old earrings that had lost its other pair. A teardrop shaped amulet now, set in white gold with a radiant blue sapphire in the middle. 'It's your grandmother's, she will bless you,' she said as she dropped it into his shirt pocket.

Ben shook his head, and huffed a small sigh.

His father giggled. 'Shall we go, while the sky is still clear?' he asked and drove away.

The MRRI was jammed as usual with the morning traffic. They made Ben squeaky and claustrophobic. Ben read the papers to keep the tender, unseen butterflies from gnawing at his stomach. Though he felt refreshed and confident of the ritualistic interview procedures, he was still nervous and it was building up like gas from his guts.

Wonder what the stars read for me today, he thought. Very cautiously, he parted the papers in the middle and flipped a few pages to where the cartoon section was. And scrolled down his eyes to where his horoscope was stationed.

VIRGO.

Something of the past will come to an end today. The meticulous Virgin must work hard but fret less. Determination pays and she will enjoy the fruit of perseverance. Lucky number 6; Lucky colour, Blue.

Blue, he murmured, and sat up straight. He took a long, deep breath.

Ben managed a little smile and looked out of the taxi, to face the rising sun.

Masalodeh

Standing at the entrance of her makeshift stall, Rajamah waited for the camphor to burn off. The early evening sun hung like a bright red lantern in the horizon, its fierce rays softened by the thick haze. The stale air was a norm, but it was now infused with the overpowering smell of cat poo.

'Inauspicious! If only the wind could direct me to it, I could flush it into the street,' Rajamah mumbled as she forced a fresh hibiscus stem between the wall and wood panel of a framed Ganesha. Kak Su, from the next stall, waved at her. Rajamah ignored her, her attention fixed on to a large green board listing out the array of kuih sold by Kak Su. Soon, the factory sirens would signal the end of shifts and she would need to get the masala vadais ready.

Her assistant, Rani, had washed the cement floor, wiped the counters, and was now pouring oil into a large wok. A tub of thick yellow batter rested on an adjoining table, waiting for the chopped onions, sliced green and dried chilies, curry leaves, spices, and lentils to be mixed in. They will be ready for purchase, just in time for the factory and office workers as they headed back home. Rajamah groaned as she spotted Kak Su walking over to her stall.

'Halo Rajam. Have you fried any masalodeh yet?'

'Not yet, Su, just getting the mixture ready.'

'Eh, that's a lot of batter,' Kak Su chirped, looking about the shop and the counters. 'Your whole elbow has gone into the tub, adoi.'

'I can use the wooden churning stick, but nothing compares to feeling the ingredients with your own hands. Only then you will know if the food will turn out right or not,' said Rajamah.

'Oh, just go by taste, you measure with hand, mind, and heart,' Kak Su said.

'Correct, Su, that's how my mother and grandmother cooked, recipes and ingredients measured by hand, memory and taste.' Rajamah giggled.

'Keep two masalodeh for me, Rajam. Later I send my helper to collect.' Kak Su turned to leave.

'Can, can, come back in half an hour.'

The preparations complete, Rajamah lifted her closed palms in prayer before turning on the stove. She cupped the mixture in her palm and daintily dropped them into the hot oil, and waited for the batter to form flat and crisp cakes as they rose to the surface.

Rani, who was sitting on the other side of the wok with a flat ladle, threw a sideway glance at Rajamah and raised an eyebrow at Kak Su. 'How come today no questions?'

Rajamah snorted. 'We'll see. She'll be back.'

Soon the two women were frying the spiced Bengal gram dhal cakes, fishing out the golden treats and leaving them on a flat strainer, before arranging them into the food containers. On a good day, Rajamah could sell about 500 pieces and make enough money to pay Rani's wages, home bills, and support her children at school and college. The stall which was secured through a government initiative to help single mothers to start small businesses was a boon when she lost her husband to a heart attack eight years ago. The financial assistance came as a startup that Rajamah used to build the small makeshift stall along the inner street in Section 3, off Old Klang Road's industrial park.

Rajamah handed out two vadais to Kak Su's assistant, just in time for the high-pitched cacophony of factory sirens to go off at a quarter past four. The street was soon bursting with the varied colours of workers' uniforms. Her stall was popular with the Bangladeshi and Nepali workers, who paid as they ate. They held the vadais, refusing the packing, and sometimes paid for each other. Rajamah manned the counter and kept an eye on the batter in the wok, while Rani packed the vadais. After a while, a familiar face appeared, the polite Encik Hassan, supervisor at the nearby paper factory. He had been her most loyal customer, who stopped by without fail a few times at least in a week.

'Aunty,' he called out and gestured for four vadais, picking one to eat.

Rajamah calculated the four pieces. 'One free for you.' She chuckled when Encik Hassan insisted on paying for the piece he was eating.

'Very delicious,' he complimented her before leaving. 'Very spicy and crisp, I love the smell too.'

A tinge of satisfaction filled Rajamah's heart. She took pride in her skill and product, which she believed was like no other. Then, another regular showed up. It was Anis and her friends, who usually lingered longer at her stall, munching on the masala vadais during tea breaks before continuing their evening shifts. When her friends left, Anis spent time with Rajamah asking about her children and exchanging news about her own life at the workers' hostel and family in the kampong. Rajamah sometimes did not charge Anis, for over the years they had formed a close bonding, warranting the word 'kakak' that Anis used to address Rajamah.

The crowd thinned when the huge, blue factory buses arrived and lined up to pick and drop off passengers. The sirens would go off again, signalling the beginning of the new shift. Then, only cars and motorcycles made random stops at the stalls strewn along the street. During this time, Rajamah would take a break and sit down to rest, drink tea, and separate out the coins and notes for counting.

Rani called out again, pointing to Kak Su, and fetched a stool.

Kak Su sat beside Rajamah, and picked up a vadai from the counter. That's the third, Rajamah made a mental count.

'Did you add pepper to this masalodeh, Rajam?'

'Pepper, yes, a bit lah, for little pungent taste,' Rajamah explained.

'But your masalodeh is soft, yet not very puffy. How do you do it, Rajam? I'm trying to make mine like yours, with soda bicarbonate. People complain they get bloated stomach, you know.' She sounded concerned.

'I also add soda, but not too much,' said Rajamah.

'How much is not too much?' Kak Su implored, to which Rajamah shrugged her shoulders. She pressed her thumb on the edge of her index finger. Kak Su nodded.

The next day Kak Su's son gave Rajamah a lift to her stall in the heavy downpour. Rani was already waiting for her, her clothes drenched in the rain.

'I thought only umbrellas got wet in the rain. Didn't you carry one?' Rajamah handed Rani a 'good morning towel' from her bag.

'Have you had lunch, Rani?'

'Yes, amma, the little one had been pestering us to take him to the new burger joint, so it was burgers today.'

'What? Burgers in those joints again?' Rajamah was alarmed.

'It was chicken burger, amma,' Rani added hesitantly, 'and fries.'

'You know very well that they have no sense between beef and chicken when they prepare your food, right, same utensils and frying pans, Rani?'

'Times are changing, amma, I agree, but a hungry stomach may not recognize where the chicken came from,' mumbled Rani. 'What goes in comes out, God is hardly interested in all that anyway, is He? The heart is what matters amma,' Rani pointed out thoughtfully.

Rajamah looked up and shook her head. 'Where in the world did you learn to talk like that Rani? I'm surprised. Hindu children eating beef-tainted burgers, adding to their karma. Thanks to parents like you Rani! Truly these are the end of times!'

Kak Su's assistants were already busy preparing for the day's sales and had heaped up rubbish from the previous day in front of their stall. Rani pointed out the half eaten and soggy masalodehs that littered the rubbish mound.

'Are they ours?'

'I'll take a look, amma.' Rani went to take a closer look.

She came back and declared, 'No, amma, they are not masala vadais.'

'When people don't seem to like what they're eating, they just throw it away,' sighed Rajamah. 'They have no respect for food, even if it is bought from their hard-earned money.'

'Yes, amma,' agreed Rani. 'But those vadais are very plain; no taste of the kadalai parupu and onions. Too much flour and soda. I won't call it a vadai at all, especially with all those cats and kittens running wild all over the stalls, all the way up to the main road. As if those make their food comparatively safer and cleaner.' She shook her head.

'Of course it can't taste like vadai, it's simply not, and people think MSG is the greatest trick! Forgoing good quality ingredients, nothing like the good old days,' lamented Rajamah as she started preparing the day's batter. They had to wait for the rain to subside before lighting the stove. Rani dropped a plastic container when Kak Su appeared once again, this time with a package in her hands.

'Try this, Rajam.' She handed a packet to Rani. 'It's roti canai. My son is joining me at the stall now.'

'Perata roti,' Rani announced as she untied the plastic bag. 'We'll eat it later,' she informed Kak Su after inspecting the content. 'Why roti canai?' Rani asked.

'Oh, he says the other stalls selling the popular Malay food—maruku, putu piring, kuih denderam, char kway tiow basah, apam balik, kuih ros, nasi lemak, lauk-lauk and all that—but there is no roti canai, our national breakfast.'

'National breakfast?' Rani interrupted.

'Yes, of course. Nasi lemak, roti canai, and teh tarik, our Malaysian favourites,' Kak Su emphasized the last word.

'Diabetes and heart failures too,' chuckled Rajamah as she handed Kak Su a hot masala vadai from the strainer.

'So if we sell roti canai, he is sure many people will want to pack this for their tea time and dinner,' explained Kak Su as she took a bite.

'Where did he learn to make roti canai?' wondered Rani.

'Now got Google. Download recipe jerr. YouTube can show how it's done. But he went to the mamak restaurant and watched them doing it, especially the flipping.' Kak Su laughed.

'You helped him with the start-up?' asked Rani. Rajamah hushed her.

'It's OK,' answered Kak Su. 'He got help from gomen. Now Wawasan 2020 era, so the gomen want more Malaysians to do business. Make sure everyone can make money, share development and goodness of the country, no rich no poor, all same-same,' she explained.

Rani butted in, 'Poor rich people, poor-poor people, same only lah, Kak Su.'

'You also can get the gomen loan, Rani,' suggested Kak Su.

'Yes, Kak Su, I'm sure I can. Maybe expand our stall large enough like yours too,' chirped Rani.

'Eh, what other spice you add to your masalodeh, Rajam? I think mine still does not match your taste. They don't sell,' she complained as she scrutinized the jagged edges of her masala vadai.

'Masala vadai,' Rani corrected her. 'Some fennel seeds will do, for sweet fragrance,' she nonchalantly said and winked at Rajamah.

'Oh, I see,' Kak Su acknowledged. 'This rain, making life difficult for us.'

Very difficult it is, Rani scoffed under her breath. 'It sure is, Kak Su, I'm sure. Come again,' she bid Kak Su goodbye.

One her way to her stall, Kak Su stopped to look up at the signboard on Rajamah's stall. She left abruptly when Rani peered over the counter. That evening, a few men arrived to climb up to Kak Su's signboard with paint and brush. When they descended, a short but very neat lettering appeared, artfully cursive but illegible to Rajamah and Rani.

Rajamah waited for Encik Hassan to explain what it was. He smiled sheepishly. 'It's for the roti canai,' he said without thinking, before leaving with a dozen masala vadais.

The rain had been incessant. It had kept the workers stranded under the covered peripheries of their factories. Few walked out to the stalls. Many made a quick dash for their buses or scuttled away to avoid getting wet.

When the rains stopped, the same men returned to Kak Su's stall, for the rain water had smudged the intricate wording they had crafted earlier on her signboard. This time they painted something in thicker bold black lines, adjacent to the masalodeh word.

'H-A-L-A-L,' Rani read out lazily as she went about her chores.

Rajamah was still able to dish out 500 vadais in the evenings. The fried cakes were still popular with the migrant workers who still did not wait for them to be packed. But the effects came unannounced. First, Encik Hassan seemed to have lost his firm gait walking up to Rajamah's stall. She initially thought he was unwell. Unlike his habit, he ordered one masala vadai, complimented and left, walking over to Kak Su's. The following day, he asked if Rajamah sold masalodeh.

'Masalodeh?' Rani cupped her mouth, in a fit of laughter.

Rajamah gave no sign of being pleased. Her insolent stare was thicker than the impending haze, which had returned undeterred by the rainy days. Encik Hassan left forty cents on the counter and walked away with one vadai, unpacked. He avoided eye contact with Rajamah thereafter, whenever he crossed the street.

'Our masala vadais are vegetarian, shall we write that on our signboard, amma?' asked Rani. 'No slaughtered product. Cats and flies included. We even pray reverently before we start the stove.'

Rajamah remained silent. 'To each his own, no need to slander,' she said after a thought. 'Get back to your work Rani. Keep your intentions clean.'

Anis, on the other hand, would walk out with her friends. They would part when they reached the stalls. While her friends busied themselves packing food from Kak Su, Anis would remain her cheerful self, packing Rajamah's masala vadais before joining them. Rani had noticed that someone usually handed her the packed food and drinks once they gathered across the street. However, such excursions were becoming rare, as Anis preferred to approach her stall to exchange pleasantries, look around, and give the I'm-not-hungry impression and leave.

A few weeks later, the haze cleared and sunshine broke through the clouds. An excited Kak Su approached Rajamah. 'Did you know?' she asked. 'There is an arch at the main road now?'

'I saw it too,' Rani said. 'Thank God it didn't fall on my head!'

'What do you mean? It's already over your head,' sniggered Rajamah.

'You never miss anything, Rani,' Kak Su waved at her playfully. 'There is a giant arch saying "GERBANG WAWASAN" at the entrance to our street. I can't believe, we are at the threshold of year 2020, new horizons,' she declared fanning herself. 'Time flies so fast.'

Rajamah let out a long slow breath. 'Still awaiting the flying cars, aren't we?' she questioned lazily. 'And look, we are riddled by money, politics and corruption, our minds and spirits defiled with greed and selfishness, everyone thinking they are great, even greater than God!' she spoke vehemently. 'What more with this new pandemic threatening to reach our shores. Shiva, Shiva!'

The women remained silent, listening to the sizzling noise of the batter in the hot wok.

'Don't worry, we still have masalodeh, Rajam,' cheered Kak Su, caressing Rajamah's elbow.

Rajamah and Rani look at each other and frown.

Like feral cats, more stalls filled the street, adding a feel of fiesta. The humble makeshift stalls with canopies were replaced with food kiosks, mobile food counters, as well as food trucks. They sold large burgers swaddled in melted cheese, fried fish balls and crunchy chicken skin, dried food, and religious paraphernalia. Local men looking strange in dreadlocks and with guitars played hand in hand with the mannequins in colourful headscarves adjoining the food stalls. Rajamah's stall now stood undisturbed at the furthest end of the street, remaining in its form of a makeshift hut, a far cry from the changing landscape.

Kak Su still made short trips to Rajamah's stall, to sample her masala vadais. This time she brought teh tarik, as her son had expanded the stall for making coffee and tea. But Rani kept them away, fearing food poisoning.

'As long as people buy masalodeh, I'm happy,' Kak Su declared. 'But they complain. Not crispy lah, smell not good lah, not tasty like the Indian masalodeh, like yours Rajam,' she said.

'They all buy from you what,' Rani blurted. 'Not from us, the original owners of masala vadai.'

'Ya lah, tu, like they have to. But they have no choice you know. Are you planning to leave, Rajam?'

'Leave?' Rajamah frowned, perplexed, 'Where to?'

'No, no, I mean, retiring, or if you plan to sell this stall, you can think of me,' she corrected.

Rani stopped frying the vadais and looked up. 'You are not getting old yourself, Kak Su?' Rani was becoming weary of Kak Su's restlessness.

'No, I'm not going anywhere, I make my living here. I'll become useless if I stayed at home,' sighed Rajamah. 'Take out the vadais, Rani, before they burn,' she called out.

'Ok, there is 500 now, amma.' Rani winked at Rajamah, before uttering a count.

'500?' Kak Su widened her eyes, astonished. 'But I still can't get it right,' she lamented. 'Are you selling until all finish?'

Rani chuckled quietly. 'Somehow we do, Kak Su.'

After Kak Su had left, Rani unplugged her mobile phone from the socket. She produced a stapler and a packet of brown food envelopes from under the counter. Rajamah joined her, and they began to pack the masala vadais as Rani read out the online orders from the screen.

'Don't forget to include the saambar and chutney. Fill the sambal ikan bilis in smaller packets.' Rajamah reminded her. 'Never knew masala vadai could go with sweetened sambal.'

'My children eat chapatti and thosai with peanut butter, amma, fruit jams too,' answered Rani. 'They detest leftover curries.'

A few customers came and went when a motorbike with a carrier stopped at the entrance. The women briefed the rider and proceeded to load the orders to be delivered out.

'I've been thinking,' said Rani.

'What is it?'

'The orders for our masala vadais are consistent. We can continue supplying to the school canteen, restaurants, and factories nearby. I'm wondering if we could sell nasi lemak,' Rani suggested.

'Nasi lemak won't sell here, but, amma, if you show me how you make the wild boar varuval, I'll prepare the coconut rice, sambal, cucumber slices, and roasted peanuts. We can

move without labels since we don't need them. We can use the
motorbike for delivery.'

'Why not?' Rajamah said. 'We can pack them here. Come
home this Sunday.'

'Nasi lemak with wild boar varuval, now that's exciting,' said
Rani. 'Chicken rendang and vegetarian too, if there is demand.'

'We call it "Nasi Lemak Wawasan".'